SIMONE SIGNORET

SIMONE SIGNORET

CATHERINE DAVID

Translated by Sally Sampson

THE OVERLOOK PRESS
WOODSTOCK • NEW YORK

First published in 1993 by
The Overlook Press
Lewis Hollow Road
Woodstock, New York 12498

Library of Congress Cataloging-in-Publication Data

David, Catherine.
  [Simone Signoret. English.]
  Simone Signoret / Catherine David : translated by Sally Sampson.
    p. cm.
  1. Signoret, Simone, 1921–1985.   2. Actors–France–Biography.
  I. Title.

PN2638.S47D3813   1993
791.43'028'092–dc20
[B]

ISBN : 0-87951-491-4

                                          92-35037
                                          CIP

ILLUSTRATIONS

INTRODUCTION

'Three chins, or is it four?' Simone Signoret asked the *Daily Mail* reporter who had come to interview her about Madame Rosa.[1] The question displays her key characteristics – courage and a sense of humour.

She saw herself as she was then, heavy, shapeless, with a face swollen by alcohol, a matron's bulging stomach, and a heart that was heavy with unspoken sorrows. When I first knew her, the end was near. Her frail body was emaciated by illness, and that legendary face was criss-crossed by a fine web of wrinkles, traces of old passions. She could hardly see any more, but newspaper articles would describe her as 'lit up from within'. Behind that pale-blue stare, the spark of life still gleamed brightly.

On the sofa in my living-room, files are spread out everywhere, marked 'Signoret', 'Signoret', 'Signoret', a mountain of papers, and literature of all kinds, left in the wake of a full life like hers. There are old press cuttings that catch one's heart: in the fifties, she was 'one of the most popular film stars', dressed in 'flannel slacks and a turtle-necked sweater'. She smoked Gauloises, and she was already an 'anti-star', 'a tough customer, but with a real heart'.

Tons of printed pages followed Simone Signoret's journey through life; I could have spent years reading them and putting them in order. My researcher, Corinne, used to deliver them, and would hand me each batch as if it were a bunch of flowers. It was like feeding a bulimic. I gorged myself on Signoret, on Mlle Simone Henriette Charlotte Kaminker, on her scent, her whole

---

[1]The elderly Jewish heroine of the film *La Vie devant soi* (1977).

1

aura. I used the same method (or lack of method) that she did when she was preparing a film role: without any preconceived ideas she'd let herself be taken over by an unknown woman, a total stranger. She would slowly *become* this other woman, she would experience her fears, desires, disappointments and prejudices; with this character – *for* this character – she would recapture the great events, and the minor ones, of her life, the agonising moments and the happy ones, the ecstasies and sorrows and the bleak grey days. 'It's almost chemical, the way you turn into that other person. I forget that I'm Signoret, I hang about the big stores, try on a raincoat that makes me look fat, I shove on old flat shoes, and when the filming starts, it's happened! The character has grown inside me, without my knowing it!'[1]

I became a Double, I changed my skin, my name, my generation. I prowled around her, letting her take me over, feel comfortable with her. She became part of my life, changing its course. Theft, possession, call it what you like, but at times I felt I was touching her, that I could hear her walking around, or could smell her scent. I carried the heavy body of this dead woman inside me like an unborn child.

I had to face the fact that this book was not going to be a scholarly compilation of biographical data; no, instead it would be the end of a long daydream in which I took over Simone's memories like a squatter. In *Nostalgia Isn't What It Used To Be*, she wrote, 'When you tell a story you usurp other people's memory.'

I have usurped her memory. Ensconced in her books and files and interviews, I listened to her ghost, I tried to guess the texture of her day-to-day life, the taste of her early-morning cup of coffee. When she woke up, did she have a furry mouth, like most chainsmokers? How many cigarettes did she smoke before emptying her ashtray into the wastepaper basket? How did she settle down in her chair when she began to write? Did she cross her legs under the table, like me? Did she now and again remember the dream she had the night before? What time was it when she poured herself her first Scotch? Were there days when she wanted

[1] *L'Express*, 26 November 1973.

to scream and shout at everybody? Sometimes I was surprised not to see her face when I looked in the mirror. My quest was not for a symbol or a legend, but for a real-life woman, who was the right age to have been my mother. A woman who had quite a life.

On the wall in front of my desk I have pinned up a photo of Simone taken during the period when she came to lunch with me, in spring 1985. She only had a few months to live. She was wearing a black tent-dress over a pale-blue shirt, which set off the colour of her damaged eyes: austere clothes, that made one forget about the wasted body underneath them. Pinned on her chest was the Solidarity badge, red on white, which she had decided to wear as long as Lech Walesa was imprisoned in Jaruzelski's jails. It was like a tiny label, a silent cry on the black material.

Her image imprinted for ever on this photograph, she's looking at me, but her gaze moves around – I swear it, it changes according to the time of day, or the light outside. It can look peaceful or desperate, tender or as severe as the frown of a Zen master. The fact is, as I sketch this portrait of her, that I'm trying my hardest to keep her looking at me. In those wonderful eyes of hers there's a sense of the absolute. Simone Signoret always let her thoughts and feelings run before her eyes like a film; the world she loved so fiercely was reflected in them. She was born curious, from the moment she opened her eyes on the world. 'Ah, so that's it! What a surprise!' She wanted to know everything: the housekeeper's first name, the colour of the walls in one's nursery. The date of one's marriage, one's political views, the last book one had read. It was as if she always had to be opening windows, exploring new worlds, replenishing her private collection of new ideas, sensations, faces, life-stories.

I can also guess at her dark side, and I will talk about it obliquely, and try to decipher its traces: the other side of the coin. The hidden counterface of generosity, her ferocity when she felt attacked or betrayed, the wounds she inflicted.

No, Simone wasn't easy. She had her views, and she would not let go of them. Peremptory in argument, stubborn as a mule – and possessive, too! Jealous, insisting that people prove their affection for her; vindictive, never forgetting a slight or insult. She had the mentality of a gang-leader, capable of brutally excluding those

3

SIMONE SIGNORET

who, in her eyes, had let the group down. While claiming to be the champion of the underdog, she could occasionally bully a terrified extra on the set like a haughty Lady Bracknell. She was a fighter inside the family as well as in public, authoritarian and unpredictable, too fond of storms and rows.

Living as she did several different lives, she had several different personalities.

You can only 'read' a face properly by the shadows that set off the lines on it. No shadows, no relief; no relief, no character. A floodlit close-up can only be one-dimensional; you cannot see the feelings. Proper lighting effects are the only way of revealing true character, because they show up the contrasts. Actresses know this, and Signoret better than any – she who once was Casque d'Or, and was past-mistress of playing up the ravages of time in the cause of good acting. She even made something splendid out of Madame Rosa's mound of chins – poor Madame Rosa, strapped into her flowery dress, which was giving a bit at the armpits!

When you write somebody's life-story, it is rather like drawing a face: you need to use thick strokes as well as tiny delicate ones, to mix light with shade. It's impossible to get the story right without lighting up the dark corners, the mistakes, the failures, the petty misdeeds. I would like to bet that this exacting but clear-minded woman would have hated the idea of being remembered as a one-dimensional figure. Simone Signoret was not a face out of a glossy magazine, but a real person, who loved whisky, and a good belly-laugh, a woman with stretch marks on her stomach, a woman who had nightmares.

And so the reader will not find a marble effigy, or unconditional hero-worship, in these pages. All I aim to do, in drawing this portrait of a woman of our times, is to give a subjective, affectionate view which I pieced together gradually during the course of a long acquaintance with my subject: a kind of personal truthfulness which only concerns me, but to which I am deeply committed.

It is not easy to write a book about a character like Simone Signoret, for special reasons that have to do with her, with her changes of role, and with the complexity of the subject, in both senses of the word 'subject'.

4

CATHERINE DAVID

In its primary sense, 'subject' means a thinking, living, doing person, with his or her psychological baggage and unique history. 'Subject: Simone', with her different identities, her enthusiasms, her political commitments, her passions, her courage, her fears, and, most enduringly, her freedom of spirit.

Then there is 'subject' in the examination sense of the word. At the Vannes *lycée*, for example, when she sat for her Baccalauréat at the beginning of the war, Simone Henriette Charlotte Kaminker got 14.5 out of 20 for her philosophy dissertation: 'Define the connections between passion and will.' A tailor-made subject for her, even at that age! You could even say that she spent all her life trying to answer this question, trying to find her own personal way of uniting these two vital forces she was blessed with at birth, with the help of the tools with which the hazards of history and life would provide her. Passion and will, desire and work; heart and head, feeling and reason. These were the two great dichotomies around which the decisions of her life revolved, the two main qualities that made her a star, and, much more than a star, an extraordinary woman.

A 'good subject', as journalists say when the features editor asks one for an article on Lou Andreas-Salomé, or a report on China. You're pleased, you know you will find out a lot, discover new worlds. It's exhilarating, but frightening too: you're never quite sure of being up to it. However many articles you may have written, each assignment is like a new journey, for journalists are eternal beginners, at least those who refuse to 'recycle' their own pieces or to replace thinking with clichés or the tired tricks of the trade.

I do not think it possible to describe a whole life; no biography can chart each day, like an archive. Strict chronology has plenty of things to commend it, it helps one to organise facts and to provide proper points of reference on which to base one's free flights of memory. But not even the most careful biographer can recapture real time, the subjective time of impressions and moods, the elastic time of lived experience.

Simone Signoret, then, is a 'good subject', because she gives the writer a great deal to think about, and opens windows on to many different kinds of landscape – the cinema, St Germain-des-Prés, the

5

French Left, romantic love, Communism, Hollywood, writing, Judaism, Human Rights, twentieth-century culture . . . Through the images that Simone Signoret has left us of the different stages of her life, we can watch the whole century unwinding like a film, from Sartre's Neuilly to Jacques Prévert's Café de Flore to the Hollywood parties with Kirk, Lee, Vivien and the others, from the conversation with Khrushchev in 1956 to Pierre Goldman's trial in 1974. Here is the century in all its complexity, showing its tragic underside as well, since Simone Signoret, born in Wiesbaden in the Rhineland occupied after World War I, came face to face with the results of the great dramas that had gone on before.

Simone Signoret's work was her life, or rather her *lives*, different lives that were interwoven like tight meshes in a tapestry: her cinema-lives may have been illusions, but for her they were just as vivid as so-called 'real' life (which is also fed by illusions). Then there were her successive lives, from young girl to woman, film extra to star; from Catherine's mother to Montand's wife; from secretary at a pro-Nazi newspaper to the woman who signed the '121' manifesto; from the Communist fellow-traveller to the champion of Human Rights. This is the story of one of the very few women of our time to have finally reached the very masculine – some might say paternalistic – status of 'the Just', of being considered a moral conscience for the nation. A wonderful subject . . .

But a taboo one. Ironically enough, Simone Signoret, the star who always insisted on remaining a human being, is protected by an impalpable aura of silence. 'Why bother to talk about her, now that she's dead?' they say. 'Leave her alone.' It is not always spelled out in so many words, but the message comes over in the end: 'Don't write this book.' One can understand the feeling of reserve and reticence, as an extreme form of fidelity. After all, for her closest friends, her 'family', Simone Signoret was, like all love-objects, a private treasure that had to be kept hidden from the public. 'I can't talk about Simone – she's my secret garden.' For the members of the clan, the 'first circle', she had stamped her own, definitive image for herself on her books and this image, or so they felt, should remain intact: 'Simone did everything well.' What more could one say?

All the same, listening to some people's recollections was like reading the newspapers in a country under political censorship. 'Simone's life-story? It was all of a piece, perfect, with no warts, no setbacks, no cracks in the mirror, no bad times, nothing like that, truly, even if you dig hard; no, she didn't drink *all* that much, no, she was never mean or unfair to people under her, no, she never had problems with Montand, they were both faithful, a model couple, no, she wasn't jealous or paranoid or possessive or exclusive. In any case, she has come clean about her mistakes, the cousin from Bratislava, Lady Macbeth and all that. She's even said her piece about Montand's affair with Marilyn. No, really, there's nothing more to say about Madame Signoret. We can't stop you from writing a book, but, truly, she's told it all already.' The file is closed, as they say in the Civil Service. On the defensive, evasive, with their embarrassed silences, cancelled appointments, polite brush-offs and empty conversations, Simone's friends did all they could to put me off.

But I won't give in to this vow of silence, this ritual embalmment, because to do so would be like saying that her life is completely over. Claiming that Simone Signoret is dead and buried is like saying that she'll never change. For in each of us, and in her perhaps more than most, there is a little sliver of immortality which lives on in the memories of those we leave behind. This is why people's images keep changing, even after they are dead. Today Simone Signoret is not the same as she was on the day of her death, 30 September 1985; her image, which also belongs to all who have seen her films and read her books, has altered, becoming both more blurred, and clearer. Mourning does its work, the lines of fate grow clearer, and a sort of balance is achieved between one stage of life and another; photos of youth jostle with those of middle and old age. Dead people are like stories you tell yourself all over again, in a new way, once you know the ending.

Signoret was 'Simone' for all of us. She could have been our sister, or a cousin, or a friend we could have confided in. She is part of the lives of the post-war generation whose dreams she fleshed out before she helped us fight our battles. She's physically part of us; we may not always be aware of it, but some of our gestures or tones of voice are copies of the way she acted. Is there any woman who has seen her films who hasn't occasionally wanted to look like her?

No, it would be quite wrong to say that Simone Signoret belongs to a different world from us. We know that is not true, because she is part of us. She is what is called a 'public figure'. But, contrary to what the gutter press may say, this does not mean that her private life should be open to all eyes. A star's private life is like a rich compost that gives her the energy she needs to do her job; everyone has the right to privacy. Private life is like a secret cave where one's personality can develop freely, where feelings are born; later it becomes a deep reservoir of inspiration for the actor's craft.

But, by definition, an actress is also a figure on display, some-body who shows herself off, offers herself to the public; and this requires a particular sort of courage. Like a great river that spreads out into many tiny separate streams, a film star infiltrates people's hearts, and lives many anonymous lives of which she is unaware. From time to time, she hears about it: a man writes her a letter telling her that his wife has not stopped crying since she saw *La Vie Devant Soi*. Simone Signoret has always been a ghostly presence in their marriage, a role-model. The wife had so identified herself with Casque d'Or that she was convinced that her husband no longer found her attractive, now that 'Marie' had become so fat and ugly . . . But nobody quite knows how these identifications work, or how to analyse the mystery of how images affect the collective imagination.

The gap between the woman and the myth is fairly large; for someone like Marilyn (if we can believe Simone Signoret's account of her) it was immeasurable. That ordinary bare-footed girl in her tight dressing-gown in Bungalow No.20 at the Beverly Hills Hotel was light-years away from the sublime siren of her best photographs. She needed three hours of preparation – make-up, brushwork, peroxide . . . In Signoret's case, things were more complex, because she was always chipping away at the myth. Just when people thought they could type-cast her, she would escape, anxious not to go over old ground, or to be cornered. Just as the public was starting to classify her as an 'actress specialising in tarts and good-time girls', she would suddenly change her image by playing the part of Elizabeth Proctor, without make-up, in *Les Sorcières de Salem*. We grew used to her icy blondes in *Thérèse Raquin* or *Les Diaboliques*, but nobody could forget *Casque d'Or*. Then she won an Oscar for her role in a film hardly seen by French viewers, the magnificent *Room at the Top*, her own favourite. And then, she began to grow fat and old, with a puffy, ravaged face that looked worse every year. Whatever happened to Casque d'Or?

The myth collapsed and the 'great lady' of French cinema began to emerge; the shattering of the myth would affect her life and sharpen its edges in an extraordinary way. She loved illusion enough to make a spectacle out of truth, and she loved truth too much not to recognise the beauty of illusion. At the same time, she was clear-eyed about it all – about herself, her joys, her sorrows and her fears. And nearly always clear-eyed about the contemporary scene, at least at the latter end of her life.

In the kitchen, she looked at me with eyes distorted by the white film that separated her from the outside world, and she did not have to pretend to be brave: she *was* brave. Like a great beast of the jungle, she was facing the gathering darkness.

At the outer edges of her vision she only had a vague sense of shapes to help her find her way in the street. She never complained ('I cope . . . But what I miss most is being able to catch Montand's eye at a dinner-party when someone says something silly, or something that we find silly, and looking at each other, and sharing the joke. Yes, I really miss that').

When Montand saw me at the Colombe D'Or in spring 1989, he gave me only half an hour ('that journalist who won't leave Simone in peace'), and was very evasive: he was excitable, even garrulous, but refused to talk about her, trying to be polite and kind, but unmistakably stone-walling. But I managed to tell him what she had said about their lost complicity, and the flash of grief she had revealed about it. And all at once, as if the room had suddenly been flooded with sunlight, his face brightened and he became tender and emotional: 'She told you that? Yes, of course, it was the hardest thing for me as well. I remember a dinner-party at Gisèle Halimi's – she's nice, Gisèle. Simone was sitting right opposite me, like you now. You know, it's the look that counts, more than sex, more than anything. It's the look that sparks off

9

love – "love at first sight". We had a habit of laughing when people said silly or pretentious things. Simone would get the giggles, she couldn't stop. It was a secret game between us, I'd look at her in a certain way and she'd start off! Then I'd pretend to want to calm her down, I'd say, "Calm down, Simone, what on earth is the matter?" I'd turn to the other guests and say, "Please forgive her, it happens now and again, she's a bit on edge at the moment, you must understand, she's filming." It was just to wind her up, you see, and she'd start off again, only more so. Yes, we had a lot of laughs together. But at the end it didn't work any longer, she couldn't see . . .'

Suddenly, he fell silent. 'Well, there's a present for you, I'll give you the story, do what you like with it. But nothing else. Please excuse me, I'm very busy with the Cannes Festival . . .' Yet another rendezvous missed, yes, of course . . . And off he went, Le Papet, striding on his long legs. From behind, in his grey suit, he looked like a wounded elephant.

CHAPTER ONE

Simone Signoret was born in 1921, but you could say that it all started at the Café De Flore in St Germain-des-Prés on a March evening in 1941, when Paris was crawling with men in uniform. At the Flore, there were no German uniforms, but intellectuals, artists, geniuses. 'By opening that door, I was entering a world that would change the rest of my life . . . The person I am today was born one evening in March 1941.' Thirty-four years later, in her memoirs, she still describes this day with undimmed enthusiasm, as a moment of revelation. In the course of one day she would find her own era, friendships and culture.

On the other hand, you could say just as confidently, with the same amount of objective truth, that the original 'great event' took play on 19 August 1949, on the terrace of the Hotel Colombe D'Or at Saint Paul-De-Vence, when she first met Yves Montand. 'And the next day he came to lunch, and in the evening I went down to Cannes to hear him sing. Finally he left with Crolla and Castella to sing somewhere else and it was dreadful. That's the way it was. In four days, we had been struck by lightning, and something indiscreet and irreversible had happened.' Can you think of a more radical rebirth than love at first sight? At the Colombe, it just happened – the archetypal, irrefutable, love at first sight, one of those meetings in which the man and woman feel that they have known each other for ever. The real thing! And life started all over again.

But, of course, everybody knows that the *real* Simone Signoret, *our* one, only came into existence when she played Casque d'Or, the blonde goddess of the outer suburbs, destined for immortal myth-status. And one remembers, too, the evening in Hollywood in 1960 when she reached the pinnacle of her fame, the top of the world. Rock Hudson called out her name, in front of a crowd of people in evening dress: 'Simone Signoret is awarded the Oscar for Best Actress for her part as Alice Aisgill in *Room at the Top.*' She nearly fell as she ran towards the dais, shell-shocked by her good fortune.

.   And yet . . . I still have a secret conviction (without which I would never have written this book) that Simone Signoret, the 'real' Simone Signoret, was only born much later, in late-middle age, when she succeeded in creating her very own role for herself, far away from the crowd. By dredging words, old ones as well as new, from the bottom of her heart, she could finally make her secret dream (long masked by her love of the cinema) come true – her dream of becoming a writer. Through writing, she could escape from narcissism, from the tyranny of her own image. Using her creative imagination, she would create herself, as not quite the same person, but not a totally different one either.

Simone Henriette Charlotte Kaminker was born secure in an unfair world, on the side of the winners in a country of losers. If her life had been a film, her first two years would have made up the early credits: you would be shown a clean, healthy, well-fed child being pushed in her expensive pram by an anxious mother on a day in 1921, in a crowd of haggard passers-by and poor-looking children, through the streets of Wiesbaden. It was no coincidence that, all her life, this little girl would side with losers and the oppressed; never again did she want to be in the shameful position of doing well by other people's misfortunes.

In 1921, with Germany bowed down by the Versailles Treaty, the consequences of the First World War were proving to be devastating for pacified Europe. Reparation payments to the Allies (symptom of a Pyrrhic victory) fed inflation, and prepared the way for the apocalypse to come. The collapse of the mark led to an economic crisis which would become worldwide, like the Great War. At the market, mothers would wheel barrows full of banknotes, still not enough to pay for even a few bottles of milk.

The occupying troops, of which Simone's father André Kaminker was part, were overseers of this historic scandal, a disgrace which would open the way to Nazism. The century's most poisonous plague was slowly incubating.

Georgette Kaminker was not a callous person; she had felt guilty about enjoying privileges she had not earned. The young mother was ashamed of being able to find meat and milk for her daughter when German children had to go hungry. She was ashamed of being well dressed and of living in a requisitioned house. She hated her husband's special mission, and held it against him for having accepted it.

Georgette Kaminker, née Signoret, had married a Jewish Army officer. For a young woman with a passion for justice, in a country still traumatised by the Dreyfus case, his Jewishness seemed like a moral guarantee. As long as she was with him, there was no chance of her straying on to the wrong side, the persecutors' side. But suddenly there she was, wife of a member of the occupying forces, condemned to enjoy the privileges of a hateful position which her husband had no scruples about exploiting: he was only doing his military duty.

In any case André Kaminker was Jewish in the same way that other people have a Breton ancestor: he never thought about it. He preferred not to think about it. Son of a Polish Jew, and an Austrian-Jewish woman, he wanted above all to be French. He had done three years' military service, and four years of fighting in the French Army, and he felt that he had payed his dues enough to join 'polite' society without people asking him awkward questions about his origins.

Possibly Georgette Kaminker, née Signoret, who was sincerely pro-Semitic, felt disappointed by her husband's constant denial of his roots. As it was, from the age of two, Simone could sense that her parents' relationship was an uneasy one. The disastrous Occupation, the first of a long series of political mistakes that would bring Hitler to power, only accentuated the misunderstandings on which the Kaminker marriage had been based from the start.

The marriage had always been a strained one; there was a canker in it somewhere. In spite of outward respectability, the couple behaved as if they had failed to create a real family. The grandparents on both sides had been against the match, and this double rejection had cast a shadow on the marriage, tarnishing its image. André's mother never accepted Georgette as a suitable daughter-in-law: for this Austrian Jewess, the 'worst thing that her son could do was to marry a non-Jew. And that's what my father did!'[1] Their love for each other was not quite enough to make the misalliance work. And their daily life was precarious, starved like a plant without proper roots.

After his exile in the Army, André Kaminker returned to civilian life in 1923. The family came back to France, and took up residence in Neuilly, eternal bastion of the French middle classes. Simone's father threw himself into a 'career of the future', advertising, or 'réclame' as it used to be called in France, a commercial expression which now sounds old-fashioned and even rather poetic. In these days of public relations and marketing, 'réclame' seems innocent, rather touching, even, like those provincial shops where a few old garments are artlessly displayed in the window, with a moth-eaten placard over the door saying 'Latest Fashions'. Simone Signoret would always be moved by shabby façades, on buildings which have never been repainted, where, under the grime, one can still vaguely make out the traces of advertisements for long-obsolete products. In these semi-obliterated names, urban archives of the old days of commerce, she found a vivid metaphor for nostalgia – that bitter-sweet word that she saw one day written in red paint on a New York wall, and used as the title for her first book. It was 'her' word. In her only novel *Adieu Volodia*, she devotes several pages to a vivid description of a vast figure of Doctor Pierre, 'toothpaste giant', painted on a wall. In the novel, children are playing under the gaze of Doctor Pierre, but their games suddenly cease as, fascinated, the children stare at the giant's enormous eye in which a tiny window has just opened.

With his boss, Étienne Damour, André Kaminker met the Prévert brothers and Marcel Carné; he brought home whiffs of modernism, poetry, film, fantasy, a tinge of surrealism . . .

---

[1] *Nostalgia Isn't What It Used To Be*, Weidenfeld and Nicolson, London, 1978.

'My father worked at the office of a deity called Damour, and wrote for a paper that looked like a chimney cowl.' By the age of four, the seeds had already been planted in little Simone's brain – names, impressions, a certain style – though they would only germinate much later, in 1941, when she would feel a sense of being at home at last with people of her own kind at the Café de Flore. If Étienne Damour had lived longer, André Kaminker would have been absorbed into that avant-garde milieu of actors, painters, writers and photographers. He would have blown gusts of fresh air into the fusty world of Neuilly-sur-Seine – echoes of literary life, eccentric friends. And probably Simone Signoret herself would have discovered the magic world of intellectuals and performing artists earlier on. But in those early days, there was just a brief flash of recognition, like a door opened and quickly closed again.

Étienne Damour died a violent death. It was a major event in Simone's life: she was five years old when she saw her father crying for the first time. She was having her first lessons in nostalgia.

Unemployed, André Kaminker was not content with just changing jobs. This resourceful character quite simply invented simultaneous translation, now such an indispensable tool of international communications. Old hands at the Quai D'Orsay still remember his extraordinary gifts. He was capable of learning a language in two or three weeks, well enough to translate a speech at a moment's notice. If there was a delegation from an exotic foreign country whose language nobody spoke, the answer was to call on André Kaminker for help. He never let one down.

He rushed around from conference to conference, and cultivated diplomats. But above all, he made himself a rare commodity. Over the years, he became an absentee father, always travelling, without much time for the family. Business trips were used as an excuse for escaping from an increasingly difficult family life. The Kaminkers seemed to float between two worlds, without any fixed points or firm plans for the future: 'We would keep on moving, the flats became bigger and bigger, but we became more and more like "displaced persons".'

Simone Signoret felt like a displaced person in Neuilly, that stagnant shore where her parents had landed by accident. The suburbs were terra incognita, a neutral zone where the tumults of history only filtered through indirectly. Neuilly must have been Simone's father's idea; he was so anxious to be respectable, such a conformist. For Georgette, it was quite the opposite: this well-heeled suburb felt like a second exile, which added to her unpleasant memories of the Rhineland. She experienced the questionable pleasure of being part of a bourgeois way of life whose outward signs she rejected as merely show.

In Simone Signoret's memories, the two sides of the family were kept carefully separate. On the Kaminker side, there were the Sunday visits to Lamartine Square, with Ceylon tea and *petits fours* served in Uncle Marcel's luxurious rooms (a 'little Austrian Jew, a Catholic convert', he had done well on the Bourse). Then there were the fashionable promenades with her father in the Allée des Acacias and the Avenue du Bois. André Kaminker showed her Boni de Castellane's fairy-tale pink castle, and was upset by her lack of enthusiasm. Already she felt alienated from her father, and the way he idolised 'important' people: a faithful reader of *Le Figaro* and *Gringoire*, he was attracted to the pure, hard Right. It was only much later that Simone Signoret would discover, very indirectly, what the word 'Jewish' meant for her – that loaded word, charged with so many intellectual and historical associations.

For a Jew of André Kaminker's generation, who had only recently escaped from the poverty of the *shtetl*, the Polish village where his family lived, the first of his line to be born in France, assimilation into middle-class society was a double victory, both over the obscurantism of his piously orthodox ancestors and over the exclusion they had suffered. To earn this passport into European 'polite' society, he forced himself to forget the archaic Judaism that had been such a feature of his youth, since it was not the fashion along the Avenue Du Bois. 'I don't know very much about my father,' she would write, 'except that he was born in France, that he had fought for France, and that being French was enormously important for him, which meant that he kept fairly quiet about his foreign ancestors: I knew that his father was Polish, but I never knew from which ghetto he came.'[1]

Because of this ignorance, when Simone made a trip to Prague much later on with Yves Montand, she was to miss a crucial rendezvous with a second cousin living in Bratislava. She had never heard of Jo Langer, or of any of the members of her family in Poland and Austria who were exterminated by the Nazis. She would bitterly regret knowing nothing of these people who were part of herself, though they had disappeared.

Superficially, what she inherited from her taciturn father was above all a feeling of anxiety, a lack of fixed attachments, which gave her (though she did not realise it) a great deal of her energy and passion. But was this feeling of transience and of not belonging the only part of the Polish-Jewish inheritance left to her by her father, in spite of her ignorance of her true roots? In spite of himself, in spite of his secretiveness, he must surely have passed on to her many other qualities, a secret identity of which she only became fully conscious at the end of her life when she would be amazed to find, hidden inside herself, a deep mine of emotions, memories and thoughts she never knew she possessed. Something has to be passed down from one person's memory to another's, from one generation to another, even if it is done in silence. Much later on, when she wrote her novel *Adieu Volodia*, she would write at length about the role of silence in the way that race memory was secretly transmitted in certain Jewish families. Simone Signoret talked about her father as if he were somebody who had lived in the same apartment, but in the next-door room. 'We didn't meet that often.' The importance of the word 'nostalgia' in her personal lexicon perhaps came from the shadowy image of this father who never knew how to tell her about his past.

Consciously, she always took the Signoret side, her mother's, and when the couple quarrelled, she always supported the latter. When her father took her to the grand apartment in Lamartine Square, she could not help thinking of her Signoret grandparents' tiny flat in the Avenue des Ternes – a hovel without electricity, which smelled of coffee and paraffin. The contrast was brutal;

[1]Preface to *Une Saison à Bratislava* by Jo Langer, Le Seuil, 1981.

it was a different world. Between a mother who took her to the Neuilly market and told her about Sacco and Vanzetti and a father drawn towards the exterior signs of social success, there did not seem to be any room for a shared universe, or any real common ground. Was there any love between them? There's no echo of it in the way their daughter describes the marriage. If there ever was any, it probably quickly evaporated. All the same, the old fires must have flared up again occasionally between them. Simone was probably unaware of this; perhaps she never asked herself the question, it was not the kind of question one asked in the Kaminker household. She was just surprised – and delighted – by the late arrival of two little brothers. 'I have never understood or tried to understand why my father and mother, who had waited nine years before having another child, then had two, one right after the other.'

But the predominant mood in this family story was insecurity, impermanence, emotional confusion. 'We lived in that immense apartment, but we never put up any wallpaper; we lived surrounded by the sizing, which was a pretty salmon colour, a bit like the lining in a piece of clothing. We were living in salmon! There had once been a beige carpet, but the previous tenants had removed it when they left, and all that remained was a leftover in a store-room. Overhead hung naked light bulbs. Next week we'd get around to lampshades . . .'

Up until the birth of her brothers, Simone had an extraordinarily close relationship with her mother. The links between the isolated woman and the young girl whose character was becoming daily stronger were exclusive, sometimes too much so.

Georgette Kaminker was the product of a lower-middle-class family with dreams of grandeur. Her own mother, a provincial dressmaker, boasted descent from an ancestor who had been guillotined in the Revolution, but forgot to talk about her father, a butcher at Valenciennes. Georgette had fallen in love with Signoret, a promising young painter from Marseilles, whose ambitions would be bitterly dashed. 'He was tall and very handsome,' his granddaughter Simone would write later on, after she too in turn had fallen in love with a tall, handsome man from

Marseilles, called Yves Montand. Alas, in spite of his artistic ambitions, handsome Grandfather Signoret had turned a blind eye to the revolutionary artistic changes of his era, and went on painting lustreless sunsets, and condemning Picasso as a charlatan. He would end his days in the little flat on the Avenue des Ternes, alone with this woman who would never forgive him for being a failure. Late in the day, the little dressmaker from Valenciennes would go on playing Madame Bovary in the squares of Neuilly; repudiating her hopeless husband, distinguished-looking with her snowy white hair, she pretended to be the wife of the famous actor Gabriel Signoret. Little did she realise that while Gabriel would quickly sink into obscurity, she herself would one day be famous by association with her granddaughter Kiki Kaminker, whom nobody as yet called Simone Signoret.

Simone's mother was an eccentric, a sort of female Don Quixote with passions and fads; she was not afraid of being made fun of, hated mediocrity, worshipped Proust and Aristide Briand, and inculcated into her daughter solid principles that mixed hygiene with morality, and bread and butter with politics.

Only daughters will know what I am talking about, especially those with elusive fathers. A close relationship with a mother who feels that she's been deserted is often just another way of sharing loneliness. It is a love-story lived out in a claustrophobic little nest, with cups of hot milk and sudden bursts of spite, where infantile pleasures alternate with longings for escape. A reassuring little nest, full of irresistible little comforts and emotional blackmail, but also a gentle but terrible prison where love and repulsion are inextricably mixed.

Docile and wild at the same time, Simone's mind and beauty developed under the eyes of an authoritarian, anxious mother who forbade roller-skates because one could hurt one's knees, refused to have a cat in the house because it could have scratched or suffocated the child, and would ask hairdressers to 'kindly sterilise their tongs', before touching a hair of her daughter's head.

In contrast, Georgette Kaminker had a high opinion of her daughter's judgement and treated her intellectually like an adult, incessantly asking her for her opinion. On a journey she would ask the six year old, 'What do you think? Shall we spend the night at Avignon? Or shall we go on?' And a few years later, when she was about to give birth to her last child Jean-Pierre, at the hospital at La Baule, she gave to Simone (who was only just eleven) the sole responsibility for looking after Alain, the little brother who had arrived two years earlier like a Christmas present, on 28 December. For Simone, aged nine, Alain's birth had been like a miracle; it awoke in her all the maternal instinct she was capable of. As she would agree later when talking about her daughter, she would never show Catherine the same devotion that she had lavished on her little brother, in those far-off days when she herself was still a child. For a few days she looked after Alain like a mother. 'I dressed him, I took him to the beach, to the clinic, I fed him – and it all seemed perfectly natural to me. People would look at me in surprise, I couldn't at all understand why.'[1]

The same year in Marseilles, an eleven-year-old urchin called Ivo Livi would leave primary school to seek work. This shared experience of having had responsibility at such a precociously early age must surely have contributed to the extraordinary alchemy that would one day link Simone Signoret's destiny with Ivo Livi's (alias Yves Montand). On the brink of puberty both these children had already had practical experience of life's difficulties, and both of them would later on derive a sense of pride and strength from it, and the memory of having been 'able to cope'.

The future Simone Signoret was already too strong a personality to identify with the images of herself that her mother tried to project on to her. She had to escape from this claustrophobic game of mirrors which so often condemns a daughter to play out her mother's destiny. Caught between the impossible alternative roles of vulnerable baby and male protector, she took a tangential escape-route by becoming strong and proud. She rejected the role of all-powerful child dreamed up for her by the unhappy woman, and instead cultivated femininity and grace.

She inherited her mother's dignity and spirit with a streak of wilfulness – plus her vengeful side in full measure. Neither woman ever forgot a wrong done to her. But the 'essential Simone', that glow from within, that sunny grace, her openness, all the qualities

[1] *Nostalgia* . . . op.cit.

that would make her a star, did not come from this lonely woman with her cramped, self-pitying lifestyle. Simone could only clear the fence by pushing her mother to one side, by freeing herself from her mother's obsessive gaze (hostile as well as loving), by escaping from this woman who had formed her childhood. Her inner light came to her from elsewhere, inherited from a deeper past.

As an adult her relationship with her mother would be distant and difficult. In 1958, Simone would mourn with her the death of Alain, the younger brother, and later she would look after her needs and care for her, right at the end, when her memory had gone. But Georgette Kaminker would stay on the sidelines, off-screen, a shadowy woman whose goodness and love had been so dangerously overprotective.

CHAPTER TWO

Simone Kaminker went to the girls' secondary school in Neuilly opposite the lycée Pasteur for boys. This was how she heard about, and vicariously experienced, the incredible effect produced by the arrival of a young philosophy teacher from Le Havre. He was an odd-looking character, always late, with his fake-fur coat, shabby shoes with holes in them, and big yellow Russian cigarettes which stank out the classrooms. He wore a turtle-necked sweater, had bulging eyes behind thick glasses, and his name was Jean-Paul Sartre. He had just written *La Nausée*, and he fascinated the well-brought-up middle-class boys. By the end of the year, most of the pupils had discovered a vocation for philosophy, however ephemeral. 'Thanks to Sartre,' claims one of them, 'I changed generations.'[1] Of course, this did not convert Neuilly, bastion of the French Right, into a Red suburb, but at least, at Sartre's feet, bourgeois youth could dream about freedom and feel the wind of History.

Simone got closer to Sartre at the Sabot Bleu, a newspaper kiosk where boys and girls met after school to flirt politely, and rebuild the world. This little clan had even decided to found a magazine called *The Hyphen*, edited by Serge Dumartin and Chris Marker. The beautiful Simone Kaminker was given the job of taking the proofs of the magazine to the printer, and the young men would quarrel over who would escort her.[2]

With these students, she discussed philosophy, Charles Trenet,

[1]Gérard Blanchet, quoted by Annie Cohen-Solal, *Sartre*, Gallimard, 1985.
[2]Cf. Annie Cohen-Solal, op.cit.

Django Reinhardt, the Hot Club and – of course – politics. In the secondary school, some of the forms contained German-Jewish girls who were escaping from Nazism. Simone had a fairly clear idea of why they were exiles, partly because her generous, impulsive mother had often taken in refugee families as guests. Georgette Kaminker never compromised with her convictions: she would return toothbrushes marked 'made in Japan' to the chemist's, because the Japanese were Hitler's allies. At seventeen, in 1938, Simone Kaminker had a seat in the best part of the house; she was well informed, and a good listener. The awakening of her political consciousness dates from this period. 'When people say, "We really didn't know what was happening in Germany," I always wonder how they managed to blindfold their eyes and stuff their ears!'[1]

In spite of being Jewish, André Kaminker was far less alert than his wife to the dangers of Nazism. In 1934, he had had the painful task of translating the Führer's ravings for the radio: 'I can still remember him coming home (for once) one evening, exhausted after having translated Hitler's first big speech at Nuremberg "live" for French radio.' He was well informed about Hitler's obsessions; but his political acumen did not always equal his talents as an interpreter. In 1938, as a member of Édouard Daladier's delegation on that fatal journey to Munich, he felt relieved by the result, like everybody else. Simone Signoret recalls with humorous exasperation the telegram that he sent his family on that dismal occasion while they were on holiday in a village in Brittany: 'The peace has been saved – Papa.' 'It impressed the locals no end that my father had been a member of that delegation of imbeciles.'

When war broke out, Simone and her mother were on holiday with the two little boys. For the second time, they had rented a big house at Saint-Gildas, in the Morbihan. The roads were choked with fleeing Parisians, and it would have been absurd to return to Neuilly in this doom-laden atmosphere. So they stayed put, and Mme Kaminker had to lodge German soldiers billeted in the holiday house. After having been an occupying officer's wife, now, by a strange twist of fate, Simone's mother found herself

[1] *Nostalgia . . .* op.cit.

cooking stews for the invaders. The stupidity of the Germans made it all the more mortifying. In her memoirs, Simone Signoret gives a hilarious account of the way in which Georgette Kaminker (a 'Breton name', for the Germans) treated the wretched Hanoverian peasants who had landed on her doorstep. They arrived one evening, settled in, and the next morning were frightened out of their wits because the sea had disappeared . . . But soon other soldiers succeeded those poor bumpkins, officers, real servants of the Reich, less rustic, more suspicious, cleverer: 'These ones knew that the tide ebbs and flows . . .'[1] They were clever enough to suspect that Kaminker could not be a Breton name. Communal life soon became impossible.

Georgette Kaminker returned to Neuilly in the winter of 1940–41, leaving Simone behind for the time being in Vannes, for her to sit her 'Bac'. The Neuilly apartment was derelict, the rent had not been paid for months; André Kaminker had left without leaving an address. She learned later that he had taken refuge in London, where he would stay for the whole war. From one day to the next, as soon as she got back to Neuilly with her *bachot* in her pocket, Simone found herself in her father's shoes as head of the family, with three children to look after – her two brothers, and a mother who had never had a job. Simone sold the Oriental carpets, argued with the bailiffs, and looked around for work.

Simone Signoret may have always secretly regretted the careless way in which she accepted a secretarial job from Jean Luchaire (father of one of her schoolfriends and an intimate friend of Otto Abetz) on his right-wing paper, *Les Nouveaux Temps*. She really didn't give the offer much serious thought: there were plenty of extenuating circumstances. Giving private lessons in English and Latin to a few boys was not enough to make ends meet.

Her little world had been limited to the leafy corners of Neuilly, and her only real dream was to star in films, to be discovered on a street corner by a 'director who just happened to be passing by'. Grim everyday realities had pushed the dreams into second place: she was having to work like a man, supporting the family. The

---

[1] *Nostalgia* . . . op.cit.

world was falling apart; in the general cataclysm, the fate of the Kaminker family was only a tiny, insignificant drama. But it was the first time that Simone would be really up against it. Her parents turned out to be weak and powerless, the chaos of their married life finally exposed. Now the family would rely on her for survival. She had broad shoulders, and extraordinary determination. She would pick up the challenge and take the test bravely, supported by her secret dream of becoming a star. But along the way, she would come up against the poisonous world of collaboration.

Ironically, it was her dream that led her to the secretarial job at *Les Nouveaux Temps*: she thought it was a 'sign' when, by chance, she caught sight of a small ad saying that the Harcourt Studio was looking for a 'personable young woman who was proficient in foreign languages'. In a period rich in euphemisms, this meant 'proficient in German'. Simone Signoret did not know a word of German, but she spoke fluent English after several trips to Sussex as a teenager. Now the 'Harcourt Studio' was a magic name; it was where the film stars went to have their photographs taken, to appear (heavily touched-up) on the front covers of magazines. 'For a girl of my age who knew nothing of the cinema, it rang out like Hollywood.' Working at the Harcourt Studio would be a step nearer to that scintillating world of the silver screen.

Hoping for a leg-up to this glamorous job at Hollywood-on-Seine, Simone Kaminker telephoned her friend Rosita Luchaire, nicknamed Zizi. Rosita Luchaire *was* a star. She had left school in the third form, announcing that she was going to be a film star, and she did become one. She turned into Corinne Luchaire in *Prison Without Bars*: a *real* star, with a fur coat, the kind that complains about having to have her clothes made by the top designers. When Simone phoned, Rosita's mother answered. She said her daughter was not there, but advised her to ring her husband, Jean Luchaire. He was still editor-in-chief of the *Petit Parisien*, but he was busy setting up a new paper, perhaps he would have a job for Simone.

Jean Luchaire did give her a job as secretarial assistant at a salary of 1,400 francs a month. He took this risk in the full knowledge of the facts: he knew, from inside information, that André Kaminker was Jewish, and that he was in London, so that his decision to hire Simone was quite courageous for a well-known collaborator in 1941. Simone Signoret is insistent that Jean Luchaire was not a pure, hard-edge collaborator, but a complicated character – 'flabby, weak, corrupt, but handsome and generous'. His sister was married to a Jewish doctor, and Jean himself gave discreet help to people who would not lift a finger to save his life when the Liberation came.

At *Les Nouveaux Temps*, where she was an 'office girl' (she answered the telephone and learned to type, which turned out to be useful), she saw many people pass through, especially women asking for help for their husbands in prison – which they received, particularly if they were attractive.

In 1945, she would force her father, after he had returned to Paris, to lodge an appeal for mercy for Luchaire, 'thanks to whom, he must remember, his little family had been able to make ends meet for a while'. But his intervention proved useless, and Luchaire died, in the style that she describes in one of the most moving pages of her memoirs: 'It was indeed in front of a firing squad, a cigarette between his lips, shouting: "Vive la France!" It was an anachronism for the internationalist he pretended to be. Still, it must have been difficult to go through with the gesture when one has just refused to be blindfolded, and is probably close to collapsing, faced with a bunch of kids who have been ordered to fire at you – and who fire.'[1]

In spite of Simone's monthly salary from the *Nouveaux Temps*, the apartment on the Avenue du Roule was seized and put up for auction. Jews who didn't pay their rent had to behave well. The family's instability had increased. 'Following due legal procedures we were evicted from our apartment by the police commissioner of Neuilly. My mother courageously accepted employment as a seamstress in charge of linens in a hospital in Valréas in the unoccupied zone, where they would lodge her and my little brothers.'[2]

Perhaps traumas like these – the anguish of the seizure and the expropriation, the months of anxiety, the false hopes and the final, inevitable, official break with the nest – are necessary to

[1] *Nostalgia* . . . op.cit.
[2] Id.

fully appreciate the privilege of having a 'Room of One's Own'. It was a major turning point in Simone's life. It was a small drama played inside a much greater tragedy, but for Simone it was a kind of liberation, and relief.

Her father was in London, but all they knew was that he spoke on BBC Radio. The family was scattered, and would never be reunited. Simone stayed in Paris on her own, free at last, living in a little room in the Rue du Cherche-Midi. She started her grown-up life in a capital city that ran on German time. She was twenty years old, merry, proud, intelligent and street-wise.

CHAPTER THREE

'Between 1940 and 1942, I had all the prerequisites – extenuating circumstances included – for becoming a prostitute. I was good-looking, poor and half-Jewish, I had my small family on my back to support, and I worked for Luchaire the collaborator's paper, *Les Nouveaux Temps* . . .'[1] One evening in March 1941, Saint-Germain intellectuals warming themselves with sips of ersatz coffee at the Café de Flore were dumbfounded to see a radiant young beauty coming into the Café with Claude Jaeger, a rebellious young rich-man's son from Switzerland who had picked her up one evening at the theatre. He had a serious, penetrating look, and – ridiculously, crazily – Simone had taken him into her confidence during that difficult time. In an impulsive moment that could have been fatal, she told this stranger everything, all about her father emigrating to London, her rather equivocal job at Luchaire's and her loneliness in the huge, devastated city.

Simone Signoret often had these intuitions, instinctive bursts of trust that impelled her to open her heart to chance acquaintances. She could not have made a better choice than Jaeger, for, working for the FTP,[2] he would become one of the leaders of the Resistance. But in the meantime, he gaily strolled about Paris, squandering his inheritance. He knew that Simone would feel at home in the Café de Flore. He was right: at the Flore she immediately recognised people of her own kind. There was Sartre, whom she already knew, but also the Prévert brothers (whom her

---

[1] Interview in *Marie-Claire*, September 1979.
[2] Francs. Tireurs. Partisans, a Communist-organised branch of the French Resistance.

father had met furtively with Damour) and Giacometti, Picasso and Soutine.

In Neuilly, in spite of Sartre and the 'comrades', History had been kept tucked away, on the fringes of real life, without really affecting middle-class behaviour – the social tea-parties, the pleated skirts, the *concierges* with their moustaches and the little maids from Brittany. At the Café de Flore, the atmosphere was saturated with historical events, people talked about them, looked excited about them: they talked about philosophy, too, politics, painting, the cinema. She was fascinated: at last, she felt, she was face to face with the contemporary world. Simone Signoret was not the type to sit back and watch the trains go by; here was a unique chance of expanding her consciousness, of learning and having fun at the same time. If this was a party, then she wasn't going to miss it!

For the first time, perhaps, reality seemed attractive. From now on, she was absolutely sure she would never feel like a displaced person again, the way she had felt for so long in Neuilly. These people at the Flore were all 'displaced persons', even more so than her – foreigners, wanderers, rebels. They were different, but they had built their art on that difference, they made a way of life, a political conscience, out of it. They would show her the way. Thanks to them, Simone Signoret discovered that her feeling of being an outsider, which had made her suffer so much, could become a trump-card, a creative stimulus, a point of departure. Right from the start she was adopted by this huge, irregular family, and it would remain hers for life. She would carry this special little world around with her everywhere she went; she would alter it, and enrich it, but its central core – the Flore – would never change. 'My friendships dating from that time were indestructible.'

It was at the Flore that the idea of being a film actress took on a solid shape, and ceased to be just a secret daydream. One reason was that once you'd become a full-time 'Floriste', you couldn't possibly continue to work for a collaborationist paper.

'A sane, balanced girl can't spend her evenings on the banquettes of the Café de Flore among people wanted by the police – some of them Jewish, many of them Communists or Trotskyites, Italian anti-fascists, Spanish Republicans, bums, jokers, penniless

SIMONE SIGNORET

poets, sharers of food-ration tickets, wandering guitarists, genial jacks-of-all-trades – when she has spent her day taking messages from Abetz to Jean Luchaire . . .'[1] So almost immediately she gave Jean Luchaire her notice, dropping the substance for the shadow with studied bravado: 'I'm leaving because, you see, Monsieur, you'll all end up being shot.' And when he teasingly asked her what she was going to do, she answered cheekily, 'I'm going to act in movies!' It was like a prayer.

Saying something like this when you're half-Jewish, in Nazi-occupied France, was not just provocative – it was foolhardy, and silly. A Kaminker had no chance of obtaining that crucial backstairs permit, the COIC[2] Card issued by the 'Propaganda Staffel' which allowed actors to be officially hired. Simone knew very well that she would get no proper speaking parts for as long as the Occupation lasted; this was confirmed when Louis Daquin, who had chosen her for a leading role, reneged on his decision without daring to tell her the reason for his change of mind. But she could be an extra or a *silhouette*, someone who had tiny speaking parts; the administration tolerated these, or rather it turned a blind eye. But then again, Simone Kaminker was not a reasonable person – or a realist. Just as when she told Claude Jaeger about all her troubles, she trusted her intuition. Saying whatever came into her head was her own special way of making things happen, of producing miracles.

At the Flore, she made friends with actors, film directors and scriptwriters, like Prévert, and the people from the October Group, Marc Allégret and his brother Yves (the future father of her daughter). They were all obsessed with film. Subjects would gradually take shape as they talked; imagination was king. Acting in films was no longer just a secret dream, a vow that you muttered under your breath in bed before putting the light out. It was a legitimate desire, a shared ambition. 'For me, everyone wanted to act, just as everyone wants to be rich, beautiful and loved; but you don't admit these things, you keep it secret.' Her comrades at the Flore did not have any such inhibitions – those who wanted

[1]*Nostalgia* . . . op.cit.
[2]*Comité d'organisation de l'industrie cinématographique*, set up by Laval in 1940.

30

to be actors said so, without false modesty. Those who wanted to be directors spent their time dreaming up their masterpieces, out loud. It was a revelation for Simone, like a window opening: for her the cinema was no longer just an entertainment industry that provided covers for *Cinémonde*, but an honourable art in its own right, fully part of the cultural scene. But also, in the meantime, an excuse for gossip and fun!

If one could not get hold of a COIC Card, the minimum requirement was a false name. 'Signoret' was her mother's maiden name, and the name of her maternal grandfather, the handsome Marseillais who liked painting sunsets. A doubly masculine name, Signoret, since it contained the Italian for the word man: *signore*. And, as things turned out, Signoret, the 'male' of the Kaminker family, would become female under this 'seignorial' name. And not just female, but a star: she would be Casque d'Or, one of the great romantic lovers of the century. A provocative, luminous, *modern* woman who would set her stamp on the history of the cinema.

Up until the Liberation, Simone Signoret collected parts as a *silhouette*. In Jean Boyer's *Boléro* her salary rose from 120 to 500 francs, thanks to the memorable cue, 'Madame, the Comtesse d'Artémise is waiting for you in the drawing room,' which gave the technicians hysterics because the chief operator's name was Artémise. Thanks to these silly little sentences, uttered after interminable hours of waiting in stifling studios, Simone managed to make ends meet. When she couldn't, the comrades would help her out. At a period when life was so tough and so full of worries, the word 'solidarity' had a real meaning, and for Simone Signoret this would amply compensate for the uncertainties of day-to-day life. All things considered, in spite of her fears and difficulties, the Occupation was an exciting time for her; it was one of the happiest periods of her life, an apprenticeship, a time of discovery. The girl from the suburbs was at last living in the heart of Paris, and finding out simultaneously about the joys of friendship and of fleeting love-affairs, in an atmosphere where danger lent an extra spice to youthful experiments.

But without being aware of it, Simone was missing out on the most important and heroic adventure of the time, and she would regret it for the rest of her life. 'I would be a liar if I told you that I was part of the Resistance. In my vocabulary, resistants were only those who truly acted, and with full consciousness of what they were doing. I did not perform a single heroic act. I did no harm, which in itself is not so bad.'[1] At the Flore and elsewhere, without knowing it, she met important resistants like Claude Jaeger and Jean Painlevé, but she would never ask her friends if they knew a way of joining the secret movement. Once she carried a suitcase full of ammunition without being aware of it; and for several months she lived with Yves Allégret in a flat in the Rue du Dragon which was used as a letter-box by the Resistance. But she did not choose any of this; it was accidental, she had not asked for it, she was not even aware of running any risk. In spite of (or maybe because of) her experiences at *Les Nouveaux Temps*, her political consciousness was hardly formed at all. She hated the Nazis, that went without saying, but it didn't occur to her to take the plunge; she had her own personal, intimate way of showing her opposition to the Germans. She was displaying the same kind of unconscious defiance as when she refused to be baptised a Protestant like her two little brothers by Pastor Ebershold. In spite of her change of name, she still kept an identity card in her handbag with the name 'Kaminker' on it. 'It was a game. Nothing heroic, because it was only useful to me in relation to an established order which I categorically rejected.' At least these little gestures helped salve her conscience at a time when others were risking their lives on the cobbled streets of Paris, a few yards from the sheltered bastion of the Café de Flore.

There were several people, like Signoret or Sartre, who lived through those dark times without compromising with the enemy, but without properly joining the active Resistance, and it seems fair to say that the memory of their fastidious inaction played a crucial role in their subsequent political commitment and even in the obstinacy and silly mistakes into which commitment would lead them. It was as if that black gap in their life-history had left them with the feeling that commitment was a categorical imperative,

[1] *Nostalgia* . . . op.cit.

and that even making mistakes was better than doing nothing. Without this haunting sense of regret, Simone Signoret might well have failed to develop her hypersensitive political antennae, which would make her not simply an actress, but one of the mouthpieces of the left-wing conscience in France.

In spite of a short eclipse after the Germans' arrival in Paris, the French cinema was thriving. As Jacques Siclier recalls, 'During the Occupation, the French appetite for entertainment – cinema, theatre or music hall – was absolutely enormous. It was a way of escaping, and, in winter, you could keep warm in the theatres.'[1] One hundred and twenty feature films were produced under the Occupation, of which none, according to Jacques Siclier, were Nazi propaganda. Let us take his word for it. Among the eighty-one film directors working at the time we find the names of Abel Gance, Marcel L'Herbier, Marc Allégret, Jacques Becker, Robert Bresson, Henri-Georges Clouzot, Sacha Guitry . . . Famous pre-war actors feature on the billboards, like Fernandel, Raimu, Robert Le Vigan, Pierre Fresnay, Ginette Leclerc, Elvire Popesco and Yvonne Printemps. A few immortal films date from those years – *The Well-Digger's Daughter, Madame Sans-Gêne, Les Enfants Du Paradis* . . .

Simone Signoret appears in the credits in films directed by Jean Boyer, Louis Daquin, Marcel Carné, André Berthomieu, Jean Faurez, Jean Tarride, Pierre et Jacques Prévert, Jean de Marguenat, Yves Allégret. They are mostly studio-productions. Simone also attended the classes of the famous Solange Sicard, who classified her as a 'comic actress' because of a slight speech-defect which made her pronounce her sibilants with a 'ch'. This famous 'ch' would later be considered as a kind of designer label, the 'Signoret sound', an extra asset like her haughty look or slightly nasal voice. Simone Signoret would never have become a star if she had not had the gift of magnifying her defects and making an advantage out of being different.

Marcel Carné gave her her first experience of proper film-making in 1942. She played one of the four 'ladies of the *château*'

---

[1] *La France de Pétain et son cinéma*, Henri Veyrier, 1981.

in *Les Visiteurs du soir*, she was a non-speaking extra, but she was on set in every scene. At last, for three months, she would be leading a real actor's life! To her delight, she discovered the pleasure of working in a group, and the complicity of an acting troupe sharing the adventure of a film. Even more to the point, the film was shot in the South of France, at Vence, close to Saint-Paul, the village that would later become her own special territory. She lodged with the extras at a *pension* called Ma Solitude, went riding in the Verdon gorges, and was on 'tu' terms with the stars, Arletty, Jules Berry, Fernand Ledoux and Marcel Herrand.

Next, she made a hilarious theatrical début at the Théâtre des Mathurins in a play by Lucien Favre, *Dieu Est Innocent*, in which she played a 'woman of the people of Thebes', for 15 francs a day. Sadly for Simone Signoret's theatrical career, the more the people of Thebes lamented, the more the actors were seized by uncontrollable giggles, especially when the stagehand in charge of the sound-effects muddled up his records and made 'aeroplane noises' rather than crowd ones. 'We would be overcome by the giggles five minutes before we were to go on, we'd be fighting them the whole time we were onstage, and we'd finally crack up as soon as we came off. Onstage, we would take up splendid Greek stances; we would cover our eyes with our forearms, and lower our heads to show grief and humiliation – and we would split our sides laughing!'[1] Simone Signoret, who could never resist a good giggle, was the only one to be caught in the act, and she was dismissed, as if she were unclean. The only mementoes of her part in the lamentations of the people of Thebes were her rented sandals, which she deliberately 'forgot' to give back, out of superstition, because Jean Gabin had worn them in a film. (They took the same size in shoes, in fact.)

A pair of sandals . . . and her first lover, Daniel Gélin. He had been picked for the part of Hémon in *Dieu Est Innocent* because of his well-shaped, sunburned legs, which provided a bit of local colour under his short Greek tunic. He was a poor but talented youth from the provinces, who had just broken away from the Conservatoire; he was intimidated by this girl of the same age as

[1]*Nostalgia . . .* op. cit.

himself, who had knocked about and was already the 'Prévert gang's muse', an *habituée* of the Café de Flore, cultivated, beautiful, exuberant and totally fearless. For him the Flore where Simone felt so at home was a fascinating but foreign world, which slightly scared him. And then, of course, he was in love with her, and she had too many attractive men-friends. 'Opposite her,' Daniel Gélin recalls, 'my lack of culture, my puny, childish physique seemed very lightweight.'[1] It would take several walks in the spring evenings for him to pluck up the courage to kiss her. After this, she brought her belongings ('a touching bra and slip, a scarf and a toothbrush') along in a hatbox to the attic where he lived five floors up in a house on the Rue Monsieur-le-Prince. It would be a short idyll – mornings spent lounging in bed, listening to Bing Crosby records, with sunlight streaming over the immense, silent city and the 'happiness you feel when you know that you're being anti-bourgeois!'. Then she left him, for another short-lived love affair with Marcel Duhamel. 'Since Daniel and I were exactly the same age,' she writes in *Nostalgia*, 'I was too old for him.' Too old, at twenty-two! A few years later, Yves Montand would come into her life, and, like Gélin, he would be exactly the same age as her. *He* did not seem to find her too old!

Marcel Duhamel was twice her age. He was a good talker and a man of the world, and he genuinely loved his wife Germaine, who was in the Free Zone during the war; he would talk about her all the time. In short, he was a heavyweight, with his forty years' experience, his paternal tenderness, his inexhaustible culture, his surrealist friends. He was a pillar of the Flore, a founding father of the October Group. Later on he would discover Henry Miller, and translate his books, and after the war, he would become one of modern literature's great benefactors by inventing the Série Noire. Simone could be as intimidating as she liked, he had met plenty of women like her. She was beginning to realise the destructive effect that her strong personality could have on certain men, and she found Marcel Duhamel reassuring for the simple reason that she did not scare him. Most probably he filled the unglamorous role of temporary father-figure – she would later use directors

[1] *Deux ou Trois Vies qui sont les Miennes*, Julliard, 1977.

as father-figures during the shooting of a film. But there were very few men who dominated her in this protective way. Yves Montand would be her equal, although there were times when she gave way to him, not from weakness but because she felt that this was the right way for a wife to behave. Simone Signoret was far from being a feminist; nevertheless she would invariably find herself at the top, leading others. For her friends she was a central figure, and as far as actors were concerned, only Jean Gabin, who played opposite her in *Le Chat*, proved a match for her.

In any case, for the time being, romance played second fiddle to the real, important events going on at the Café de Flore, in the streets of Saint-Germain-des-Prés, and from time to time in the film studios. The Flore contingent even took off on a trip to the South-West, near Dax, for the shooting of a film by the Prévert brothers, called *Adieu Léonard*. 'What luck to be young, with those people, and in that production where there wasn't the slightest discrimination between actors, technicians and stars.'[1] The little extra made friends with Pierre Brasseur, Carette, and Charles Trenet.

With Yves Allégret, her lover of the moment who was eagerly awaiting her return from Dax, the flirtation between the Flore and the cinema would blossom into a real marriage, although it would not be celebrated officially until 1948, two years after the birth of little Catherine. When he met Simone, Yves Allégret was a married man, with a son called Gilles. Separated from his wife for two years, he was part of the group called 'Les Croque-Fruits', pillars of pre-war Saint-Germain-des-Prés who went down to Marseilles at the time of the Nazi take-over, hoping to escape from France into Spain or Portugal; trapped in the Free Zone, they took on jobs in a boiled-sweet factory, but, gradually consumed by longing for the big city, they crept back to Paris, preceded by a flurry of rumours. 'Jacques is coming!' (Meaning Prévert.) 'Yves is on his way!' (Allégret.) Yves had been one of Trotsky's secretaries at Barbizon. But, above all, he was the director Marc Allégret's younger brother, destined for the cinema (though his first film had been destroyed in a laboratory fire).

[1]*Nostalgia . . .* op.cit.

CATHERINE DAVID

The STO[1] were looking for Yves, and so, on D-Day, he took Simone and her friends Serge Reggiani, Daniel Gélin and Danièle Delorme off to La Sapinière, the house in the Haute-Marne that belonged to his father, Pastor Allégret. In this country retreat, they savoured the joys of the Liberation of Paris from afar, and it was there that, one fine day, they met their first Americans, and eagerly asked them for news of Louis Armstrong, George Gershwin and Clark Gable. A budding actress, a promising young director . . . their future was a starry one.

---

[1] *Service Travail Obligatoire*, a Vichy law which provided a workforce for the Germans.

CHAPTER FOUR

In *Cinémonde* on 2 April 1954, there is a profile of Simone Signoret put together by a certain 'G.B.': it starts with a description of the shooting years before Yves Allégret's *Les Démons de l'aube*, on the outskirts of Marseilles. The mysterious G.B. (an excellent journalist) describes the rising star of the French screen as she appeared at the time of the Liberation.

'She was a typical young actress,' wrote G.B., 'a tough little thing, spunky and tremendously Parisian; she used to sit for hours on a spit of rock above the sea, interminably sewing. She was curious about everything, and she read a great deal more than is usual for young ladies who feel they are destined to appear on screen. She was greedy for everything, in a nice way, and she'd fall avidly on anything that could tell her something she didn't know about a painter or a musician or a favourite film director. At the same time, her ideas were pretty dogmatic, and we knew at once that nothing would make her change them.

'Partly for her own benefit, partly for others, she used to recite chunks of Jarry, Lautréamont, Max Jacob or Prévert. After this we'd go for a dip in the sea, until an assistant came along to get her out of the water: it was "her" scene. In her bathing-suit or blue jeans, with her hair pulled back and no make-up, she was just like anyone else, a comrade among many others.

'When, a bit later on, she came under the cameras, I could hardly recognise her. Where was the tomboy who swam and played games with us? Instead, here was a siren with hollow cheeks, a pouting mouth like ripe fruit, slanting eyes. Even her walk was different: before, it had been casual, now it was quasi-provocative.

A barmaid in a soldiers' dive, she was supposed in this scene to kiss a young simpleton who couldn't pluck up the courage to do his manly duty. A classic scene, apparently without much scope for variation, which is why, on set, we all suddenly had a sense of revelation: she was born for the cinema, there were no two ways about it, her performance was like a second birth. A sensual little animal, a cat down to her claws and purr, she transformed that kiss into one of the most straightforwardly erotic moments of contemporary cinema . . . From that day on, the sailors would look at her with new eyes and ingratiating smiles, and would unfurl the red ribbons on their berets for her benefit.

'But next day she put on her blue jeans and espadrilles again, lit a Gauloise, and asked for her round of cheap red wine.'

What G.B. does not say is that this alluring young woman was pregnant by her director. In *Les Démons de l'aube*, Yves Allégret had given her her first proper speaking role, even if it was still just a bit-part; he had also given her a child. Eight days after the film was released, Simone Signoret gave birth to Catherine. She was a wanted child, all the more so since, a year ago, there had been another baby, conceived in the middle of the war, who had not survived. But Catherine's arrival coincided with the spectacular take-off of her mother's career. Simone's world was suddenly opening up. People were grabbing at her, she was in demand, but she had this big stomach, this baby which had to be pampered. The film world was after her, they wanted her for big parts. She had dreamed about this for so long; but what about Catherine? Her mind was in a turmoil.

Three weeks after the birth, she was due to have a test-screening for a film directed by Marcel Blisthène, called *Macadam*. She was breast-feeding Catherine, but she still believed that she could combine everything. She asked, therefore, if she could be tested between noon and three o'clock, in between feeds. Of course, she was there all day, and got the main part in the film, fighting back the milk as she did it. The conclusion was inevitable: an actress cannot be an ordinary mother. It was best to give up motherhood at once, and to face the facts. And so she would not be for her daughter what Georgette Kaminker had been for her, a constant, supportive maternal presence. She was sorry, but that was life;

she could not give up the cinema. For the first time, she was being offered the starring role. She pressed her swollen breasts, out of joy. She had already been a mother, a long time ago, when she had looked after her little brother, so that she knew she was capable of maternal feeling. But she no longer had the time for it, she had to follow her vocation. They were calling her, they were shouting for her, her dream was coming true, the secret dream that she used to whisper to herself in bed before she went to sleep: 'I'm going to be an actress, I'm going to be in films, I'm going to be a star.'

In *Macadam*, Simone Signoret found herself on an equal footing with actors of the very first rank: Françoise Rosay, Andrée Clément, Paul Meurisse. It was a disjointed tale, with jewel-thefts, denunciations, and serial-killings in Montmartre. She played the part of Gisèle, a girl of easy virtue who isn't quite a professional tart. A killer's mistress, Gisèle falls in love with an innocent, dreamy handkerchief salesman whom her wicked lover has sent her to seduce. Changed by true love, she tips the scales in favour of the 'good guys'. Simone Signoret's newly minted talent blossomed thanks to this transformation. She clearly had a gift for expressing love: one believed in her; she glowed. This intensity wasn't part of her acting; it came from an inner truth, deep within her. As Daniel Gélin writes in his memoirs: 'Simone was made for love, like the inevitability of the seasons, the rhythm of the tides, the divinity of the sun or the brotherhood of the earth. Love was her true vocation.' One day, one man, Yves Montand, would become the sole object of this vocation.

On a cover of *Cinévie* dated 12 November 1946, a close-up of her face looks almost Cubist, because of all the retouching that has been done. The caption runs: 'Simone Signoret falls in love in *Macadam*.' Look at her: a wax doll. There's a fringe of perfectly spaced eyelashes over her eyelid, making a delicate rim around the jewel-like eye. Her gaze is lost in the mists of a deathless ecstasy; her hair falls in sculpted waves around the oval of her face. Her mouth is like a cherry, ready for eating. Her eyebrows are neatly plucked, and look like two birds trapped in full flight at the base of her forehead. You have to concentrate to find any likeness between this improvised photographic plate, and the real Simone Signoret.

It was a curious fashion, inherited from pre-war films, a fashion that superimposed the mask of the myth so strongly on the woman's face that the latter almost disappeared: as if the main purpose were not to show faces, but to hide them.

Simone Signoret and others like her would shatter this mask. She enjoyed showing her real face, which was so well structured, and so intensely expressive, that make-up hardly seemed to touch it. The surface was beautiful, but there was something else there, deep down inside: energy, vigour, a zest for life. All this came through not only in her look, but in her squarish cheeks, the sensuality of her mouth and her serenely curving brow, and made her inimitable and, in a way, unalterable. The photograph in *Cinévie* is an exception. Simone Signoret had no need of a mask.

She would not be afraid of continuing to show her face, with all its dreadful ravages, up until the age when no retouching, however artistic, could have erased the wrinkles.

But it was always the same face.

I have always wanted to believe that it is possible to live several lives in one, and that a new life can start for each of us right up until the last minute of our existence, if only we can learn to face the future without fear. Simone Signoret developed to the highest degree a talent for renewing life, for rekindling passion, for starting the adventure all over again. She never seemed to be frightened, or, if she was, she would never hold back, for she was propelled by intensely powerful feelings derived from childhood. Her curiosity remained on the alert until the very end. That she succeeded more than most in living several different existences to the full must be due to her profound sense of inner stability, which, like a fixed lodestar, helped her to change without losing her way. It was always there, like a nightlight in the dark.

This limitless self-renewal was also a professional duty for an actress like Signoret. The lives of her screen-characters – her 'lodgers', as she called them – added to her own experiences and enriched them. She threw herself into her parts, and, like the real one, her fictional self was different every time. She would prepare herself psychologically, she would let the 'other', the woman in the film, settle in and make her nest in her clothes, her furniture, her body. Her choice of costume was a crucial part of this phase, and it is no accident that she made Sonia and Olga, the two heroines of *Adieu Volodia*, theatrical dressmakers.

For Simone Signoret, acting was above all dressing up, like a little girl at play. 'I was, I am, I will be, I hope, somebody who keeps on dressing up, like a repertory actress who is offered lots of different jobs, and is amazed that she's still wanted.' She believed in the reality of outward show, and she knew better than anyone how accurately appearances can indicate what is going on inside. She knew how a mask betrays the personality, or clothes one's state of mind, how a look reveals the inner soul and a voice the music that is playing within.

Choosing the right dress, handbag, hairstyle and make-up, without cheating or trying to make oneself beautiful if the part did not require it: this was all-important. The Casque d'Or whom cinema-goers remember as a dazzling apparition owes an enormous amount to details, accessories and hairstyle, to the way her hair was piled up, and her short fringe was carefully teased over that radiant face. Hair was the director Jacques Becker's first priority: 'He took me straight to the hairdresser for a platinum-blonde job, announcing that he would collect me at noon to check that the colour was right. After that we'd have lunch, then we'd go and see about the costumes, after which we'd order the shoes . . . Jacques bent over the roots of my hair like Pasteur over his microscope.'[1] At the other end of the spectrum, one thinks of poor Jeanne's too-short raincoat in René Allio's *Rude journée pour la Reine*, and the clumsy parting in her grey hair, her flat shoes, flower-patterned apron and her frizzy perm.

Simone Signoret would talk very freely about the crucial importance of costume, saying that the reason why actors make so much fuss about it is not capriciousness (as is too often thought) but a genuine desire to do the job properly; they want to become the 'other', the ghostly stranger who has to be born in their body. In *Adieu Volodia*, she describes in almost obsessive detail how the actors who came to get their costumes at Masques et Bergamasques were thrilled when they 'suddenly recognised, on a new costume,

[1]*Nostalgia* . . . op.cit.

for a new part, a scrap of material, wisp of lace or two or three ornamental buttons that they'd already worn in other parts. It was like finding mementoes of an old love-affair, and they loved it.' Just as she had loved the idea of wearing Jean Gabin's sandals in the theatre.

One day, while she was playing in *Les Diaboliques*, she spotted an extra from Jean Renoir's *French Cancan* on the next-door set, wearing one of Casque D'Or's dresses. For a moment Simone felt betrayed and dispossessed, as if this young woman had stolen her dress, the dress that was hers in another life, and along with it a part of herself.

For Simone Signoret, the cinema was not a self-indulgent game, but a deep commitment, renewed every time she took on a new part.'You ask her to lie down in a bath, telling her she's underwater. Leave her there for two minutes, and you'll come back and find her drowned.'[1] She entered a film role with her eyes wide open, like a child venturing into one of Mary Poppins' magic pictures, longing to fill the unbridgeable gap that separates human beings from each other, longing to get outside herself and to find out what goes on inside another person's mind, body or memory. Becoming somebody else is also a way of getting to know oneself better, at a distance – much better than looking in the mirror.

But there was still something unchanging in her, an incomparable 'something', a depth of character, a mysterious quality called 'presence' that drew one's attention as soon as she appeared on screen, that made her the centre of her circle of friends, and, in the France of the last twenty years, turned her into a symbol of the dramas and pleasures of her generation. She was true to herself and to her secret inner feelings, but she also felt compelled to open herself to others: it was probably this tension that made her so strong.

Some human beings, right from the start, seem all of a piece because of the nature of their ambition: they settle into a single track and tirelessly dig the same furrow, until, with luck, they produce a river, a torrent, a finished work. They stride through the

---

[1]Jean-Louis Trintignant, *Un homme à sa fenêtre*, Simoën, 1977.

jungle of possibilities, pushing back the branches and discarding any materials that are not relevant. We describe these lucky people as simply having a 'vocation'; we envy them and respect their single-mindedness.

Others are open to the frightening range of choices and different lifestyles, and tirelessly travel from one world to another, from literature to politics, from the stage to poetry, from daydreaming to public fame, as if they had to get to know the whole world, and live every kind of human experience, their own and other people's. They seem to practise diversity like a sort of ascetic religion, a 'diaspora' of knowledge. Simone Signoret was one of these explorers: in espadrilles or high-heels, she wanted to know and to try everything. At this point, when her career seemed set on a brilliant course, she was drunk on the elixir of discovery.

'That did it, I was off and running! Things picked up: it didn't occur to me then that one could make a film without a firm contract for the next one.' After *Macadam*, she came together again with Marcel Herrand, whom she had got to know during the shooting of *Visiteurs du soir*. Draped in a cowl, he played Fantômas in a modernist version, with helicopters, electronic gadgets and death-rays. His daughter, Simone Signoret, ran down a long corridor filled with bones: 'The glaring light from a projector aimed at her and at the bones around her made her pale hair sparkle, and made the look in her eyes almost supernatural, by violently accentuating the pure lines of her face,' wrote a journalist who was present on the set.

But it was *Dédée d'Anvers* in 1947 that would make her a full-time star. In a role specially written for her by Jacques Sigurd and Yves Allégret, she enlarged her range, but stayed in the same register as in *Les Démons de l'aube*. For, once again, she plays a streetwalker transformed by love.

The rain is falling on grey Anvers, an industrial port where northern melancholy casts a pall over the silhouettes of passers-by and the faces of the girls splashing through the puddles. Over in a prostitutes' bar, beautiful Dédée is trying to coach a good-natured pimp, played by Bernard Blier. But she is out of place, she's not made for the job, she has too much dignity, too much class. When her protector maltreats her, she does nothing to resist. But one morning, a ship comes into the harbour. Standing on the bridge, a man steers it in – Marcel Pagliero, the very picture of *gravitas*. Dédée's eyes meet his as the foghorn wails like a signal, and a great love is born. Dédée decides to change her life, to leave this dismal town and escape across the sea with her new love. But her pimp has other ideas. He steals into the harbour under cover of darkness and there, amid the huge silent cargo-boats, he shoots a bullet into the back of the man who has stolen the goose that laid the golden eggs.

'With *Dédée d'Anvers*, Simone Signoret has finally found the part she was looking for, which immediately raises her up with the first rank of French screen actresses. If she doesn't waste her talent, she will go far,' wrote the *Paris-Presse* film critic, expressing the general view. For Simone Signoret, the wager had been won: she was talented, people loved her, but above all, they found her different. She didn't belong with the china-doll types of star who featured in magazines; she was unique, everybody felt it and noticed it. Was it her disdainful moue, or the pride that she showed in every gesture? Perhaps; her acting style was hers, and hers only. Totally identifying with her screen character, she did everything by a look, an imperceptible shrug of the shoulders, a quickened step, or the shadow of a smile. Anything would do. What made Simone Signoret so different from the others was her extraordinary economy of methods and the secret passion that animated her.

It was up to her to prove that she was not one of those actresses without creative flair who repeat themselves over and over again and always play the same character. She knew there was a danger of being 'typecast as a tart', and she already had a fairly clear idea of what she would *not* do. 'There are some things that nobody can force me to do. No means no. In life, I haven't done all I would have liked to do, but I've never done anything I didn't want to!'[1]

Those down-to-earth working-class parts became a trademark. Right up until *Madame le Juge* in the eighties, she would retain the 'common touch', a streak of populism. Her '*grande dame*' roles were

---

[1] Interview in *Elle* magazine, 21 January 1985.

few and far between. In Stanley Kramer's *Ship of Fools* she played a countess, but a morphine addict. In *Rude journée pour la Reine*, she's a queen, but only in a cleaning-woman's imagination. Even Thérèse Humbert, the empress, only reigns over Paris because of a gigantic confidence-trick. And Lady Macbeth, whom she played at the Royal Court Theatre in London, was the biggest setback of her whole career.

And, looking back, it is hard to imagine her playing ingénues or terrified virgins. The middle-class girl from Neuilly looked, and felt, like a Parisian street-kid. She was drawn to anything working class or left wing, and, the sexual side apart, this would be the key to her original attraction to Yves Montand. As a popular singer who made ordinary, humble people dream, he was bound to appeal to her. She had a natural taste for raillery, for street-slang and low life, for cheap red wine, the kind that stains, and Gauloises Caporal. All these were her symbols of belonging to the big family of the Left, her way of being up-to-date, at a time when intellectuals, beguiled by the myth of the proletariat, would construct a whole lifestyle out of a political idea, to disguise their middle-class backgrounds. But for Simone, it was also a spontaneous reaction, dating back to her father's vain attempts to interest her in Boni de Castellane. She had never been impressed by middle-class trappings: she preferred bric-à-brac to period furniture, and basic table manners to dainty teacups held with the little finger crooked. Her attitudes and clothes were dictated by her idea of the Left, of culture and the Modern, but she had also inherited some of her mother's intransigence: Georgette Kaminker had remained faithful to her modest origins, and had always refused to let her husband lure her into well-heeled respectability.

During the next year, she worked with Marcel Herrand, Paul Meurisse and Danièle Delorme on Maurice Tourneur's last film, *Impasse des Deux-Anges*. It would be torn apart by the critics, but the setback did no harm to her image: 'Her silences are just as important as her words,' wrote Jean-Jacques Gautier in *Le Figaro*. 'She acts with her mouth, her eyes and her skin. In this film her temperament is much more powerful than her role.'

The love-affair with Yves Allégret was still going strong; he offered her her first role as a 'baddy' in *Manèges*. This time she

CATHERINE DAVID

is no longer a 'tart with a heart of gold', but a 'metaphysical whore', to use Georges Sadoul's[1] expression. Dora is malevolent down to the ends of her pretty painted nails, manipulated by a devilish mother, Jane Marken, who encourages her to bleed her lovelorn, simple-minded husband, Bernard Blier, dry. 'I naïvely took on Dora in *Manèges* – that monster, that bitch, that liar, that real whore without a pavement or a pimp – cooked up by Sigurd and Allégret,' she writes in *Nostalgia Isn't What It Used To Be.*

When *Manèges* came out, she was amazed that people in the street gave her black looks. They hated her for treating poor Bernard Blier so badly; it was quite different from the friendly smiles she had received after *Dédée D'Anvers*. She was discovering how hard it was for actors to disassociate themselves from their parts in the public's eye. Identification was irresistible, and she would later tell how even Yves Montand was surprised by how hostile he felt towards an actor who played the villain in one of his films. 'If people adored Dédée, it was because of her misfortunes – that poor creature, so sweet, so generous, basically a victim of society. If I'd understood that at the time, I'd only have played sympathetic characters, and would have deprived myself of a great deal of pleasure.'[2] Later on, in Clouzot's *Les Diaboliques*, she would repeat the *Manèges* experience a hundredfold. But she was fond of her characters, even the nastiest ones. What counted was the film as a whole: 'I can easily play a Gestapo informer in an anti-fascist film, but I can't play a model mother or a proud mistress in a fascist film.'[3]

With *Dédée D'Anvers*, the new star's fame crossed the Atlantic. The film's success in New York attracted the attention of the big Californian studios to the Signoret-Allégret couple. After lengthy discussions, Simone Signoret signed a four-year contract with Howard Hughes for one film a year, to be mutually agreed. This was preferential treatment when the norm was the notorious 'lion's share' seven-year contract, which tied the actor's hands and feet to the producer's whims. But fate was to reduce the contract to a mere

[1] A Communist critic, who wrote for *Les Lettres Françaises.*
[2] Interview in *Le Nouvel Observateur*, 27 March 1982.
[3] *Nostalgia . . .* op.cit.

47

scrap of paper. Nobody could have foreseen it, but *Manèges* would be the last film that Signoret and Allégret would make together. Her conquest of America was still to come.

After they had finished shooting *Manèges*, she took Catherine and Gilles, Allégret's son, with her to recuperate at Saint-Paul-de-Vence at the idyllic Colombe D'Or which she had gazed at so enviously when they were making *Visiteurs du soir*. Now she could afford it, she belonged to the magic world of the stars. At last, she could devote herself to her daughter – at least, for several days . . .

CHAPTER FIVE

A man has appeared in front of her on the terrace, amidst the flowers and doves under the wide blue sky, the Provençal tiles and the dry branches twisting up towards the sky. He too is a celebrity – Yves Montand, the rising star of the French music hall. On stage, he is dynamite: young girls faint away as they listen to him. Housewives, workmen, children, all join in the same communion of adoration. He is a great shambling figure with a wide smile that makes his ears shoot up into his bushy hair, an elongated, endless, elastic acrobat's body, a loping stride, bright eyes, a forehead as wide as a field, and the warm voice of a Marseilles crooner with class.

19 August 1949: one of those dates that mark the end of one era and the beginning of another.

The post-war period was ending, wounds were starting to heal, the future seemed radiant, and children were being born in hundreds of thousands in a France where reconstruction was in full swing; it was a magical time for songs and laughter, for falling in love. Yves Montand was a son of the people who charmed the middle classes because 'he was the perfect incarnation of the cheerful mechanic with dirty hands and a pure heart'.[1] He had a self-made man's halo of prestige, coming as he did from the Marseilles slums, from a family of Italian immigrants who had settled in La Cabucelle, a poor quarter where only a genius could imagine any other way of life. He invented himself out of almost nothing – a Fred Astaire song, a Trenet tune, a desire to break into

[1]*Le Chant d'un homme* by Richard Cannavo and Henri Quiqueré, Robert Laffont, 1981.

49

song, to dance, to make women laugh. He did not go to secondary school; he learned only from the street. The Livi family, anti-fascist peasants, fled from Tuscany to escape Mussolini's myrmidons. Ivo, the little Italian, grew up among the dockers, wandering about the port; he worked in a factory at the age of eleven, and in a hairdresser's salon at thirteen. But he was a singing bird, and, gradually, swept along by his dream and by the energy of youth, Ivo Livi became the romantic singer Yves Montand. He made his début at seventeen in a derelict barn in the suburbs of Marseilles, in front of fifty peanut-munching housewives on an improvised stage 'made of planks and mason's trestles which were used as scaffolding during the week'. In wartime, he 'busked' during the intervals in cinema-theatres.

One day in 1944, he received a notice from the STO, and escaped in his own fashion, by moving to Paris. There he performed his own kind of Resistance, circus-style, by singing cowboy songs like *The Plains of the Far West* or *He Sold Hot Dogs on Times Square*. He would come on stage brazenly shouting 'Hello, boys!' to provoke the odd bewildered German in the audience. Then a miracle happened: he met Edith Piaf. She was already famous; she filled the Moulin-Rouge every night and was looking for a singer to impersonate an American star in her act. The first impression was disastrous. She mistrusted this professional seducer, she did not like his 'greedy, bully-boy style'. But he sang for her, and like everybody else she was won over by the charm of this overgrown youth with his precise but airy gestures. He found her attractive, with a great sense of humour, a free-spirited, cheerful woman, very different from the tragic Piaf of the last years. 'She was great fun, and loved a good laugh. At the time that I met her, she was very, very pretty. Other people probably didn't get to know her properly until near the end of her life, when she had gone completely to pieces from the drugs she took after her motor accident.'[1]

For three years they sang together, as lovers and working partners. And she became his inspiration. She sensibly advised him to give up American songs; they were out of date, the world

[1]*Le Chant d'un homme*, op.cit.

4222

was splitting into two blocs, and the United States was no longer top dog. 'Choose songs for tomorrow, not just today.' They went on long trips in an open car; Montand's repertoire increased and diversified. His friend Prévert wrote lyrics which Kosma set to music. One day, Prévert introduced Francis Lemarque, a penniless young man who did not know Montand but spent his time writing songs for him, just for him, after hearing him sing only once. He would write Montand dozens of songs, and the two would become inseparable.

But Edith Piaf, the tragic actress, knew how to be cruel. When she left him, overnight, after three years of love and fun, she knew that she had finished her task as Pygmalion. She had refined and perfected him, changed the provincial youth into a Parisian, the housewives' heart-throb into a romantic crooner. She wrote songs for him and changed his 'look', she modernised his repertoire – in short, she launched him. Partly thanks to her help and advice, he became famous. But now that they were equals on stage, filled the same houses and made the same audiences laugh or cry, he did not need her any more. What she had loved in him, apart from the sexual attraction, was precisely that unfinished quality, his rough-and-ready side, his beginner's pent-up energy. He listened to her, transformed himself and gradually became his own master. With nothing more to teach him, she could no longer love him.

In the wake of the break-up, she wrote some wonderful, crowd-pulling songs. She needed heartbreak to stretch her range. It was one or the other – passion or tragedy. She rejected long-drawn-out endings, where passion expires like embers in an abandoned stove, where love fades into friendship. Drama was the stuff of Piaf's life, and when it was not spontaneous she would manufacture it. 'Unconsciously, it was the only way she had of singing as amazingly as she did. She sang marvellously when she was in love, and she sang marvellously when she was in pieces.'[1] Montand suffered too, but resigned himself to the inevitable. He consoled himself with the 'groupies' who would fall into his arms after each concert: nothing serious, just a diversion to bolster his ego and prove his powers as a Don Juan.

[1] *Le Chant d'un homme*, op.cit.

Wherever Montand went, in his famous brown suit, tieless, he would sing to packed audiences and bring the house down. But appalling stagefright overcame him every evening, as he waited for the curtain to go up. From six o'clock, he was inaccessible, self-enclosed. Colleagues tried to protect him, and avoided speaking to him, while he sweated with terror. He would wipe his hands and forehead, and talk to himself. He would say that stagefright was a necessary evil, that Jacques Brel would vomit before going on stage.

'A red curtain goes up in front of a black one,' wrote Prévert. 'With his eyes, his dazzling smile, the movements of his hands, he sketches his own set . . .' His lightness of touch was the result of single-minded, desperate effort. He would spend hours doing his scales in front of a mirror, with his cane and top hat. He had guts. Every evening, standing alone on stage facing the dark mass of the public, he was on the edge of the abyss: 'The complicated thing about this job is that every second you have to re-invent instinct. Every night, every second, for every movement or tone of voice, you have to re-invent what you've done a thousand times before.'[1] He had a way of mingling laughter with tears, nostalgia with hope, tenderness with anger . . . Above all, he had an inborn knack of making every woman in the audience think that he was singing for her alone.

On that summer night, he was twenty-eight. Sophisticated yet adventurous, he was ready for new experiences. It was his day off; on a tour of the Côte d'Azur, he had come to dine at the Colombe d'Or with his guitarist Henri Crolla, an old *habitué* of the Flore, and his pianist Bob Castella.

'There is a sun-drenched courtyard, old houses with tiles like fish-scales, a circle of hills: it's Provence, and even the wind is kind and still. In the centre of the courtyard, surrounded by doves, is a young woman with ash-blonde hair.

'She's wearing blue trousers and an open-necked shirt. She's smiling like the girls in the Italian Old Masters. I know that her name is Simone Signoret, I've never seen her films, I've never met

[1]*Le Chant d'un homme*, op.cit.

her, but I know that I'm going to walk towards her, trying not to disturb the doves, and say a few words to make her turn towards me, just a few words, without frightening the doves . . .'[1]

The doves did not move. Time was suspended.

Freeze-frame: love at first sight in the noonday sun. The ladykiller is touched to the heart by this luminous, fresh young woman, who embodies all the graces. The bloom of youth, the halo of fame, the outspokenness, the intelligence . . . they are all there. She excites him, daunts him. Her face is on the cover of the film magazines, but she's also read all the books, she's an intellectual. Don Juan is as shy as a virgin. But he hides it, and comes on like a conqueror, charming, irresistible, making her laugh and playing the fool. Quickly the first attraction makes way for love – deep, innocent, overwhelming love. They talk, they hold hands, kiss. They are insatiable; the Colombe d'Or has turned into a love-nest. 'It was a wonderful day,' Montand continues, 'and I'll never get tired of going over the details with my magnifying glass – her blonde hair, the burning sun and the exact moment when Simone watched me coming towards her . . .'

In the hotel, everybody was confused – children, management, guests. Yves and Simone were not thirty yet, but they had outgrown crushes. They knew that it was not just another flash in the pan. Soon Montand would lay down his conditions: an ultimatum, with no appeal. It was all or nothing, he wanted her for himself alone, for life. He would be a real Italian husband, possessive and jealous. Simone would not hesitate. Allégret was no match against her certainty: she had to live with Montand. If he had been less demanding, he might have lost her. In taking over all of her, in 'ravishing' her, in both senses, he tightened his grip. Confronted with the expression of such an overwhelming desire, she embraced his love like a religious faith.

Yves Montand was a solitary, bear-like creature, focused on his work, his career and his musicians. By contrast, Simone Signoret spent her time making friends. She already had a little world around her: and she brought this world of her friends to him like a part of herself.

[1]*Le Chant d'un homme*, op. cit.

53

SIMONE SIGNORET

Simone Signoret would carry on Piaf's work. She was the same age, a woman of character and culture. But the more she dominated him intellectually, the more she played the submissive, adoring female. He was the master, she would follow him anywhere. This man should be boss. Anyone who did not like Montand was now barred from her presence. At the centre of the circle, the court, there were now two, the king and the queen. The Place Dauphine where they were to set up house in Paris would be secretly rechristened by their friends as the 'Place Yves-et-Simone'. But instead of blinding her, love would open her eyes, make her attentive to the weaknesses of this much-loved man who was also vulnerable and narcissistic, capable of being immoderate, clumsy and naïve. She would protect him from himself. Steering with a pilot's expertise, with maternal loyalty and tact, she would help him to face new challenges in politics, cinema and fame. This inveterate womaniser would owe much to a few exceptional women.

Their love was a public event, from the very start. It started in full force, in broad daylight, on the terrace of a hotel filled with friends – 'the only four-star hotel where the bar is a village pub'[1] – and it would always bear the stamp of its spectacular beginning. 'If I had met Montand in a foreign town, far from everyone I knew, or anyone who knew Montand or Allégret, there wouldn't have been witnesses; we wouldn't have lived our story under many eyes, which magnified everything.'

The glowing couple stood for all our romantic dreams: love, youth, beauty, fame, under the blue sky of Provence, among the doves. And this great love-affair would become a myth for a whole generation. For – miraculously – it lasted! That was the official version. And there was some reality in the fiction of a perfect union which helped make them a glorious national heritage – a pair of guardian angels. The truth is still uncertain. Only they could have told it and yet – did they know, do we ever really know the truth about the story while we are living it?

A few days later, Yves Allégret was expected at the Colombe d'Or, to rejoin his wife and children. She could not lie to him:

[1] *Nostalgia . . .* op.cit.

everything was already clear. Simone had no wish for him to learn the truth via the anxious looks of their friends. It was up to her, and she did not flinch from the painful task. She went, alone, down the road to meet him and to tell him the bad news. But however veiled her look, she could not disguise her exultation.

CHAPTER SIX

From now on, there was no question of either of them going to America. 'Without Montand, you couldn't have made me go from the Porte de Vincennes to the Porte d'Asnières. As for America . . .'[1] Bringing her suitcases but not Catherine, who stayed with her father for the time being, Simone installed herself in Neuilly, where Montand had a small flat. She was not enthusiastic about returning to her childhood haunts: too many memories lurked under those shrubberies. And in the bedroom she could still detect the lingering perfume of the pretty girls who had been the bachelor's night-companions. The maid would come in and announce in cheeky tones that 'Mademoiselle Josette rang again at four o'clock'. They needed a proper home, a new place.

They were inseparable: she followed him on tour – all she wanted to do – and even forgot the cinema. She loved her new job. To tremble for him each night; to hover in the corridors during the show; to inspect the women in the audience, and guess how star-struck they were; to devour him with her eyes, then later fold him, sweaty and exhausted, in her arms – she had never experienced such pleasure. The man who made hearts throb in darkened halls was hers alone. She savoured the growing adoration for this demi-god of the music hall. That other women loved him was exciting. But she would not share him – far from it. The film actress, José Artur, recalls a concert of Montand's at the Alcazar in Marseilles in the early fifties: 'Yves Montand announced "Amour, Mon Cher Amour". Up in the gods, the

[1]*Nostalgia* . . . op.cit.

56

lovelorn, sweetly lubricious voice of a very young girl let out a long sigh, like an orgasm. Simone looked up and, with exquisite refinement, murmured, "Bitch!" under her breath. That was when I really started to like her!'[1] At that stage, Simone considered a healthy jealousy to be an essential component of love. Later, after the Marilyn episode, she would have to adjust her theory to circumstances. Jealousy would no longer be the proud possessiveness of a triumphant, beloved mistress, but a secret wound that refused to heal.

For now, she saw herself as a perpetual groupie, a 'little woman' in ecstasy in the shadow of the singer. 'As for America . . .' Yves Montand had made the mistake of signing one of the notorious seven-year contracts with Warner Brothers. Breaking it was difficult. But, in any case, a year later, it was the Americans who would not want either Simone Signoret or Yves Montand. They had become Red devils, because they had signed the Stockholm Petition. Two great lions had just entered the political arena. Despairing of winning the war against Japan, who was sending Kamikaze pilots to bomb American warships, Harry Truman pressed the red button and Hiroshima was wiped off the map. Born out of Hitler's lust for destruction, the bomb would bring in a new age in which humanity could destroy itself. Intellectuals saw the bomb, along with the Nazi concentration camps, as representing absolute evil. But they still desperately hoped they could make it disappaear, and ban it. That was the aim of the Stockholm Petition.

Since the bomb was American, they launched the protest against the USA. It was a far cry from the Occupation, when singing cowboy songs had been Yves Montand's way of supporting the Resistance. Besides, the country was deteriorating. The frustrations of the Cold War and Senator McCarthy's machinations had produced the anti-Communist witch-hunt that gripped the United States like a fever. Anyone who, at any stage of life, had harboured sinister left-wing sympathies was considered suspect. It was enough to have given a dollar or two, before the war, to an appeal for the Republican side in Spain, to be questioned and

[1] *Micro de nuit*, Stock, 1974.

harried by the all-powerful Committee for Un-American Activities. Informing was encouraged, and paid for. Reeling from the shock of denunciations, including one by Elia Kazan, Hollywood was in a major crisis. Joseph Losey, Jules Dassin and John Berry would emigrate for ever; Dashiell Hammett, author of *The Maltese Falcon*, was in prison. Soon, under the agonised gaze of his wife, Marilyn Monroe, Arthur Miller would have to reply to a series of incredible interrogations. Julius and Ethel Rosenberg, accused of spying for the Russians, were executed without proper evidence, after a travesty of a trial.

Meanwhile, on the other side of the globe, under the magic rod of the 'people's little Father', other liberators, other heroes of the battle against the Nazis were building a better world, where they proclaimed the workers were finally in control of their own destiny, and where Justice and Equality had replaced oppression. As if to prove it, the European countries that had been freed from the Nazi yoke by the brave Red Army were converted one by one to the new ideas. On one side, the heroes of Stalingrad, the millions of dead sacrificed to the war against Hitler. On the other, the nation that had bombed Hiroshima. On the one side, a classless society, whose aims were the abolition of the State and a tomorrow without fear, with the hope of redeeming mankind through the march of History. On the other, the capitalist jungle and the scramble for profit, the rule of the dollar, social inequality, colonial imperialism. How could one possibly get it wrong?

The Stockholm Petition, 'priority action' for the French Communist Party of the period, collected 273 million signatures throughout the world (which admittedly included a block of 115 million Soviet names). In France, several millions of people willingly signed what they saw as a petition for world peace. Among them were people of every political hue. Some of them, like Maurice Chevalier or Fernandel, would later publicly regret having lent their names to what the right-wing press branded as a Communist propaganda exercise. But for other, more politically aware people, like Gérard Philipe, Picasso, Roger Vailland, Claude Roy or François Périer, the Stockholm Petition was an opportunity for taking up a moral position.

For Simone Signoret, the ground had already been prepared by her mother's political convictions. But her first real meeting with the Left dates back to the Flore days. It was a heterogeneous, intellectual Left, as much the product of anarchism and Trotskyism as of Stalinist orthodoxy: a tribe, a clan, an adoptive family. But for Yves Montand the Left was *the* family, his real one, his anti-fascist father, his trade-unionist brother, a CGT[1] militant since 1933. When he took his young fiancée to meet his parents in La Cabucelle, she saw working-class life from the inside for the first time in her life. 'It was the first time that I sat down at a table among people who had all worked in factories for most of their lives.'[2] She could now measure the size of the chasms that Montand had had to cross, from La Cabucelle to the théâtre de l'Étoile. She had met plenty of leftists, but from an abstract, idealistic left. In Marseilles, she would penetrate the slum where her lover had grown up: 'The sirens of the gasworks, the gut factory and the docks were the chronometers of the whole district.'

For the rest of their lives Simone Signoret and Yves Montand would take up strong positions on major contemporary problems. Acting on sudden whims and gusts of emotion, they would agitate, mobilise themselves and take up cudgels on behalf of the underprivileged of this earth. Even if they got it slightly wrong . . . In the fifties, while the French Army was floundering in the mud of Indo-China and the Americans were bombing Korea, it went without saying that men and women of goodwill would follow the Left, and the workers' party. Later, they would learn the truth about the sinister reality of the so-called 'socialist paradises', and, with some agony of mind, they would finally detach themselves from an unquestioning loyalty which could no longer be a substitute for a political conscience. From then on, they would only commit themselves to individual cases, leaving ideological references behind. But, for now, there was no room for doubt. Faith in Stalinism, conqueror of the Nazi monster, liberator of peoples and defender of the exploited proletariat, was

[1]Confédération Générale de Travail, a trade union.
[2]*Nostalgia* . . . op.cit.

an irrefutable dogma. 'When Jacques Prévert warned me against Stalinism, I told myself, "Jacques is a poet." He never pressed me. He knew that he was dealing with a bigot, and that there is no arguing with bigots.'[1]

Signoret and Montand were not card-carrying members of the French Communist Party. 'We're engaged, but we're not getting married.' It was a difficult position. The pressure on them to join was very strong, particularly from Julien Livi, the trade-unionist brother. Many important intellectuals were Communists, like Aragon, whose books Simone Signoret had read with passionate interest. It was honourable and prestigious to belong to the party of the 20 million dead. Nevertheless, Signoret and Montand were not paid-up; they wanted to be committed, but free. Politically, they were convinced, and confident, but they found the cultural recipes of Socialist realism hard to stomach. Jdanov's directives on artistic subject-matter, those boring films about the building of cement factories in the Ukraine, the heroic paintings of Fougeron, the obligatory downgrading of jazz and Hemingway – they found all this hard to swallow, in spite of their goodwill. After all, entertainment was their profession. The fact that Fred Astaire was a product of capitalism did not diminish his talent. They felt it, they knew it, they could never completely forget it. Joining the Communist Party would mean accepting a cultural policy which made a dogma out of artistic banality, and branded artistic freedom as a crime against the proletariat. So they chose to stay in the background, while trying hard to believe that the cultural question was only a minor problem resulting from the superstructure, secondary to the fundamental question of transforming the methods of production. They did not as yet know that in Communist dictatorships cultural rigidity is an infallible sign of serious political sickness. And so, with occasional reticence, they toed the official party line, and would continue to, through thick and thin, until after 1956.

That is how, like Sartre, they came to join the ranks of the informal band of fellow-travellers: those reserve-troops of artists and intellectuals who would mount the battlements at times of

[1] *Le Chant d'un homme*, op.cit.

crisis to uphold Stanlinism, French-style. In the strategy of the Communist Party, they performed a precise function. In official communiqués, they had no right to be called 'comrades'; they were 'friends' of the Party. They were irreplaceable mouthpieces, because they had more credibility than the militants of the inner sanctum. Moreover, since they felt vaguely guilty about their mental reservations, and worried about being *petit bourgeois*, they would compensate by being extra-enthusiastic.

As far as public opinion went, Montand and Signoret were Communists with no fine distinctions. Everybody, the Communist Party as well as the Right, conspired to cast them in the part. 'I have a feeling of having been exploited,' Yves Montand would say later, 'of having been used to advertise an idea, just like a shampoo or an apéritif.' They certainly let themselves be used, with a willingness that was worrying. When *Le Figaro* accused them of being Communists, they did not contradict it, 'so as not to give the impression of denying an accusation'. When, at a dinner party, they heard someone refer to concentration camps in the Soviet Union, they would get up from the table and leave, in indignation. Like almost everybody else they were taken in by the one-dimensional images, Mitchourinian peasant women with plump cheeks, strong-armed Stakhanovites and men of marble. And they themselves stayed marble-cool, rather courageously, when the right-wing Press sneered at Montand ('the designer-Kominformist') for driving a Bentley, or at Signoret for 'selling *L'Huma-Dimanche* in a mink coat'.

They were resigned to not going to America, having been denied an entry visa. After being courted by Howard Hughes and Warner Brothers, they were thrown back into the Communist inferno. Yet it was hard to come to terms with it. For actors of their generation, Hollywood was the original myth, the modern dream, Cinema with a capital 'C'. They felt sad about it, but they rationalised it, and were even proud of sacrificing such tainted pleasures in the name of the radiant future.

Eventually they would read a different meaning into the course of history; meanwhile, they were living a great romantic adventure. By accident they had found their dream-house, an old bookshop which they would christen the 'caravan', in memory of Cocteau's *Les Enfants Terribles*.

On the Ile de la Cité is a little triangle planted with trees and surrounded by ancient buildings, a corner of the old 'village' Paris tucked between the Pont-Neuf, where Henri IV preens himself on his bronze horse, and the Palais de Justice. Simone had wanted to live on this corner for a long time, ever since the war. During the Flore period, when she was walking with friends one evening along the Quai des Orfèvres, bordering the island, she looked up at the proud, shaded façades and said, 'One day, I'll live here.'

It was not the only time she had foretold her own future aloud. When she left *Les Nouveaux Temps*, she had told Jean Luchaire that she was going to be in films, as if saying it would make it come true. It was a question of willpower. By proclaiming herself a future film actress, she committed herself – which was sacred. So she became a film actress. In the same way, she found an apartment in one of those quiet buildings where she had announced she would live.

The 'caravan' would become a place for meetings, shared confidences and laughter, where news and gossip circulated, where memories were stored; and also, much later, a solitary refuge, a place for writing and meditation.

Meanwhile, Simone Signoret was distractedly working in three films, including a masterpiece, *La Ronde*, by Max Ophuls, the director with a 'philosophical smile'.[1] She was excited to find herself acting in a film with Danièle Darrieux, whom she had admired since childhood. Montand stayed with her all the time, spending the day in her dressing-room and sitting in on costume-fittings. The besotted lover must have been overwhelming for a director. But the shrewd Ophuls had it under control.

Next she made *Le Traqué*, an American thriller directed by Frank Tuttle and Borys Lewin, and a melodrama with a Russian flavour in which she played a pianist haunted by a Tchaikovsky tune. *Ombres et Lumières* was the only film she was ashamed of (there was another, *Les Granges brûlées*, but for tortuous reasons she refused to talk about it); but in spite of this, it would be a wild success in the Soviet Union.

---

[1] Quoted in *Simone Signoret* by Joëlle Montserrat, PAC, 1983.

But none of this really mattered. Basically, she was convinced that she no longer wanted to work for the cinema. The world was full of causes to defend. And Montand was enough to make her happy. The last thing to cross her mind was that the cinema would transform her into a goddess of the Parisian suburbs, called Casque d'Or.

CHAPTER SEVEN

'It's thin, very thin.' The Belgian journalist shook his head, embarrassed at having to tell the sad truth to poor little Signoret, standing in front of him with her eyes full of hope. One critic had to come out with it. In Brussels, twelve critics had just attended the first screening of Jacques Becker's first film, *Casque d'Or*. The reaction had been unfavourable.

It was a disaster, a fiasco. A director's nightmare, a monumental flop. Such are the pitfalls of the critic's hazardous profession.

At its world première in Belgium, Becker's masterpiece lasted four days. Paris was even more painful. The critics were in for the kill: in concert, they smugly denounced the 'vulgarity of the dialogue and the photography', the skimpy plot and the old-fashioned costumes. They hated the wonderful Serge Reggiani even more than they hated Claude Dauphin, Raymond Bussières, Loleh Bellon, or Simone Signoret. His spontaneity, simplicity and vulnerability did not come across; he was too moving, too realistic for the critics of the early-fifties, because he did not conform to their idea of a sturdy manual worker. After *Casque d'Or*, Reggiani would stay in limbo for several years. Becker's vision was too fresh, too faithful to historical realism not to be disconcerting. Viewers accustomed to classical tunics or Louis XV costumes, New-Look-style, could not identify with this authentic recreation of the underworld at the turn of the century. Jacques Becker was an innovator because of his historian's scruples, his love of detail, and his precision. His journey back in time was not nostalgic; he did not cheat. And from this intense realism, this quest for the truth, sprang *Casque d'Or*'s poetry, which has made it a classic. Becker's

CATHERINE DAVID

vision was too truthful, too free from stereotypes for its time. The film would have to wait until stereotypes changed. Only the next generation would see the work clearly in its timeless dimension.

For this film, Simone Signoret had the 'special kind of protective-ness one feels towards the misunderstood, towards children who start off badly in life but turn out to be late developers'.[1] *Casque d'Or* is a puzzle in cinema history. It is always difficult to explain why people misunderstood a masterpiece at the time. With hindsight, their way of looking changes, and perspectives shift. How could they not appreciate what dazzles us today? The nostalgia of the banks of the river Marne; the tragic story which transforms petty backstreet crooks into Racinian heroes; the simplicity of sets where every little detail counts, from the choice of landscape to the feathery fringe of Marie, the 'lady of the night' of the Ange Gabriel Inn, Signoret at the top of her creative form. Inspired by the paintings of Renoir and Toulouse-Lautrec, the images of Casque d'Or have a freshness, a luminous clarity which makes them unforgettable. To quote Georges Sadoul, the only critic of the time who was sympathetic to the ill-starred film, 'Not only does Jacques Becker follow the finest plastic traditions of French fine arts; he has also recaptured the realistic poetry of Paris and her suburbs, a secret which seemed lost since Louis Feuillade's *Vampires* and *Fantômas*.' Yet Sadoul would criticise *Casque d'Or* in *Les Lettres Françaises*, for supposedly political reasons: should not these wonderful parts have been given to solid, trade-union militants?

Casque d'Or's career would seem to have parallels with that of impressionist painting. Becker's film, like paintings by Auguste Renoir or Monet, reveals minute attention to light, and to tricks of lighting which can transform a human face. *Casque d'Or* is a black-and-white film, but it permeates the memory like a symphony of colours.

The title ('golden helmet') was inspired. With this in mind, the eyes are immediately transfixed by Marie's 'helmet', that mass of hair proudly piled up on her head like a shining dome. Simone Signoret's face supports it like a frame. Her hair intensifies the look

[1] *France-Soir*, 4 May 1973.

65

in her eyes, which makes her mouth look larger, and reflects the light. And softly enveloping all this is the happiness of love. It is impossible to understand Simone Signoret if one forgets that she was that perfect woman, with her inner glow. She carried Marie's image with her, engraved like a secret medallion. And once she no longer looked like Casque d'Or, she no longer cared about growing old. She would never scale such heights again; or so she thought.

The plot was indirectly inspired by the true story of a certain Amélie Hélie, known as Casque d'Or, a prostitute in the Point-du-Jour quarter at the turn of the century; the mistress of a robber called Manda, head of the band of Apaches who used to hold up passers-by at la Folie-Méricourt. Settling an old score, Manda had stabbed his ex-lieutenant, Dominique Leca, who was now head of a rival gang, and his rival for Casque d'Or's affections. In 1902, the two thugs had been condemned to penal servitude, and Casque d'Or, who had been made famous by this flattering news story, briefly took up a career as a cabaret singer, while her two former protectors did time at the penal colony at Cayenne.

It was an old project, one of those sea-serpents that recur in cinema circles. Before the war Duvivier, then Clouzot, then Yves Allégret, had dreamed of filming this tale of gang-warfare in the suburbs of the Belle Époque. The exotic populism of the working-class suburbs and their pleasure-gardens seduced a film maker of the period as it had seduced the Impressionists. The romanticism of ordinary artisans touched a chord.

Jacques Becker had transformed it, to make a love-story. He centred everything on the passion between Manda and Casque d'Or, doomed lovers hounded by the jealous hatred of Leca, the wine merchant (Claude Dauphin). After inciting Manda to kill Casque d'Or's former protector in a duel of honour, Leca denounces to the police an innocent man who happens to be Manda's best friend. Then he tells Manda, hiding with Casque d'Or in a country cottage, that his friend has been accused of the murder.

After four days of happiness in their thatched dream-cottage, Manda gives himself up to the police. He will be guillotined. In the final scene, Casque d'Or watches her lover's execution from a window. Back-lit, rebellious tendrils of hair escape from her golden chignon, and catch the light for a last time.

Those who watched the shoot realised that it was no ordinary film. It was like a party, with a sort of collective gracefulness. Even the elements were favourable. Jacques Becker needed a light mist over the fields, and fog rolled in that morning. Next day, he wanted sunshine, and so the sun shone. The actors lodged in a little country hotel which could have been part of the film-set, with porcelain basins in the bedrooms and 'a kitchen garden with the "conveniences" at the far end'.[1] And they were all present at that key moment in life when love reveals itself in its glory. 'Jacques was in love with Annette, and his love of love filtered through the images. I was in love with Montand and Manda reaped the benefits. And since Manda was Serge, it was deliciously incestuous to pretend to a different kind of love, when we had loved each other so much for such a long time. And Jacques loved us all.'

Casque d'Or was lit up by all this love. But it was a dark film, a tragedy; it struck a wrong note during the frivolous fifties. The spectre of post-war privation was disappearing, economic growth was dizzy, the cellars of Saint-Germain-des-Prés were packed with people, Françoise Sagan was writing *Bonjour tristesse*, the *dolce vita*, whisky and sports-cars were in fashion. Forget the rest.

Nobody was ready for *Casque d'Or*, that black diamond.

It would not be shown again in Paris until ten years later, wreathed in world acclaim. It had been a triumph in Germany and in Italy; in Britain, it had received a British Film Academy Award. But Jacques Becker, who had become one of the closest friends of Simone Signoret and Yves Montand, had died in November 1959, without knowing that his film would become a film-club classic.

Nevertheless, Simone had to take herself in hand to make it. For it was the first time since their meeting that she had been separated from Montand. When Becker summoned her in March 1951, she was keeping Montand company in the Camargue, where he was shooting Clouzot's *The Wages of Fear* with Charles Vanel. Clouzot had been begging Montand to accept the part for several weeks before he made up his mind. Montand had burnt his fingers

[1] *Nostalgia . . .* op.cit.

with his first experience of the cinema in *Les Portes de la nuit*, a film by Prévert and Carné, in which, without much conviction, he had played a part turned down by Gabin. But he still did not consider himself a proper actor. When he sang on the music-hall stage, he was playing himself, in control of script and rhythm. He was not yet sure of being ready to submit to the demands of a director. But finally everything went smoothly, he was reassured about his capabilities, and, soon, in the evenings, there he was in the hotel restaurant playing silly games with Vanel. Simone had the holiday of her dreams, went shopping in Nîmes with Vera Clouzot and clashed with Clouzot in interminable political arguments which would soon turn sour. Later, during the shooting of *Les Diaboliques*, Clouzot and Signoret would grow to hate each other.

Going away, leaving Montand: it was like being torn apart. She sobbed as she packed her case and kissed the crew goodbye. Montand took her to the station at Nïmes to catch the train to rejoin Becker. The train came in, and all at once she stopped crying. She made no attempt to pick up her suitcase, but, hands on hips, glared at the train with a defiant look. She felt she was loyal to her legend, to Dédée d'Anvers, to her image of intransigent woman-in-love; like giving a 'V' sign to the rest of the world. The train slowed down and stopped; two minutes later, it moved out again. As in a dream – or a second-rate melodrama – she was planted on the platform, an allegory of Love triumphing over life's obstacles. She watched the train move away into the distance.

She had won. She would not make *Casque d'Or*; so what? She was staying with Montand, in her natural place in the world's order. She would return to the haberdashery counter at the Dames de France in Nîmes with Vera Clouzot, and that would be it. Becker would find somebody else, she was not irreplaceable. She saw herself as the heroine of a great love-story. Lightheartedly, she was renouncing a lifelong dream, of the first big part that would make her a star.

For the next morning, she no longer felt so proud. She dropped her swaggering act. The fact was, Casque d'Or was a fantastic part. She had not made a film for a year and a half. People would forget her . . . And then, Montand didn't seem so keen on her giving up her career to be with him. He was flattered, of course, who wouldn't be? But he didn't want a doormat; he wanted his 'woman' to stay as she was when he met her, a film star. He was happy about her success, he took her seriously. He wanted to admire her unreservedly, to know that she was desired by other men, and envied by women – courted, radiant. And then, in a typically masculine way, he needed her absence to prove to himself that he really loved her. It probably wasn't such a bad idea for her to go away. Their friends had been surprised to see her reappear after all those solemn goodbyes; they had made a fuss of her and congratulated her on her courage, but she could see they were embarrassed, and dared not tell her what they really thought: that she had just made the biggest blunder of her life . . .

Jacques Becker would wait until the next evening to telephone her. After two days of suspense, she was like a cat on hot bricks. She was prepared to argue, and to answer back; but he was more subtle. He did not shout as she had expected; on the contrary, he congratulated her. 'Yes, a true love like yours has to be tended *very* carefully. You're absolutely right, darling.' Then he mentioned the names of two actresses who would be fine in the part.

The next morning, Casque d'Or was sitting in the train bound for Paris.

In that adventure, Signoret would win the immortality of the stars. Millions of women would want to look like her; her face would be a symbol of beauty, love and fantasy for a certain period. But she would also emerge from that extraordinary film feeling she had made a decisive step forward in her craft. For it was while shooting *Casque d'Or* that she first became aware of the phenomenon of an actor's dissociation or dual personality, a mysterious process which no amount of academic commentaries can really explain. How do actors forget themselves, and disappear behind the character that they are playing? She had never thought about it much; she acted by instinct, which had always been a good guide, in real life as well as professionally. But this time there were the boots . . .

'My usual dresser is sick and her replacement hasn't the faintest idea of costume continuity. She dresses me, she puts on my corset, hands me the various things I ask for. I had two pairs of boots for the film: one superb pair made of grey suede with black patent leather, and another pair of very ordinary brown leather. My dresser hands me the grey ones, at which point I say, "Oh, no, I'm going to wear those this evening." "Why? Are we going to film tonight?" "No, skip it, it doesn't matter . . ." I realised that I was getting dressed in a bistro-owner's bedroom beside a piece of wasteland in Belleville, to go out in a moment and say to Manda, my friend Serge Reggiani, that is, "Come this evening; I'll wait for you at l'Ange Gabriel . . ." It wasn't me that I was dressing – Montand's wife-to-be, Catherine's mother – but Marie, who was already thinking ahead to what she would wear that evening to go out with Manda . . . a scene we filmed three weeks later at the Billancourt Studios, where the Ange Gabriel set was in the process of being constructed.

'It was very strange. I found that things were happening to me that I had no control over, which seemed to come nei- ther from my mind nor from my will. Consequently I was someone else. Then it hit me and I said, "This must be what they call dissociation! Whole books have been written about it." '[1]

Simone Signoret would often say that she did not like analysing her work. It was necessary, in order to interpret a part properly, to identify totally with the character, but she refused to think too much about it, or to intellectualise the fusion of emotions. It was a spontaneous identification, desired rather than willed. Theories seemed colourless and sterile compared with that complex trans- formation which involved her whole being. She was Marie, she was a double, she had two identities, two passports: one for fantasy, one for reality. That night, Marie was going dancing, and all at once Marie's life had spilled out into Simone's, though she would not film the dance-hall scene until three weeks later. Fantasy was encroaching on real life, imagination was taking control: 'It is the answer to all those naïve questions people often ask you: "How do you manage to cry? . . ." It's not hard

[1] *Nostalgia . . .* op.cit.

to cry when you're unhappy: if my character is unhappy she cries, and I cry!'

But all her joy from that unique film did not help her solve her personal contradictions. She was the prototype of the modern woman who, day after day, is faced with the difficult privilege of living several different lives at once. The time was over when an 'actress' would lead a life apart, in the *demi-monde*. There was Catherine, her daughter, whom she had neglected since the 'crooner' had burst in on the family holiday. She remembered her mother who never went away, but was always there to make her her afternoon tea or take her to piano lessons. Leaving Catherine with her father was no solution: Catherine came to live with her, and she would grow up with these two 'sacred monsters', between the 'caravan' and the elementary school in the rue du Jardinet, a pretty building tucked away down cobbled alleyways lined with old aristocratic mansions. A school surrounded by palaces and trees, where she would win a crop of prizes. But Catherine was mainly brought up not by Simone, but by the family of Montand's brother, who lived on the floor above with his wife and children.

Simone would console herself for neglecting her daughter by seeing it as the reverse side of the coin. For Catherine had the good fortune to be brought up among artists, exciting people, famous people, eccentrics, Montand, Becker, Semprun, Prévert, Carné, Gérard Philipe, Serge Reggiani, Danièle Delorme . . . At least her daughter would not have an ordinary childhood. But Simone could sense that Catherine missed her mother. If she gave up the cinema, she could at least look after Catherine properly.

But, above all, she could be with Montand all the time. She would take pains to fabricate this new image of herself as a self-effacing wife knitting by the fire; to forget the real Simone, the screen goddess, the fighter, the ambitious go-getter.

In December 1951, Yves Montand and Simone Signoret were married in the town hall of Saint-Paul-de-Vence. It was a country wedding, with Prévert as best man. The doves came, just like the first time, and, from Vallauris, Picasso sent his greetings and a drawing done with the first felt pens to come on the French market.

Later Simone Signoret would realise that, far from threatening her marriage, continuing her career had helped safeguard it. But, for the moment, she was in a rebellious mood. After *Casque d'Or*, she attracted attention by telling the Press she was giving up the cinema.

And she firmly turned down every proposal. In any case, *Casque d'Or* had not had the success it deserved, and she had no reason to court another set-back. They would have to do without her; she had better things to do. She even turned down the Hakim brothers, with their big producer's cigars, who offered her a most attractive part. It was Zola's *Thérèse Raquin*, with Marcel Carné directing. Simone Signoret was keen on Zola, and it was with Carné that she had discovered the pleasures of film-making in 1942 at the time of *Les Visiteurs du soir*. As for the character of Thérèse herself, the provincial heroine martyred by a puny husband, whose passion for a handsome Italian would end in murder, Zola might have written it for her. There was plenty to think about.

Carné too had hesitated for a long time. Jacques Feyder, his master, had already made *Thérèse Raquin* into a silent film in Berlin in 1927. Feyder had scrupulously followed Zola's plot, but Carné thought it lacked dramatic impact. In the novel, the guilty lovers, Thérèse and Laurent, are hounded by the murdered husband's ghost. Carné had the bright idea of replacing the ghost with a blackmailer. From then on, the story makes sense. Raf Vallone played Laurent, Thérèse's lover, an irresistible Italian lorry-driver. The blackmailer was assigned to Roland Lesaffre, one of Carné's old friends. Only Simone was missing. But she was adamant. Huddled in her 'caravan', she was knitting a scarf for her husband, stitch by stitch.

In *Nostalgia Isn't What It Used To Be*, she jokingly describes the little domestic scene that finally tipped the scales. Searching for a scrap of paper, Montand lost his temper. 'Why are you still there, knitting?' 'Because I want to be here. If I weren't here I'd be working.' 'That's easily said! In order to work, somebody's got to offer you a part.' (. . .) 'In order to work, somebody's got to

offer you a part? I could be in the middle of making *Thérèse!*' 'They
didn't really want you for Thérèse. By the way, I hear that X is
about to accept.'[1] Cut to the quick, she put her knitting down and
slowly walked towards the phone. With a beating heart, she called
the Hakim brothers, trembling with fear lest they might indeed
have hired somebody else. Next day, she signed the contract for
Thérèse Raquin.

It was the last time she would try to go back. She accepted
the omens. 'Once again we would be miserable when separated
and then come back together and discover a miraculous reunion
without a flaw.' It would be hard to go on cherishing the illusion of
a soft cocoon of togetherness, and of evenings spent nodding by
the fire. She had to face it: she was no longer credible in her own
eyes in a secondary role. She was too fond of playing the actress,
of dressing up and pretending, of being taken in hand, pampered
and guided. She adored working in a team, the fun of the evenings
during a shoot, the intense friendships when you work together,
and the cosy knowledge that everybody else has stagefright too.
She loved the limelight. 'Let those who have never savoured that
magic crowning, when the lights come on in the auditorium, cast
the first stone.'[2] For her, the cinema was no longer the play-acting
of a girl who pulls up her eyelids to look like Danielle Darrieux.
It was a way of life, a passion. Still better – it was her profession.
She was no more ready for retirement than Montand was.

Carné transposed *Thérèse Raquin* to modern times, to the fifties.
It was the first leading part in which Simone Signoret abandoned
her usual character, the tart with a heart of gold. With her grey
cardigan and black dress, her hair severely pulled back, her pale
face and the smouldering passion in her eyes, Simone Signoret's
Thérèse Raquin is fascinating – a volcano under ice.

Thérèse acts as nurse to a peevish husband, Camille (Jacques
Duby), himself the willing slave of his old mother (Sylvie), a
female monster who harries her daughter-in-law with an implac-
able hatred which ferments in the closed world of the provincial
lower-middle classes. Obsessed by her passion for Laurent (Raf

[1]*Nostalgia . . . op.cit.*
[2]Id.

73

Vallone), Thérèse nevertheless refuses to run away with him. And so Laurent becomes part of the little circle around Camille and his mother (Sylvie), playing a claustrophobic game of cat and mouse in a dingy front parlour where you can almost smell the mothballs and beeswax polish. Depicting these family scenes, Carné's realism comes close to caricature.

But Camille takes Thérèse to Paris, to keep an eye on her. Hearing about their departure, Laurent sneaks on to the train. Thinking her husband is asleep in the carriage, Thérèse creeps out to join her lover. Camille follows her, and, after a violent quarrel with Laurent, he is thrown out of the open door of the carriage. Nobody saw Laurent getting on the train, and Thérèse assures the police that she was asleep during the whole journey and did not see her husband leave the carriage. She returns home, and calmly confronts her mother-in-law, who realises the truth but can no longer speak. She is a paraplegic after a stroke.

It would have been a perfect crime if there had not been a witness in the carriage. He is Roland Lesaffre, a smarmy thug and petty blackmailer, the character invented by Carné to replace the ghost in Zola's novel. Laurent and Thérèse accede to his demands, and give him money. They are free to escape. But the blackmailer is run over by a lorry whose driver loses control. The villain does not reach the hotel in time to stop the maid from posting his letter informing against the couple.

In spite of Carné's alterations to Zola's original text, *Thérèse Raquin* was well received. Endless arguments about adapting literary works for the cinema were still to come. At the Venice Biennale of 1953, *Thérèse Raquin* was awarded the Golden Lion. In *France-Soir*, Jean Dutourd described Simone Signoret as a 'female Jean Gabin'. He was right. They took the same size in shoes, they were of the same calibre. In 1987 an opinion poll in *Paris-Match* listed Gabin and Signoret among the twelve most significant French personalities of the century, beside General de Gaulle, Doctor Albert Schweitzer, Picasso and Pagnol.

CHAPTER EIGHT

My first piano-teacher was called Maurice Martenot, an elderly man with a little moustache full of white hairs and bristly at the ends. My mother would always take me to the lesson, which, for the first few years at least, took place in the school founded by two sisters, Ginette and Madeleine, in the Rue Saint-Pierre in Neuilly, in a little red-brick house built round a courtyard planted with trees. I admired Monsieur Martenot immensely, because I had heard that he was the inventor of the only instrument capable, like the human voice, of moving from one note to another without a break. When, much later, I accidentally heard a radio recording of a concerto for 'Martenot waves', I felt a mixture of pleasure and disappointment. That fabulous instrument sounded inhuman, tinny, and inexpressive. Since then, musicians have achieved much better effects through electronics. Martenot was undeniably a pioneer, and a remarkable musician as well as an attentive, patient teacher. He addressed children, particularly little girls, by the formal '*vous*'. When my mother asked him why, he replied that little girls grew up, and that it was not appropriate for a piano-teacher to call his pupils '*tu*' once they had turned into young ladies. Of course I was very proud of being called '*vous*'. He never raised his voice, and never scolded me when I arrived with my heart beating because I had not practised enough during the week. His gentleness inspired respect. He used to say that what counted most for him in his work with children was teaching them to take pleasure in music. For me he was a true master, an initiator.

My surprise and emotion were therefore great when, at another stage, I met him again in *Nostalgia Isn't What It Used To Be*: not as the worthy Monsieur Martenot, but as a passionate young inventor. When Simone Signoret was at school in Neuilly, she took music lessons at the Cours Martenot: 'It was run by two sisters, Madeleine and Geneviève' (in my day, people only talked of 'Ginette', by now an elderly spinster who still held sway over the local children in the big hall downstairs) 'in a private house on the Rue Saint-Pierre. They had invented a very attractive method, with musical games and finger exercises that I still know how to do!'[1] I, too, can remember the card-decks that represented musical intervals, and how we played *picquet* with them. 'They had a younger brother who had been in the signal corps during the war. We sometimes saw him racing through the garden, like a madman, wearing a white smock. He worked in a shed at the end of the garden, from which emanated terrible sounds: transfigured human voices, strange noises. He was working on an invention, which finally saw the light of day; it was called the Martenot waves. Suddenly, the Cours Martenot was famous. On Thursdays, one would meet the girls from the Catholic school . . .'

Chance may be blind, but one can hardly help reading a meaning into coincidences like this. Starting from different points in time, two persons' memories interconnect, and superimpose images of the same man at two periods of his life. Tiny little things can connect – a conversation with a taxi-driver, a smile exchanged with a lady knitting in the Métro, or a ball thrown back over the wire to children playing. Simone Signoret adored chance meetings; she invited confidences, she had the gift of empathy with casual acquaintances – her hairdresser, the porter at her London hotel, the film-technician on the set, the visitors dining at the next-door table under the lime trees at her local restaurant.

Monsieur Martenot counted for far more in my life than in hers; for her he was just a romantic character, a point of reference. She mentions the Cours Martenot because it was the only place in Neuilly where she met middle-class children who were not 'displaced persons', well-bred little girls who wore white for

[1] *Nostalgia* . . . op.cit.

CATHERINE DAVID

their first communion, and whose mothers organised elegant tea-parties. Of this chance tripartite meeting, Monsieur Martenot will know nothing, nor will Simone Signoret, since I forgot to tell her about it when we saw each other. As for me, I remain the only surviving witness of a meeting which only took place in my imagination; though I invented it, I treasure its memory, because while I was writing this book it felt like a secret sign.

Simone Signoret would often talk about the countless different strands in life which sometimes bunch together, like balls of wool, and over the years help to weave strong links and durable friendships. 'It's not chains that make a marriage last, but the thousands and thousands of threads that sew people together.'[1] And because she longed, more than most, for loves and friendships to last for ever, as if cast in bronze, she was obsessed with tiny details; for her, nothing was too insignificant – the chance meetings, gangways, openings through which human lives interconnect and memories blend with one another.

And of course, inevitably, she attracted this kind of connection in her own life. She seemed to have the gift of attracting coincidences. 'When you're dealing with Simone Signoret, you have to expect the wildest kinds of coincidence or chance meeting. I'm quite certain that Simone is a goddess of coincidences, of meaningful accidents; she's a kind of guru of ordinary, everyday life.'[2] These few lines of Jorge Semprun's are one of the nicest tributes paid to Signoret. Since first getting to know her, Semprun had picked up the habit of believing in coincidences: when he had a sudden urge to read the pages about Aragon in *Nostalgia* (devastating ones), he was hardly surprised when he heard the news of the old poet's death over the radio that very night.

Semprun no longer felt surprise, but he continued to marvel when a taxi-driver recognised Montand in New York in December 1981, after having heard him sing in Moscow in 1956. 'We were amazed, Simone and I: stupefied, even. We looked at this Russian who had heard Montand sing in Moscow – perhaps at the Ouljniki Stadium. Perhaps he was one of those tiny silhouettes one can just

[1]*Daily Mail*, 4 July 1978.
[2]*Montand, la vie continue*, Denoël, 1983.

77

make out on the photo I've already mentioned, the one you can still see at the Place Dauphine. He must have been a little kid, in 1956, given his age now. I wasn't too surprised at this coincidence happening once Simone reappeared in our lives. Things like this kept on happening all the time with her. I ought to have been used to it; but it was amazing all the same, strangely significant . . . Those lives that had intersected twice, in Moscow and New York, would probably never cross each other again. It was up to us to treasure this sign in our memories.' For this, he could trust Simone. She never forgot. She would hoard mementoes and keepsakes by the drawerful, tidying them away with other fragments of her life collected while filming, or away on her travels.

Sometimes coincidences would proliferate around her, in a way that usually only happens in dreams. In the villa at Autheuil, during those fateful five days when she went over the story of her life, like a rosary, with Maurice Pons in front of the tape-recorder turning under the tutelary eye of Dominique Roussillon, there were 'tea-breaks', moments when the machine would stop and Signoret would feel she was out of reach of the 'mechanical ears', free to wander away from the tracks of chronology, and to dream aloud. Simone Signoret did not like tape-recorders, because they replaced live memory with a recording. She distrusted this artificial, stupid kind of fidelity, which kept all the nervous mannerisms of speech, the 'ums' and 'ers', or interjections like, 'Damn, I can't remember his name,' or, 'No, no, I've got it wrong!' When Dominique Roussillon turned off the spying little red light, Simone would breathe again. She had been speaking for hours; now they could really *talk*.

During one of those breaks, she told them about the extraordinary day, in the seventies, when her childhood memories had lit up again like a necklace of stars. Everything had started during the projection of a film directed by her lifelong friend, Chris Marker, about the concert given by Montand on behalf of the Chilean refugees, *La Solitude d'un chanteur de fond*. When she arrived, in the corridor, she met René Vauthier, a film maker who had just made a documentary about the death of her younger brother, Alain Kaminker. Alain had been drowned in December

1958 off the island of Sein where he was directing a film on the life of the fishermen. Alain was the little brother who had arrived like a Christmas present when she was a little girl of nine years old, on 28 December 1930, and who had awoken all her maternal instinct.

Alain had become a director, the only member of the Kaminker family to follow a career that brought him close to 'la Grande Simone'. He had died a few days before his twenty-eighth birthday. 'Now the little half-Jew, made Protestant by Pastor Ebershold "so his papers would be in order" lies in the very Catholic sailors' cemetery of the Ile des Veuves (the Widows' Isle),' his elder sister writes soberly in *Nostalgia*.

In the corridor, René Vauthier told her about his documentary, *Death of a Film-Maker*, in which the islanders gave their recollections of the young man who had disappeared in the storm that had taken the lives of so many of their own people. This chance meeting had overwhelmed her, as did anything that evoked Alain and his senseless death.

Then, in the afternoon, Chris Marker came round to see her at the Place Dauphine. He was very agitated. He had just been talking with a bookseller friend whose shop was full of knick-knacks. He was looking for a birthday present for her, and had asked the bookseller for a blue clog ('Sabot Bleu'). In the intimate code of their old friendship, this was a way of evoking the newspaper kiosk in Neuilly, the famous Sabot Bleu where the boys from the lycée Pasteur and the girls from the secondary school would meet to discuss how to change the world. 'We walked and we talked; one of the main subjects of conversation was Charles Trenet . . . We also talked about the books we thought were important – *Dusty Answer* and *Sparkenbrooke*.'[1] The bookseller did not have a blue clog, but, hearing that Chris Marker had just made a film about Montand, he immediately started talking about Signoret. He had known her when she was very young, he had lived in the same house as her, in Neuilly. Chris Marker had thought that this coincidence would make a perfect birthday present, as precious as a blue clog.

[1] Novels by Rosamond Lehmann and Charles Morgan respectively.

SIMONE SIGNORET

That very evening, she visited Montand, who was making a film in the studios at Épinay. The crew were having a drink at the end of the day's work, and she thought she recognised a rather elderly man who was looking at her and smiling. She went towards him, and he hugged her, with the words, 'Hello, Kiki Kaminker!' It was years since anyone had called her Kiki. It was Zuber, the photographer who had worked at Étienne Damour's office with her father, and had taken the only photos of the family in which one could see all four of them, Kiki-Simone, her mother, and her two little brothers, Alain and Jean-Pierre. And so the day that had started with Alain, the young director drowned in the high seas, ended with the moving sight of the same Alain at the age of three, dressed in a sailor suit.

For most of the time, the mind is like a dark crypt, where the light of memory only penetrates in a hazy way. For Simone Signoret, forgetfulness was tragedy, a wound, a crime against the living past. She would not accept it. She was a fighter, and she would fight to push back the frontiers of memory, to accumulate traces and benchmarks, and wherever she went, she would plant little white marker-pebbles like Hansel and Gretel – words on a page, objects on a shelf, or photographs in a frame. In her novel, *Adieu Volodia*, one can see the crucial role of the 'Cadre des Nôtres', the family picture, that mosaic of images which, for her heroes, symbolised the different stages of the long journey from Poland and the Ukraine. Everyone who knew the 'caravan' in the Place Dauphine will remember the way the souvenirs were piled up on the mantelpiece – roubles, dollars, photos. In the 'Cadre des Nôtres', as on the mantelpiece in the 'caravan', souvenirs continue to be passed round, past meetings are repeated, and lead to new ones, as if the traces of the past are living their own silent life.

Simone Signoret nursed a secret dream of an all-retentive memory that, like the memory of a character in one of Borges' short stories, could retain the trace of every leaf seen in the forest, of every word spoken, of every dream, night and gesture at every moment. She kept everything, little bits of paper people had scribbled messages on, the odd gift from one of her fans, the photograph of a young Greek waving a carnation shortly before his assassination.

She had an overloaded memory that was daunting. 'A real furniture store', an inexhaustible source of stories, names, dates, old jokes, faces, details, events. In her profession, she was lucky: she could remember her parts with disconcerting ease: 'It's not hard to memorise a script (if it's a good one) because they're the same words the character would say in that situation.' She would remember strangers she had met long ago and chatted briefly with: 'We actors are made up of all the places we've been to. Like everybody else. And of the life we've led . . . And we're also the product of all the different social worlds we've touched on, of houses we've been into because we were shooting a film on the other side of the street. "Madame, can I change in your kitchen?" We have our own travelling habits. I don't know much about the museums in a foreign country, but I'll have a mass of information and gossip about people – why they are there, where they've come from.'[1] Without this prodigious memory, her first book, *Nostalgia Isn't What It Used To Be*, would probably have been just another talented but rather ordinary piece of writing, the memoirs of yet another actress, with all the limitations of the *genre*. The precision of her memories enabled her to make it a true contemporary chronicle, a saga of the French intelligentsia from 1941 until today, in which several generations of actors, political activists, journalists and writers would recognise themselves. But she still had not exhausted her reserves and her novel *Adieu Volodia* would secretly draw on the same sources.

At the end of the novel, after his parents have been dead for a long time, killed in a railway accident, the hero, Maurice Guttman, spends hallucinatory nights immersed in the deep waters of his memory. Sipping a glass of spirits, he plunges in 'like a deep-sea diver who has pinpointed his buried treasures and knows that he will find them intact, but has no intention of bringing them back to the surface, since there is no way that they can survive in the air above'.

[1] Interview with Mathieu Lindon, *Libération*, 1985.

Simone Signoret describes Maurice's voyages into his own mind with the precision of someone who has herself burrowed deeply, with methodical ferocity, into these secret regions. 'He would choose a theme, and did not allow himself to stray from it. For example, it could be the image of all the clothes he had ever seen his parents wearing at every age of his own life. He would count them, and, if he had forgotten one, would start all over again, because forgetting one garment meant skipping a date. New clothes always went with an important new date. Sometimes, too, he would hesitate, above all with girls' dresses, he was no longer sure if it was Sonia or Olga that he could picture in a flowered blue dress, in such and such a setting, because they often lent each other their clothes. He would pursue his investigations like a sleuth looking for signs and pieces of evidence, who lines up his exhibits.' Simone Signoret could probably memorise all her mother's dresses. When she talks of an 'investigation', and the 'obstinacy of a sleuth', she attributes her own detective instinct to Maurice – her passion for getting it exactly right.

But what Simone Signoret valued most of all was what she called 'shared memory'. When she had lived through an event with someone else, she could not bear him to remember things differently. 'Sometimes Montand doesn't remember things, because he hasn't listened, because he's concentrating on something else; this doesn't matter to him at all, but it does to me, enormously so . . . And sometimes it takes on huge proportions . . . But often it's just a question of tiny little things, tiny details. It's quite true that, when someone describes a recollection or a story, and has a woman wearing a blue dress when she was wearing red, it drives me crazy . . . I realise it's absurd, but I can't do anything about it, I'm like that. When people don't share something completely with me, at the same time as me, I feel as if a part of myself has been stolen.'[1]

She could spend hours on her investigations, trying to pare them down, verifying them, and asking questions. She would feel a terrible, childish rage when the other person's memory proved

[1] Interview with Pierre Démeron, *Marie-Claire*, September 1979.

defective. In *Adieu Volodia*, when Maurice realises that his friend Zaza does not remember his telling her Volodia's story because she had her first proper date on that day, he feels a terrible sense of betrayal.

It was by evoking the 'nostalgia of shared memory' that she finally succeeded in finishing her memoirs. She had learned, from experience, that her desire for total accuracy could never wholly be fulfilled, either with her friends and family, or with her contemporaries: 'One person's memories never really fit with another's.' She was inconsolable. Parents' memories are different from children's, and not even lovers share the same memories of their secret pleasures. The failure was not hers; it was human nature's fault, its inability to create proper, indissoluble bonds between people. It was the failure of a Utopia in which she had always needed to believe.

CHAPTER NINE

After *Thérèse Raquin*, Simone Signoret was finally able to go back to being a performer's wife. Montand was singing at the Théâtre de l'Étoile; for the first time, he held the stage alone every night.

Over a six-month period, from October 1953 until April 1954, left-wingers outraged by the war in Indo-China would come to hear Montand sing as if they were attending a political rally at La Mutualité; they would demand 'committed' songs, 'Le Dormeur du Val' or 'Quand un Soldat', which was banned on radio at the time. Yet Montand would still alternate political protest-songs with his ordinary repertoire, while feeling slightly guilty about gaily striking up 'bourgeois' refrains like 'C'est Si Bon' or 'Une Demoiselle sur une Balançoire'. These were solemn times, after all.

For the Right, he was Public Enemy Number One. Parachutists sent him threatening letters; Biaggi, a pro-fascist lawyer, sat in the front row of the auditorium with twenty bully-boys instructed to spread out a newspaper and read it throughout the show. It was the beginning of the period when billboards would be smeared with tar, and stink-bombs and tear-gas canisters were thrown into the auditorium. But, supported by Simone and his own beliefs, Montand held his ground. Of course, he was personally courageous, but the brutal stupidity of the Right lent wind to his sails.

He had faith in the popular mood. Stalin had died on 5 March 1953, but his memory still lingered in the minds of the Left. The favourite slogan 'US Go Home' was blazoned on the walls. Eisenhower was considered a fascist; the Korean War and the

84

Rosenberg trial were scandals to justify maximum protests from intellectuals.

French intellectuals were not yet very uneasy about the events in Prague the year before. In an iniquitous trial, a carbon copy of the trial of the Hungarian Rajk, Rudolf Slansky and ten of his 'accomplices' were condemned to death and hanged. The Czech Press ferociously welcomed the execution of this 'loathsome band of spies and lackeys of imperialism, international traitors, who for a handful of dollars serve the British Secret Service, the Gestapo and the CIA; all equally willingly.'[1] The trials in Czechoslovakia were so well-rigged that hardly anybody was outraged.

In Moscow the façade of Stalinism was beginning to show some cracks. The 'white coats', the Jewish doctors accused of trying to assassinate Stalin, had been rehabilitated. But the French intellectuals who had denounced the anti-Semitism of the American judges in the Rosenberg trial turned a blind eye to the flagrant anti-Semitism of the Soviet bosses. 'Who can make a Western fellow-traveller understand that for more than a quarter of a century the Russians have been living under a whole group of all-powerful McCarthys, untouchable, absolute rulers with control over their life and death?'[2] It was a question which a far-off cousin of Simone Signoret's, whose existence she did not even suspect, would ask herself agonisingly every day in Czechoslovakia; but in Paris in the fifties, nobody could hear it. Ho Chi Minh was the hero of the day. Aragon was writing *The Communists*, and insulting Paul Nizan's memory for not having accepted the Hitler-Stalin Pact in 1940. Sartre declared that 'we must not let Billancourt despair' and Paul Eluard demonstrated that poets were not free from political cant: 'I am too concerned with the innocent proclaiming their innocence to spend time on the guilty proclaiming their guilt.' Montand would endorse this with both hands.

He was not the only one. 'We were totally well-meaning, but totally misled,' writes Emmanuel Le Roy Ladurie.[3] As fervently

[1] Quoted by Jo Langer in *Une Saison à Bratislava*, op.cit.
[2] Jo Langer, *Une Saison à Bratislava*, op.cit.
[3] *Paris-Montpellier*, Gallimard, 1982.

as the militants, the fellow-travellers – those 'intellectual virgins' – would defend their imagined paradise with a relentless schizophrenia, even if they had read, like Le Roy Ladurie, the devastating testimonies of Boris Souvarine, Victor Serge and Léon Trotsky, or Arthur Koestler's novel *Darkness at Noon*. 'In fact, reading Koestler actually increased my loyalty to the Party,' Le Roy Ladurie admits, looking back in stupefaction.

Over six months, 200,000 spectators would throng to the Théâtre de l'Étoile. Such is fame; but it also earned Montand a small fortune, with which he bought the house at Autheuil, in the Eure region, which would become the couple's third refuge, after la Place Dauphine and the Colombe d'Or. Every life-story has its own special geography, towns, houses, or crossroads, where lines meet. Simone Signoret's geography was triangular, and her journeys – from Neuilly to Saint-Germain-des-Prés, from Moscow to Hollywood – would fan out from those fixed points, three houses to which she would always return to restore her strength, and touch base. The Hotel Colombe d'Or was the first of these magic places; then the flat in the Place Dauphine, and finally the big, warm white house in a leafy garden, casually furnished with bric-à-brac from antique shops. Here, she could put down roots which she needed more than most.

Montand and Signoret would keep open house at Autheuil, like a sort of commune. 'Some weekends there would be nearly twenty guests, a full house. Children and dogs were admitted, even sought after. To have a bedroom on the first floor, you had to be old, very famous or a first-time guest. I slept on the second floor, because I wasn't either old or famous, and I went there every weekend,' recalls José Artur in *Micro de nuit*. 'On the same floor as me, I saw François Périer, Françoise Arnoul, Roger Pigaut, Serge Reggiani, Pierre Mondy and Jacques Becker . . . We'd play "Ambassadors", liar dice, the "*bachot* game" and volley-ball; we bathed, and we even washed. I would bring along unsaleable records by singers we couldn't stand, and we'd use them as airgun-targets.' Using the money from *Les Diaboliques*, Simone would build a swimming-pool. But this fun-palace was also a workplace. Montand had a piano there, a corner where he could rehearse his shows. Autheuil was where

CATHERINE DAVID

Simone Signoret later wrote most of her books, and where she died.

When Henri-Georges Clouzot brought her the script of *Les Diaboliques*, she had just committed herself to acting, with Montand, in *The Crucible*, a play by Arthur Miller which they had heard about from Elvire Popesco, but also from Jules Dassin and John Berry, two French directors who had been victims of the McCarthy witch-hunt. In New York, *The Crucible* had a cool reception. The public was not ready for the message of a play that, through the story of John and Elizabeth Proctor, a seventeenth-century Puritan couple who were victims of a witch-hunt, denounced the all-too-topical trial of the two Jewish scientists, Julius and Ethel Rosenberg.

But on the very day that the Rosenbergs were electrocuted in Sing Sing jail, part of the New York audience had stood up in silent protest at the hanging of John Proctor at the end of the play. From that minute's silence until today, performances of *The Crucible* throughout the world can be seen as symbols of protest against fanaticism and intolerance. 'I can almost tell what the political situation in a country is when the play is suddenly a hit there,' writes Arthur Miller in *Timebends*. 'It is either a warning of tyranny on the way or a reminder of tyranny just past.'[1] And he tells how in Shanghai in 1980 the play served as a metaphor for the trials of the Cultural Revolution.

For Simone Signoret, it was an exciting project, which finally brought all the different strands together – Montand, politics and her career. It was also a huge professional risk. Her own experience in the theatre, as one of the 'people of Thebes' in the crowd scenes at the Théâtre des Mathurins, had ended hilariously but pathetically. She was not at ease on stage; her voice did not carry. In films, she had 'learned to reduce my effects to a minimum, to use a glance or gesture to convey meaning'. The Théâtre Sarah-Bernhardt seemed enormous. It was a 'first' for Montand, too. A priori, there was no evidence that

[1] *Timebends*, Methuen, 1987.

'a music-hall singer and a movie star were capable of playing a tragedy'.[1]

She was in a state of nervous tension when Clouzot called her. Their relations were up and down, to say the least. During the shoot of *The Wages of Fear* they had had acrimonious arguments. 'Clouzot had no sense of humour, but of course, he didn't know it. Knowing you haven't got a sense of humour means you already have one, which wasn't the case with him.' He had a tyrant's reputation with his actors, particularly with 'actors who think for themselves', and, having already established that Signoret was strong-willed and hardly conciliatory, he was prepared for the worst: 'Clouzot was as suspicious of my flaws as I was suspicious of his.' But he admired her talent and Véra, his wife, adored Signoret. She had to play the other female part, she was not a professional actress, and she counted on Simone's friendly presence for reassurance. 'Simone Signoret describes how Clouzot made her suffer during the making of *Les Diaboliques*,' writes Paul Meurisse, ironically, 'but it had to happen; they were friends.'

The actual shoot would take two months, but sixteen hellish weeks were required to complete a film as packed with nervous tension as the crew who worked on it. The drama came to a head with the start of rehearsals for *The Crucible*, which lasted four months: 'After a period of unbearable nervous tension came a period of pure hell, and then the apocalypse . . . I went straight from murderess to New England Puritan, without any transition, and the next day I would be a murderess again at the Saint-Maurice Studios, where the director, his wife and I were no longer on speaking terms.'[2] Like everyone else, Paul Meurisse would have hateful memories of making *Les Diaboliques*, and of Clouzot insulting him by telling him that he was incapable of rolling his eyes up so that only the whites were showing.

But the result was extraordinary. 'The film was a triumph. It spread terror through the cinema aisles,' writes Paul Meurisse. Even Véra Clouzot, whom Meurisse rated as insignificant,

[1] *Nostalgia* . . . op.cit.
[2] Id.

transmits her only-too-real agonies of anxiety in her role of pale-skinned tropical beauty. Clouzot was past-master at creating an atmosphere of malevolence, as he had already proved in *L'Assassin Habite au 21* and *Le Corbeau*. At a time when Hitchcock was starting to work in Technicolor, Clouzot remained loyal to the mysteries of black-and-white for this sleazy tale of a faked crime, adapted from a novel by Boileau-Narcejac.

In a boys' boarding school, the headmaster (Paul Meurisse) sadistically bullies his wife (Véra Clouzot), a rich, delicate South American heiress. He is having an affair with one of his teachers (Simone Signoret), a handsome, tough woman who stands stockily on her stiletto heels. Between the pathetic heiress and the mistress, who is shocked by her lover's treatment of his wife, there springs up a female solidarity which develops into a murder plot. The sequence in which Paul Meurisse is drowned in a bathtub, and his body is then carried downstairs in a wicker hamper, is one of those few scenes in cinema history to which buffs return with continual pleasure. In a roller at the very end of the film, Clouzot asks the audience not to reveal the ending, and, although the movie has now become somewhat creaky, the advice still holds good, and I will reveal no more about this murky tale.

Simone Signoret had never had so much work. Adapted by Marcel Aymé and produced by Raymond Rouleau, performances of *The Crucible* began in December 1954 and continued without a break until summer. Arthur Miller was under a State Department travel ban because of 'ideological subversion', and could not come to Paris. Nicole Courcel, who played the part of the seductive witch, made the front cover of *Paris-Match*, while, in *Les Nouvelles Littéraires*, Gabriel Marcel compared Simone Signoret with a Holbein portrait. Robert Kemp of *Le Monde* found her 'Sophoclean'. In the role of a Puritan frozen in a betrayed wife's grief, she recalled her earlier range in *Thérèse Raquin*. Her fire smouldered inwardly, and her passion was all the stronger for being almost invisible, hidden, trapped in the strait-jacket of convention.

'At the third performance, Sartre came to see the play. He came to our dressing-room, saying, "This play was for me. Why didn't I do the adaptation?" We told him to keep a better eye on his secretariat.'[1] His 'secretariat' consisted of Jean Cau, whose future political position would be diametrically opposed to Sartre's. When Cau was first given the play to read, he took it on himself, in Sartre's name, but without consulting him, to turn down the offer of an adaptation. Sartre would later climb on the bandwagon by writing the script for the film based on the play.

Sadly, this was not Sartre's most productive period. After having conceived existentialism, and set the tone for the self-styled French intelligentsia of the Left, Sartre, like many others in the early fifties, had been preoccupied with militant protest. He knew more than most about the existence of the Russian labour camps, which he had denounced two years earlier in his literary magazine, *Les Temps Modernes*. But somehow the gulags were a low priority in a political era when the process of decolonisation was just beginning, and would soon transform the world.

French paratroopers were on the offensive in Indo-China, before Algeria, while at home trade-unionists of the CGT were indicted for 'demoralising the nation'. Antoine Pinay[2] was the mouthpiece for the French Right, America was deep in the mire of McCarthyism. On the opposite side, the Communist bloc, in spite of 'hiccups', seemed to pave the way to progress. In spite of his reservations, Sartre chose his camp, and played the fellow-traveller with the French Communist Party much as the waiter in his novel *La Nausée* plays at being a waiter, or as the cat in Mallarmé's poem plays at being a cat. 'He became a guarantor for Communism, a surety, a proselyte, a passenger, a pedlar, a travelling salesman.'[3] In his 300-page film-script for *Les Sorcières de Salem*, he superimposed an ideological gloss on Miller's original play, which diminished its universal dimension. 'Jean-Paul Sartre's screenplay, however, seemed to me to toss an arbitrary Marxist mesh over the story that led to a few absurdities. Sartre related the witchcraft outbreak to a struggle between rich and poor peasants, but in reality victims like Rebecca Nurse were in the class of relatively large landowners.'[4]

The film was co-produced by the DEFA, the East German

---

[1]*Nostalgia* . . . op.cit.
[2]Prime Minister of the French Fourth Republic.
[3]Annie Cohen-Solal, *Sartre: 1950–1980*, op.cit.
[4]*Timebends*, op.cit.

state production company which had already, the year before, invited Simone Signoret to act in Brecht's *Mother Courage*, staged by the Berliner Ensemble. The first trip to East Berlin had given her the opportunity of testing out her theories against reality in a Communist country. Unlike Bernard Blier, who was on the same trip, she had stoically refused to live in the lap of luxury in a West Berlin hotel. The wall had not as yet gone up, and Blier would make the double journey daily from one side of the frontier to another. But Simone, as usual, was keen to push things to the limit, and to fit action to theory. 'In a very childish fashion, I really believed that throughout the Eastern bloc everything was exchangeable. I thought everything was traded. I thought I would find Chinese pineapples that had been swapped for Polish coal, splendid Zeiss spectacles exchanged for Ukrainian wheat, Russian caviar exchanged for Hungarian uranium.'[1] The blinkers of a left-wing intellectual enabled her to understand and forgive everything. Her convictions withstood the little inconveniences of daily life, like telephones not working, or barbed-wire and guard-dogs at the border. She did not think to ask why, when the filming was suddenly interrupted: without any explanation, Brecht's wife Hélène Weigel backed out, although the film was already half-finished. There were plenty of mysteries in that part of the world.

So, after a short interlude – when she unwillingly went off to Mexico to act in Buñuel's *La Mort en ce Jardin* with her old friend Charles Vanel – Simone Signoret welcomed the idea of returning to East Berlin for the filming of *Les Sorcières de Salem*, which would come out in Paris in the spring of 1957. But meanwhile, a major event had happened in her life: Yves Montand's grand tour of Eastern Europe. It put her convictions to the test. But she would take years to realise how she and Montand had been manipulated as pawns in a political chess-game.

Delusion had reached its peak. In June 1956, *Le Monde* published Khrushchev's speech to the 20th Party Congress, which he had delivered in February. The First Secretary lifted the veil off the excesses of Stalinism, and the 16 million dead. He declared that the

[1] *Nostalgia . . . op.cit.*

paths to socialism were specific to each country, and that the final victory 'would not be achieved by armed intervention by socialist countries in the internal affairs of other states'. In the USSR, Poland and Hungary, thousands of people wanted to believe that a new era was beginning. Hope blossomed, even in the gulags. From his Slovakian prison, a certain Oskar Langer, who had been condemned to twenty-two years of solitary confinement, and of whose existence Simone Signoret was still unaware, wrote to his wife: 'This man who has finally stood up to talk freely is an honest, humane person. The times and circumstances that turned honest individuals into cowards are over.'[1]

Embarrassed by the frankness of these revelations, French Communists would implicitly cast doubt on the contents by describing the speech as 'attributed to Khrushchev'. More subtly, several fellow-travellers used the Secretary-General's frankness to praise the formidable self-criticism of the Soviet system. It was another typical example of intellectual back-turning by a system of thought that seemed prepared to swallow anything for the sake of the 'great socialist tomorrow'.

Events in Poland in October seemed to confirm the arrival of a new era. A four-day confrontation between striking workers and Soviet tanks led to a peaceful outcome when Gomulka, the former bugbear of Stalinism, returned to power. Hungarians, too, were at boiling-point; a solemn parade took place in memory of Rajk's execution, and the Party leaders officially admitted that his trial had been faked. In Budapest they upturned the huge statue of Stalin, and Imre Nagy and János Kádár seemed united, hand in hand with the government, in their support for the new populist movement. But the populist dawn proved all too short-lived.

On 4 November, Soviet tanks opened fire in Budapest. Thousands were killed, and Khrushchev's *perestroïka* died an immediate death. In Hungary there would be no Polish-style compromise. The man who had been preparing to play the role of a Hungarian Gomulka, Imre Nagy, president of the Hungarian Republican Council, appealed to world opinion: 'Soviet troops have attacked Budapest with the clear aim of overturning the

[1] *Une Saison à Bratislava*, op.cit.

92

democratic Hungarian government. Our troops are fighting back.'
Two years later, Nagy would be hanged on the orders of János
Kádár, who had claimed to be his ally.

It was all too much. Brutally awakened from his ideological
slumbers, Sartre would set the tone: 'I entirely and unreservedly
condemn the Soviet aggression. Without directly blaming the
Russian people as a whole, I repeat that the present Soviet government has committed a crime . . . And, for me, the crime is
not only the armoured attack on Budapest, but the fact that it
was made possible by twelve years of terror and blind stupidity.
I mean by this that it will never be possible to resume relations
with the men who are running the French Communist Party at
this moment.'[1]

For Yves Montand and Simone Signoret, who had been blithely
wondering in East Berlin what clothes they should pack to face
the freezing weather in Moscow, the invasion of Hungary was
a personal catastrophe. By a stroke of bad luck, Montand's tour,
which should have started in October, had been postponed for
a month owing to bureaucratic delays in the filming of *Les
Sorcières de Salem*. If the film had been completed sooner, if the
director, Raymond Rouleau, had been less of a perfectionist, if the
shooting-script had not been endlessly altered, they would have
set off for the Soviet Union before the Hungarian débâcle, none
of their friends would have dreamed of criticising them and their
trip would not have turned into an affair of State.

'For Montand and me, November 1956 was the most absurd, the
most cruel, the saddest and most instructive month of our twenty-
seven years of life together,' Simone Signoret would write in her
memoirs.[2] The French Right was exultant: at last, events were
confirming their darkest prognoses. Biaggi, Tixier-Vignancour and
Georges Bidault[3] paraded up the Champs-Élysées in triumph.
French intellectuals on the Left were grief-stricken and in disarray.
They felt that they had been used as stool-pigeons. They retreated
in disorder, and the Peace Movement was formed. In the *Nouvel*

---

[1]Annie Cohen-Solal, *Sartre*, op.cit.
[2]*Nostalgia . . .* op.cit.
[3]Well-known French lawyers on the Right.

Observateur, Jacques-Francis Rolland protested against the 'brutal, servile position of the French Communist Party in the Budapest catastrophe', and the 'slavishness of the intelligentsia'.

To go or not to go? The question applied more to Montand than to Signoret, since it was his tour that was at stake, and he had given his word to Obratzov, the director of the Moscow Puppet Theatre. Honouring his engagement would look like underwriting the Hungarian massacre; but if he stayed in Paris he might appear to be admitting to the right-wingers, who had vilified him for so long, that he had been wrong. Pressures were mounting on both sides. 'Paris had two shock battalions. Their objectives were clear, but their tears were crocodile tears,'[1] wrote Simone Signoret. Without taking sides, Sartre would sum up their dilemma succinctly: 'If you go, you support the Russians. If you stay, you support the fascists.'

The main confusion was in distinguishing between right and wrong, which had seemed so clear up until now. In order to stand by his promises, by his father and his left-wing ideals, Montand was now forced to serve a cause that he and his friends could no longer believe in; he was compelled to be a sham, to put on an act, to tell lies. He was caught in a double bind. And because he was a public figure, he could not resolve the contradiction in the privacy of his own heart.

For Yves Montand the popular singer, class conflict had never been merely an ideological chimera; it was a personal experience, a *mélange* of strange smells, petty deprivations, patches of wasteground, of ill-fitting shoes, patched-up clothes, inadequate meals and unresolved yearnings. His whole career had been based on this working-class image, on loyalty to the weak and oppressed. At a time when the French Communist Party had more than 30 per cent of the electorate behind it and was still the party of the masses, to cancel his tour was to make a savage break with his background, for which he was not in the least prepared.

On 3 December, with a heavy heart, Montand wrote Obratzov an embarrassed letter, explaining that he would keep his promise in spite of the 'profound distress felt by a great number of

[1] *Nostalgia* . . . op.cit.

French people because of the Hungarian drama'. Referring to the Algerian War and the Suez Expedition, he presented himself, rather bizarrely, as an emissary of world peace, determined to 'try to prevent by any means a return to the Cold War, and consequently the possibility of any war'. In the confused context of that time, the strong streak of megalomania in Montand's formula was probably less apparent. By bowing to the flattering illusion that world peace somehow hinged on his personal decisions, Montand justified in his own eyes a decision that he had reluctantly made when, for the first time, he no longer knew what he *had* to think.

Many of Montand's later political stands – like the virulence with which he denounced the persistent elements of Stalinism under Brezhnev and Andropov – only make sense in the light of this earlier trauma. He had a score to settle with himself. If he had not been such a blinkered Stalinist, he might not, later, have acted with quite so much enthusiasm in Costa-Gavras's *L'Aveu*, a film for which he lost over twenty pounds in weight in six weeks.

Everything was distorted by the political in-fighting. In an ideological struggle whose stakes they did not fully understand, Montand and Signoret found themselves back in the front line of a battle for which they no longer had the heart. Montand had decided to make a clean break, to go abroad, to weigh anchor. He may have felt 'heavy at heart', but he was secretly relieved to extricate himself from the claustrophobia of the Parisian fuss, and to take a few months' respite from the public debate about his state of mind. In spite of everything, the trip sounded exciting, and he vaguely hoped to be of some use over there.

In 1978 a psychoanalytical conference on the theme of 'the unconscious' was organised at Tbilisi, in Georgia. In a country where the works of Freud were only available in certain libraries, it was the first time that the subject would be discussed with Western psychoanalysts. In the months before the conference, the psychoanalytical community in France was riven by debates similar to those that took place before Montand's and Signoret's departure in 1956. For a psychoanalyst going to the USSR in the late seventies ran the risk of appearing to sanction the policy of 'psychiatric internment', whereby dissidents were considered mentally ill, and would occasionally be made so, by the use of neurolepsy and ECT. Many of the analysts and psychiatrists invited to participate in this historic get-together with their Soviet colleagues refused the invitation. But others accepted, out of a conviction that, in a country where free speech is censored, nothing can be more desirable for the inhabitants of that country than an exchange of views, even if it is restricted to an official group. The conference took place, and gave rise to fascinating discussions and exchanges of ideas. Now we know that it had a liberating influence, with long-term effects that laid the foundations for *perestroïka* in the field of psychiatry. The Montands' trip probably had the same kind of long-term effect, though the context was entirely different.

CHAPTER TEN

When she described their trip to Eastern Europe in *Nostalgia Isn't What It Used To Be*, in lingering, almost voluptuous detail, Simone Signoret was stealing some of Montand's thunder. After all, it was *his* tour, *his* triumph, and she had just gone along for the ride. But in those sixty pages she describes a joint triumph, and never once puts herself in second place.

There was quite possibly a secret rivalry, probably subconscious, which led them to be constantly shifting the balance from one to the other in the public eye. Their relationship seemed to need this see-saw element; they took turns in the limelight. They would climb the ladder of fame together, rung by rung: one would never get in front of the other. It would have been dangerous if Montand had become a prince consort, or Signoret just a has-been. They were the same age, both strong characters; she brought her culture and intelligence, while he shared his experience of life and the professional baggage of showbusiness. So the balance was about equal, if variable, despite ceaseless efforts by the Press to find out which of the two super-celebrities wore the trousers, which dominated the other, which gave way or which shouted louder in their quarrels. Nothing sells better than an article about the balance of power between a famous man and a famous woman.

On the trip to Eastern Europe, she would limit her role to the performer's wife. The Russians only knew of her through Henri Calef's second-rate film, *Ombres et Lumières*, the story of a pianist who goes mad while playing a Tchaikovsky concerto. At leisure for once, she promised to record everything they saw. However awkwardly they departed, it was Russia, the mother country of socialism, that they were preparing to discover. However much they knew or suspected, the idea still made their hearts skip a beat. They had talked and dreamed for so long about this better world; it was a heady adventure. Simone Signoret would savour every moment, and would relish every episode with the *frisson* of a child playing truant.

Faultless in the part of a performer's perfect wife, with her suitcase packed full with fur-lined boots and outfits from Hermès, she bought sables at GUM, made friends with their interpreters, enthused about Russian folklore, samovars and her chats with ordinary people, and navigated the corridors of power with all the self-assurance of an upper-middle-class lady from Neuilly, and the clear conscience of one who knows that she is in the right.

She would reassure herself by paying attention to the 'little' people at the bottom of the system, and by noting the sad, enigmatic looks that followed them when they visited the factories in their Parisian finery. They brought Ilia Ehrenbourg his favourite goat's cheese, sent by Claude Roy; they asked the Russian top brass awkward questions about Hungary or McCarthyism, which, oddly enough, did not seem to bother the Soviets, though it was a favourite stalking-horse for Party members in the West. Unconsciously, her vigilance had the effect of blinding her all the more to the truth; she was content to note the outward drama without imagining, or asking questions about, its inner meaning. She did not see the poverty, the economic decline or the secret police. She noticed the sad looks, and took careful note, as if understanding them was only secondary.

She had not had so much fun since the old Flore days. 'Moscow by Night' was full of attractions. She went to the ballet, where the Russian dancers danced superbly, and spent fascinating evenings with the interpreters, who enjoyed unburdening themselves and disclosing, off-duty, their inside knowledge of Soviet society. Montand sang at the Oudjniki Stadium to a spellbound audience of 20,000 spectators. Never had he been applauded with quite such enthusiasm or intensity. In their longing for the West, Soviet audiences hero-worshipped the French singer who was supposed to be praising the paradise in which they themselves were suffocating. He brought them gusts of fresh air, and tenderness; he bathed them in kindness.

The famous dinner with Khrushchev was one of the high points of Simone Signoret's life: her discovery of the Café Flore, her first meeting with Montand, *Casque d'Or*, winning the Oscar, the publication of her books – and then her meeting with the rulers of the Russian Empire.

The evening had begun at the Bolshoi with Madame Sadoul, the French critic's wife, who thought they were watching her great friend Plessetskaïa perform when in fact she was dancing in Kiev that evening. The two women laughed over the mistake, while Montand was singing in the Tchaikovsky Theatre to a full house, as on every other night. For once, Simone was spending her evening elsewhere. The two French ladies had crossed Moscow behind the grey satin curtains of an enormous Zim. 'Wrapped and hatted in pastel mink', Simone Signoret was luckily wearing her black Hermès suit.

For, in the middle of the second act, they came for her, and took her back in style to the Tchaikovsky Theatre, where she was sneaked into the wings. Only when she arrived did she realise why this evening was so special. There, arrayed in a box like onions, were Khrushchev, Molotov, Mikoyan, Bulganin and Malenkov. They had come to hear the French fellow-traveller sing. They had liked his performance, and they applauded enthusiastically. Montand was moved but worried about their coming to shake his hand in his dressing-room.

But they brought him an extraordinary message: Yves Montand and his wife were cordially invited to have supper with the rulers of a country whose tanks had just stamped out liberty in Hungary. To quote Montand's own words, 'I was over there in conditions where I had nothing more to lose.' A refusal was unthinkable. Amazed, flattered, they accepted on the spot. But they decided to use this unique opportunity to unburden themselves and to tell Khrushchev what they really thought. A way, perhaps, to justify their trip to themselves and to prove their courage and acumen. They could return to Paris without blushing, feeling they had been of some use, having talked things out with Khrushchev. Without much difficulty, they

SIMONE SIGNORET

convinced themselves of their sacred mission of representing the intellectuals of the French Left, and of conveying their anxiety to the very man who had caused it and who could very well sympathise (so they thought) with their arguments.

After the formalities, they immediately grasped the nettle, explaining their hesitation about coming, and mentioning Hungary. They assured the master of the Kremlin that in France the fascists had not been the only ones to denounce the Soviet invasion, and that many people of goodwill, like themselves, did not understand, and asked questions. They were astounded by their own audacity. What was at issue, they explained to Khrushchev, listening with a smile, were the revolutionary aspirations of millions who felt betrayed. They waxed still more passionate, believing they were keeping cool; they pleaded the cause of world revolution, of the proletariat and the 'radiant future' – two actors teaching morality to the dinosaurs of Soviet power. Just for one evening, they were the Emperor's privy counsellors, the guests of the Tsar. They had convinced themselves that perhaps the fate of Hungary and of world peace hinged on the force of their convictions. They were on tenterhooks.

Khrushchev replied to their cut and thrust with good humour, and an occasional chuckle. That was his style; the image of kindly old stager. He justified the tanks with a jolly shrug, not much moved by their finer feelings. He reiterated that it had been the Hungarian people who had appealed to their Soviet big brother. To confront the fascist counter-revolutionaries, the masses had begged the Kremlin to intervene; he had only done his duty, however painful. The outcome is well known: Khrushchev did not feel threatened by these showbusiness people; he was enjoying himself, he was charmed by them, he had spent a delightful evening, a change from the official Kremlin parties. The Ukrainian peasant also made the most of his tête-à-tête with the glamorous Parisienne; he had taste, an eye for beauty. He admired her elegance, her refinement, her Hermès suit . . .

Simone Signoret was, it was said, kept as ignorant as Catherine the Great when she was shown round villages of smiling, well-dressed peasants while the rest of the country was starving. In later years, she was agonised by guilt about her negligence, and realised she had been taken in by the very people whose faults she claimed to be unmasking. To be fair, she never ceased trying to make up for her short-sightedness.

CHAPTER ELEVEN

'She passed before me like a flash of lightning, elegant, regal, hurried, but with her head held so high that I still had time to notice signs of contrariness, nervousness and boredom on her proud face.'[1] It was in Prague, in the foyer of the Hotel Alkron, at the beginning of 1957. Jo Langer was a lonely, driven woman whose husband was festering in a Slovakian labour camp; the effect of her flamboyant cousin arriving in grand style, in a cavalcade of official government limousines, can be imagined: hope, anxiety, and unease.

Yves Montand was due first to sing in Prague, then to give a concert in Bratislava, the Slovakian capital where Jo Langer lived. She took her courage in both hands and telephoned Simone, her cousin from France. She said she had read in the Press that their arrival was expected in Bratislava, and she keenly hoped to meet them there. Simone was at her most evasive – absent-minded, hard to pin down, very much the star. 'Family when you're on tour – what a bore!' Irritated by the sense of urgency in the voice of her unknown cousin, she immediately 'classified her as one of those tiresome people who are desperate to discover a family link with celebrities, just to impress their neighbours'.[2] In any case, officials had warned her that the Bratislava concert would probably be cancelled. On this endless tour, so much the better.

Without allowing herself to be upset, Jo Langer decided to catch the first train from Bratislava to Prague, and found herself,

[1] *Une Saison à Bratislava*, op.cit.
[2] *Nostalgia . . .* op.cit.

shivering with both terror and hope, in the foyer of the Hotel Alkron. 'I didn't intend to ask her to do very much – only for her to slip one of the officials a little question, about Oskar, just like that, innocently, at the end of a banquet or cocktail party. There would probably have been such a panic that it might have been enough to get Oskar freed, on the quiet.' Then Simone suddenly arrived on Montand's arm. They came out of the lift, surrounded by a cloud of buzzing officials, and headed towards the hotel's grand dining-room. They hurried past Jo Langer, a few feet away; she just had time to smell Simone's expensive perfume. But she dared not go up to them; she felt under surveillance, and departed as swiftly as she had come. In despair, she took the train back to Bratislava, to a hell that would last for several more years.

Jo Langer was the granddaughter of the sister of Simone's paternal grandmother, Ernestine, nicknamed Tiny, the Austrian-Jewish bigot who had never come to terms with her son's marriage to Georgette Kaminker. Simone had only had sporadic contact with this grandmother who used to bring cinnamon-flavoured pastries, and occasionally would take her on a Sunday to 'sniff the fresh air of the cinema'. She could not remember her ever having mentioned any Hungarian cousin. Jo Langer belonged to a world of silence, the unknown country of her father's family.

But Jo Langer, eleven years older, knew very well who little Kiki Kaminker was, and had followed every stage in her brilliant career from afar: which was why, when the Press announced the arrival of Yves Montand and his wife, she had decided to show herself; not because she longed to 'impress her neighbours', but because it was a question of life and death. Jo Langer knew something of the power that fame can bestow, particularly in a country that has broken down, and in which a small item of truth can cause cracks in the edifice of the State. She had an intuition – correct, but premature – of the energy that a celebrity like Simone Signoret could deploy, to support a cause like hers.

But the Czech authorities were on their guard. The government was well aware of the potential dangers for its image if the two cousins were to meet. From the moment that the train crossed the German-Czech frontier, Montand and Signoret had been escorted by 'two gentlemen, with their arms full of red carnations'.

SIMONE SIGNORET

Carnations were a bad omen . . . Simone Signoret unreservedly believed in the French actors' suspicion that carnations bring bad luck. The two gentlemen asked Montand if he would agree to add two extra gala-concerts to his programme, for the police and the Army. Montand politely refused; he was exhausted but he did not say that nobody would dream of asking such a favour in his own country. The two gentlemen, worried about him feeling so tired, suggested – very casually – that it might be best to cancel the Bratislava concert, which suited him well enough since he really was feeling exhausted. 'Today I can truly maintain that, during that week in February 1957 in Prague, everything was put into place, or sometimes displaced, so that a meeting between the wife of the political prisoner Oskar Langer and her cousin, the wife of the singer Yves Montand, would be impossible.'[1]

Born in 1912 in Hungary, Jo Langer had married Oskar Langer, a Slovakian economist and a Communist of the pure, hard kind. In 1938, after the Anschluss, they set off for the United States where they lived for eight years. It was not an easy exile; for Oskar Langer, Chicago was never any more than a transit asylum, where he lived through a temporary purgatory. He had a single obsession, to return to his own country to build socialism there. In 1946, he felt happy at last: a letter had come from his old comrade Karol Bacilek, secretary of the Central Committee of the Slovakian Communist Party, finally summoning him back to his homeland. Karol Bacilek was the same man who would 'become Chief of Police a few years later and have the rare privilege of delivering to the State executioners eleven of his nearest and dearest ex-comrades, plus several hundred other ex-comrades whom he did not know quite so well'.[2]

Oskar Langer was one of those committed Communists who insisted, against all the evidence, on believing in the 'radiant future' of Stalinism. In America at the time of the Hitler-Stalin Pact when he had received letters from old German Communist comrades who had left the Party after seeing the Swastika gaily floating

[1]*Nostalgia . . .* op.cit.
[2]*Une Saison à Bratislava*, op.cit.

over Moscow airport, he had forbidden his wife to answer them. Even when she told him that she herself had wept over eyewitness accounts of the Moscow trials of the thirties, he refused to discuss them. His certainty was unshakeable.

In August 1952, after six years of honest, loyal service, the faithful comrade was arrested by the secret police. He was not alone: many of the old Party members had already been arrested, and Oskar Langer knew that he was under surveillance. Going out with his wife and two daughters, one in her pram, he had narrowly escaped an assassination attempt. Two big black cars had borne down on them in the street, and they had only saved themselves by taking flight, leaving the pram to bounce along the cobbles like the pram on the steps in the film *Battleship Potemkin*.

Oskar Langer was Jewish, and, worse, he had lived in the United States. He was thus doubly suspect as a Zionist agent. But for him Judaism was no more than an archaism, condemned by History. As his wife would later write, with some cruelty, 'He was one of those Communists who so hate being Jewish that they would kill a Jewish beggar rather than give him a crumb of bread.' In spite of the police surveillance and the murder-attempt, his faith in Communism stayed intact. In bed at night, he continued to defend the Party, explaining to his wife that the 'fate of individuals is of secondary importance'. What of his old comrades, then, arrested, judged and condemned to death? They had probably committed serious mistakes, crimes, even. In any case, they had confessed. 'If they prove their innocence, they will be released,' he would say, without dreaming that he himself would soon be a victim of the same fiendish logic.

Three months later, in November, a special edition of *Pravda* announced the opening of the trial of the 'conspirators against the State led by Rudolf Slansky'. Among the names of the prosecution witnesses was Oskar Langer's. He accused himself of holding on to his American nationality so as to be able to return to the USA if his activities were unmasked. His wife well knew that he had in fact given up his US passport three years before. He testified that he had returned to Czechoslovakia in order to take part in the Zionist plot orchestrated by Slansky and aimed at overturning the Socialist régime. When, many years later, he managed to send Jo

Langer his first clandestine letter, she was not surprised to learn that his statement had been dictated to him, from the first line to the last. He had had to learn it by heart. Out of the fourteen defendants in the Slansky trial, eleven would be condemned to death and hanged.

Among the three survivors was Artur London, future author of *L'Aveu*[1] (*The Confession*). He had been sentenced to 'only' eleven years' penal servitude, having received preferential treatment thanks to his wife, the sister-in-law of Raymond Guyot, a member of the Central Committee of the French Communist Party.

Oskar Langer's trial would take place a year later, behind closed doors. He was condemned to twenty-two years' penal servitude for high treason and espionage. From then on, Jo Langer would run the usual gamut of miseries and humiliations reserved for the wives of political prisoners, alone with her children in a country of informers and liars, knocking on every door in her efforts to have her husband freed, and coming up against the closed faces of her old friends. 'Nobody knew where he was. At that precise moment, they were probably beating him up. How else could they make him guilty enough to justify the sentence? . . . And there was I, mother of two children whom I had to feed and bring up fatherless in a society where we were pariahs, and the police were on my heels . . .'[2]

In spite of the pressures, and the confessions, Jo Langer did not doubt for an instant her husband's loyalty and total innocence, in contrast to Lise London who, in a moment of madness, had convinced herself of Artur London's guilt, and had called for his execution in an open letter. But Jo Langer was not politically naïve; she was always more sceptical and clear-minded than her husband. Remembering what she had read about the Moscow trials, she was less susceptible than most to the rigged evidence of extorted confessions. And, paradoxically, she was all the more convinced of his innocence because their partnership had not been a harmonious one. There had already been problems in America, where one

[1]Gallimard, 1968.
[2]*Une Saison à Bratislava*, op.cit.

of the main bones of contention had been Oskar Langer's blind loyalty to the Communist orthodoxy. She had all the more reason to be certain that a man like him was incapable of betraying anyone he felt to be one of his own kind. Moreover, she possessed hard proof of his innocence: 'There I was, the wife of an absent man whom I had once loved, whom I did not perhaps love any longer, but with whom I was more closely linked than ever by pity and loyalty.'

In following the trajectory of Simone Signoret's life, a few women, real or imaginary, emerge who have to confront the question of marital solidarity in moments of high drama. When John Proctor is condemned to be hanged in *The Crucible*, his wife stays by the side of a husband who has humiliated and betrayed her, loyal, in spite of everything, unto death. This was the only conceivable attitude for Simone Signoret. Later, when Costa-Gavras offered her the part of Lise London, she would hesitate for a long time. Solidarity with Montand was one of the cornerstones of her life; she had no wish to portray the character of a woman who was capable, even in a moment of madness, of believing in the guilt of a man with whom she had shared everything – militant action, resistance, the threat of deportation. 'In *L'Aveu*, Simone Signoret would have to act out the only scenario that she would have been incapable of performing in real life: the part of a wife who can bring herself not only to believe in her husband's guilt but to proclaim aloud, to disown him in public.'[1]

In 1963, appalled by the execution of Julián Grimau, a Spanish Communist who had just been shot by Franco's myrmidons 'under the glare of the car headlights, at dawn', she asked Jorge Semprun to put her in touch with the dead man's widow, Angela Grimau. She then introduced the latter to her friend Pierre Lazareff, and as a result, Angela Grimau was able to talk about her husband in a special news programme on television. Her broadcast moved the entire French nation. But, two years later, Simone Signoret by chance met Angela Grimau again. Her friend Jorge Semprun had just been expelled from the Spanish Communist Party; she

[1] Jorge Semprun, *Montand, la vie continue*, op. cit.

asked Angela, who owed so much to Semprun, what she thought about the expulsion. Angela Grimau muttered something about loyalty to the Party mattering more than any personal friendships, whatever the circumstances. Simone Signoret could not get over the shock of seeing the Party's fierce bigotry reflected in the eyes of 'that simple, loyal woman'.[1] Later, she may well have thought of Angela Grimau when she read this sentence in Jo Langer's book, which she herself translated: 'Socialism has a long track record of physical assassinations, but it beats all records in the assassination of souls and consciences.'[2]

On the first page of *Nostalgia Isn't What It Used To Be*, in a sort of prologue, Simone Signoret writes, 'What I call my "conscience" is in fact the way that half-a-dozen people look at me. And these half-dozen are all men. It's very odd: I don't feel women's eyes on me very much.' She might not have written these lines if she had thought back to Jo Langer's anonymous gaze fixed on her that day in 1957 in the foyer of the Hotel Alkron.

'I knew nothing at all about Simone's inner convictions, but my own conviction whispered to me that if I could only find a way of being alone with her for a moment to tell her about Oskar still being in prison, she would listen to me, believe me, and try to help me. It was unthinkable that, after having discovered all that she must have discovered, about Budapest, the rigged show-trials in all the Socialist Republics, all the lies, she would not have believed my story.'[3] But Simone Signoret had not yet discovered all these things. Of course there had been all that hesitation before they left, and the tanks invading Hungary, and those sad looks and those enigmatic signs – thousands of little details. But she was far from imagining what this unknown cousin could have told her: 'We did not have the remotest suspicion that, three and a half years after Stalin's death, there were still people in prison who would not be rehabilitated until 1964.'

This meeting-that-never-was, so like a scene from a film, proved a turning point in Simone Signoret's life. Jo Langer did her an

---

[1] Jorge Semprun, *Montand, la vie continue*, op.cit.
[2] *Une Saison à Bratislava*, op.cit.
[3] Id.

inestimable service in implanting in her the seeds of self-doubt, and in shaking that daunting self-assurance which was always a characteristic even before she became famous. Whatever else may have been said about Simone Signoret, one thing is sure: she could acknowledge her mistakes. When she described that terrible misunderstanding, that failure to help a person in danger, she made no apologies.

Yet she would turn a deaf ear to her cousin for quite a long time to come. Nine years later, in London, where she was playing Lady Macbeth, Jo Langer came to see her at the Savoy Hotel. Oskar Langer had been freed and rehabilitated, but had died a few months later, as a result of his long martyrdom. 'He had paid with his life for those ten years of penal servitude. His whole organism had worn out, destroyed by his continual hunger strikes.'[1]

This time Jo Langer felt less intimidated. She had managed to get out of Czechoslovakia for a few days; though she had no money at all in her pockets, she had not come to ask her grand cousin for any favours. All she wanted was simply to explain, to tell her story and open her heart to a friend. 'But above all to take the opportunity of talking at last with a specimen of a family whose survival I could not understand: by this I meant French left-wing intellectuals.'

Simone Signoret did not interrupt her for a while. She was in a hurry, she was anxious to rehearse, once again for the thousandth time, a speech that she found particularly difficult. She knew that she had been crazy to accept the part, but she was still trying to cobble the pieces back together. Nevertheless, she allowed Jo Langer to start her story, but, when she got to her husband's arrest in 1952, Simone could not help trying to be clever. She asked her, 'Don't you think that, if you had stayed in New York, your husband, as a Communist, would have run the risk of the same kind of treatment from the Americans?' The ghost of Joe McCarthy had knocked once again; and once again, Jo Langer went away telling herself that left-wing intellectuals were still just as blinkered as ever.

It was only in 1969, after the crushing of the Prague Spring, when Jo Langer had left Czechoslovakia for good to live in Sweden, that Simone Signoret would read Artur London's *L'Aveu*

[1] *Une Saison à Bratislava*, Simone Signoret's preface, op.cit.

and Slansky's wife's autobiography one after the other, and finally understand what had happened to Oskar Langer. She would suddenly realise, with a dreadful sense of the irrevocable, that she had probably had it in her power to get him freed, and thus to save his life.

And it would not be until 1973, in Paris, seventeen years after the failed rendezvous in Prague, that the two cousins would really come to know each other properly: 'It was wonderful, to be able to do what I might never have been able to do. Listen to her and hug her.'[1] She would do much more than that. In 1981 Jo Langer's book, *Une Saison à Bratislava*, would be published by Le Seuil, translated by Simone Signoret herself in collaboration with Éric Vigne, the historian. For Simone it was a last attempt to repair the irreparable and a way of owning up to her mistake.

But she had not finished making amends to Jo Langer. Still later, the failed meeting in the Hotel Alkron would serve as inspiration for the central scene in her novel *Adieu Volodia*. For Élie and Sonia Guttman, Jewish emigrants from the Ukraine living in the Rue de la Mare in Paris, Volodia was the 'friend, cousin, almost a brother' who for years they had assumed to be dead. He would reappear for a split-second in their lives in 1927, just long enough for a smile, at the 'café-restaurant des Trois-Marches in the Place Dauphine, opposite the Palais de Justice'. Another meeting-that-never-was: for even if Volodia was present in the flesh at Les Trois-Marches, well dressed and smiling, in reality, like Jo Langer, he was enclosed in an invisible ghetto, under the watchful eye of the interpreter Dimitri, who was probably a KGB agent. It was like a nightmare. Élie and Volodia embraced, 'cheek against cheek, with their eyes closed, so fiercely, and for so long, that they grew dizzy and had to hang on to each other so as not to fall down like drunks on the café floor'.

But Dimitri the *apparatchik* took control of the conversation in his comically literal French, and after a few polite phrases and an exchange of addresses, the visitors from the Ukraine said their

[1]*Nostalgia* . . . op.cit.

farewells and headed back to the gulag from which they had only escaped for long enough to play this little charade.

Simone Signoret placed this scene at the centre of her talkative, warm-hearted novel – a bleak and terrible scene, full of silence and constraint, like a black hole in the lives of her protagonists – which tells us all we need about how far she had travelled since that day in 1957 when she had not noticed the anguished gaze of a woman watching the only people who could have helped her, as they disappeared out of sight.

CHAPTER TWELVE

By the time Montand and Signoret returned to Paris after their grand tour in Eastern Europe, still dazed by images of collective farms and cheering crowds, most of the fuss had died away. The public had other things to think about than the goings-on of this famous couple. Professionally, Simone Signoret was standing still: nobody came looking for her any more. She was in the wilderness. The *Zeitgeist*, fashion, politics – everything seemed to conspire against her, to make her a has-been. 'The future belonged to very young girls and pretty young women.' New-wave directors, from Godard to Truffaut, burned to breathe new life into the 'seventh muse', and saw her talent as old hat, and in general film people stopped thinking of her, so as 'to keep in with the Americans'. In short, she was out of the race. Domestic happiness at home with her husband was the only course left open; but their passion had cooled somewhat, and she was not all that eager to settle down to be a housewife.

An English film-maker, Peter Glenville, would come to the rescue, offering her the part of Alice Aisgill in *Room at the Top*. And then, Yves Montand was invited to sing at the Henry Miller theatre on Broadway. Three years after 'playing' the Soviet Empire, they got ready to discover the New World.

For Simone Signoret, America had at first been like a fairy-tale land of dreams. Her maternal grandmother had been there to visit a cousin from Valenciennes who had struck it lucky in the USA, and she had told Kiki Kaminker all about New York in 1890, the skyscrapers, the heady whiff of excitement in the air. Later, Simone would discover the American cinema and the glamour of

Hollywood, the smooth ageless faces of stars like Fred Astaire and Duke Ellington. But she met her first real Americans at the time of the Liberation, in the big Allégret house where she had 'taken to the *maquis*' with Serge Reggiani, Danièle Delorme, Daniel Gélin and Yves Allégret. 'It was raining, it must have been eleven in the morning. All the Americans were busily eating the same thing, a sort of bright-red pâté, they were sunburned, handsome and not at all Wagnerian-looking. There were Gary Coopers, Paul Munis, Spencer Tracys, John Garfields, Donald Ducks. They laughed a lot.'

America meant fun, parties, spangles, Vincente Minnelli ballets, floodlit fountains, Cyd Charisse's legs, *joie de vivre*. America spelt Adventure, pioneering, Western films, gallops across the great outdoors. America was the homeland of the cinema, the factory where myths were made, the firmament of the stars, the Mount Olympus where the shadowy gods from the silver screen lived. It was the land of innocence, the land of infinite possibilities, of plains stretching away into the future, where the Red Indians described by her grandmother drank firewater, and found themselves defenceless against their white attackers. In Elia Kazan's *America, America*, America was the promised land, an untarnished place – the virgin soil where people's lives would be completely transformed, where the good of each man worked for the good of all.

During the Cold War, this delightful picture was challenged by a vision of another earthly paradise, full of sturdy workers, determined to stamp out man's oppression by man. The Stalinist mythology imposed its own totems, bare-armed athletes holding up their trowels in front of a brick wall, vast allegorical pictures of the armed proletariat pursuing the capitalists with righteous anger. And Stalin's face, with its defensive moustache, piercing eyes, and high collar. These arid visions were intended to be inspiring, but they had none of the charm and freshness of their American rivals.

Simone Signoret and Yves Montand had been barred from the USA, and America was no longer a dream-country for them, but a dishonoured one, a jungle, a continent crawling with huge fascist beasts. There was no need for Simone Signoret to break her four-year contract with Warner Brothers; they no longer wanted her. Stoically she was preparing to make the best of it when the longed-for visa suddenly arrived. It was a restricted visa, known as a 'waiver', a mean-minded gesture to the 'Red devils'. But the door was open.

It was a typical New York September, with the tarmac melting under the Indian summer sun. Manhattan was just as it was in the movies, poetic, hard, with metal staircases running up the sides of the buildings and awnings over the doorways of the grand apartment blocks. Simone noted how close the quarters were to each other, and the proximity of poverty and the majestic skyline of the skyscrapers. They installed themselves at the Algonquin, Mecca of the American intelligentsia, in the heart of Broadway. Staying in the next-door room were Oscar Peterson and Ella Fitzgerald. *Room at the Top* was doing excellent business in the New York cinemas; the taxi-drivers recognised Simone Signoret, and called her Alice Aisgill, like the heroine of the film: 'In Paris, Montand was Montand, and I was I, and we were husband and wife. In Moscow, I had been Montand's wife. In New York, before the opening, my main worry was that people would take Montand for an actress's husband.' She was always so anxious to preserve the balance.

She was soon to be reassured. A few weeks later, Montand would be as famous as Maurice Chevalier; but before this, he rehearsed his show with feverish energy, in spite of appalling toothache. Journalists asked him why it had taken him so long to come to America; Simone translated the questions and answers, performing her father's old job as an interpreter. Montand could not speak a single word of English; sweating blood, he learned phonetically, memorising short versions of his songs in English, which would charm his warm-hearted fans.

On Broadway, all is won or lost on the first night. At 2 a.m., reading the stop-press headlines, Montand knew that he'd won: the French singer had become the toast of New York City, and the great adventure had begun. He was invited to appear on Dinah Shore's famous TV show; soon, he would make *Let's Make Love* with George Cukor and Marilyn Monroe. Meanwhile, in the cinemas, Alice Aisgill stayed in the limelight.

CATHERINE DAVID

After Broadway, it was on to Hollywood and its sensual mirages, the party thrown by Kirk Douglas and his French wife, Anne, competing with the reception organised by Richard Nixon in a downtown hotel. Walt Disney came, and Jack Warner, and 'the Coopers, the Kellys, the Pecks, the Wilders, the Hathaways, George Cukor, Dean Martin'. Once again, Yves Montand and Simone Signoret found themselves rubbing shoulders with the great. They had come to the USA for three weeks, but Simone Signoret would stay there for several months, and Montand for nearly a whole year. When they returned, they would both be international stars; they would also have survived the first serious crisis of their life together.

'Hollywood is just like Le Vésinet!'[1] Simone Signoret told Jean Cau one day, and he was delighted by the comparison; but it was only a joke. All her life, she may well have refused to behave like a star, to strut around with the official panoply of fame; but nevertheless she was in her element with Henry Fonda, Gary Cooper, Lauren Bacall and Vivien Leigh. Now she was part of the family photo, in the first row. And the judges for the Oscar would choose her over the heads of the other nominees – Elizabeth Taylor, Audrey Hepburn, Katharine Hepburn and Doris Day.

She had come a long way. In the French film world, she was an actress at the end of her career. Salvation came from Britain. *Room at the Top* was a film adaptation of John Braine's novel, the bestseller of the year in Great Britain. The part of Alice had been jealously sought after by British actresses: 'Intelligent, generous, understanding, maternal, sexually liberated, without any class prejudices.'

Directed by Jack Clayton, the story unfolds in Bradford, Yorkshire, a region where fog mingles with the factory-smoke and young people hang about with nowhere to go. These are the same 'angry young men' who, a few years later, would transform their revolt into a cultural revolution and conquer the world with their songs. In this working-class version of *La Traviata*, Laurence Harvey plays an ambitious but weak-willed young man, agonisingly split between his decision to marry a rich young heiress

[1] A middle-class suburb of Paris.

115

and his doomed love for a heart-breaking Frenchwoman of forty, isolated in her cold Anglo-Saxon exile.

The character of Alice has a great gentleness about her, striking an unusual note for Simone Signoret. Alice Aisgill is fragile, with no defences against betrayal, and no protection against love. At the end of the film, after four days of happiness – as in *Casque d'Or* – she is abandoned in a cowardly way by her fickle lover, and she commits suicide. For the first time, nobody asked Simone to be faithful to her own image, to register haughty disdain or arrogance, or to show the 'wildcat' side she had made such good use of in *Dédée d'Anvers* or *Casque d'Or*. She no longer needed to be strong; at last she could draw in her claws and show a vulnerable side, give her sensuality full rein, in all the dazzling sex-appeal of her maturity. The Oscar judges were right: *Room at the Top* is one of her best films.

It probably needed an outsider's, a foreigner's, eye to bring about this metamorphosis, for her image to break free from its French stereotype ('the Signoret tradition') and her screen career to get going again. In New York, she realised with surprise that nobody had seen *Casque d'Or*, apart from the odd film buff from Greenwich Village.

In *Room at the Top*, she is also faced with the unfairness of ageing. The part of this 'older woman' whose great love-affair turns into tragedy became a crucial marker for Simone's mid-life; *Room at the Top* was the peak point of her career. Winning the Oscar was her revenge on the French film-makers who had thought they could do without her; thanks to the Oscar, she could impress Montand; thanks to the Oscar, she could start filming again in the best conditions, choosing her own subjects, and she would savour the pleasures of acting to the full.

People may remember the incredible photographs of the Oscar ceremony that appeared in *Libération* on the day of her death. In it we see Simone in the crowd of spectators in their glamorous party clothes – waiting, hoping; she's not sitting back in her seat, like the others, but leaning forward towards the stage, as if towards Heaven. Her face is tilted backwards, in ecstasy – like a lover offering herself to the kiss of fame, she's clasping her breasts with both hands, her bare shoulders gleaming from the deep 'V' of her *décolletage*. She's at her peak, as woman and as artist, with her 'robust charm and curly hair the colour of Chablis', as the American newspapers put it. She listens as the names of the prizewinners are read out like a litany: Oscar for best short film, *Poisson Rouge*; Oscar for the best foreign film, *Orfeo Negro*. The French cinema was forging ahead that year in Hollywood. Introduced by his dream-hero, Fred Astaire, Yves Montand takes the stage and sings; he's a wild success. 'Good!' she tells herself, 'at least one member of the family has done well!' Finally, Rock Hudson opens the fateful envelope and cries out: 'Simone Signoret!' 'Then,' as she later told Jean Cau, 'I heard a roaring noise which grew into the most frightening ovation I'd ever heard in my life! I felt as though I'd been bludgeoned like an ox! I got up – I rushed to the platform, in tears, running like a madwoman. Goodbye, cool head and self-control . . . My nerves were in shreds. The shouting made me feel weak at the knees. In the mist I could see dear old Montand sobbing away as if he'd just buried his twelve best friends. And then I had that golden thing in my arms. I was struck dumb. That's all. Afterwards, it was bedlam – TV cameras from all over the world, waves of journalists . . .'

In one instant, in the dazzling flash of the cameras, she saw the past recaptured all in one go in her mind's eye, like a photograph developed in a fraction of a second. And there was Montand, holding out his arms, and America, at her feet. After Claudette Colbert, she was the second French actress to experience this heady triumph.

But Simone was no fool. She knew perfectly well that there were 'political' reasons, which had nothing to do with talent, behind her rise to fame as a Hollywood superstar. The American film world was at last breathing again after the long McCarthy years, and by giving the Oscar to this subversive Frenchwoman who had signed the Stockholm Petition and, as everybody knew, had close, almost family, ties with the French Communist Party and had been for many years *persona non grata* on Federal soil, Hollywood was advertising its joy at the return of free expression. For the Los Angeles judges, her Oscar was like a final challenge hurled at the defeated Right – a cry of freedom. 'The Americans wanted to prove to themselves that McCarthy really was dead . . . I felt this in the way that they worded their congratulatory telegrams. They were celebrating their own victory.'

Alas, *Room at the Top* was never given its proper due in France, though it received other awards apart from the Oscar. The British Academy gave Signoret the prize for best English-language actress of the year, and at Cannes, André Malraux handed her the Palme d'Or for best actress. But French audiences did not recognise their 'very own' Simone in the typically English setting of Clayton's film; they missed her gutsiness, and her broad Parisian accent, and were unmoved by the subtle sound of the Yorkshire working-class dialect. But above all, they were not particularly bowled over by the story of an adulterous affair between a middle-aged woman and a younger man (still considered daring in the Anglo-Saxon countries). '*Room at the Top* didn't scandalise anybody in Paris by showing lovers in bed together; the theme of a maturing woman, cousin to Stendhal's Léa and Mme de Rênal, experiencing her last, unhappy love-affair with an ambitious young man, didn't seem particularly shocking.'

In the seventies, *Room at the Top* was shown on French television. On the day, Maurice Pons telephoned Simone. Since he'd never seen the film she had talked so much about, would she allow him to come along and watch it with her? He expected to find her surrounded by friends, having a party and drinking champagne to celebrate the tenth anniversary of her Oscar. But when he arrived, he was stunned to find her in her 'caravan', about to watch her favourite film, her 'Oscar', alone. No other friend had thought of calling her; she was alone with her nostalgia.

Marilyn Monroe never won an Oscar.

In Hollywood, they called her 'the goddess', like Gloria Swanson and Greta Garbo. Millions of men dreamed about her beauty, her laugh, her painted lips and her glorious body. When she appeared in public in all her cosmetic splendour, dressed up as 'Marilyn', with her carefully-contrived blondeness, her low-cut tops and frills, revolution broke out, traffic jams, apoplexy! Today adolescent boys still idolise the goddess's image as a feminine ideal, the perfect incarnation of sex. But this unbelievable face, the most famous face in the world – so famous that a few strokes of the pen are enough to evoke it on T-shirts, plates, or electronic games – was a mask, a miracle of the art of make-up.

There was none of the 'real' Marilyn in this façade. Since the cinema was invented and stars appeared, there was never such a discrepancy between an actress and her image. Marilyn's sensual perfection was all her own invention, a work of art created by herself. But behind the look, beneath the legend, there was nothing but a frightened, abandoned child. She knew that she was only an impostor, and the knowledge hurt her deeply.

She did not really feel suited to the job of superstar. She considered herself colourless, talentless, and plain. The only thing she was really proud of was a series of photographs in which she aped the faces and postures of other actresses. Because she despised herself, people around her responded in kind. Nobody can be the most desirable woman in the world without attracting jealousy; and the spitefulness of others reflected her own lack of self-esteem. On set, she felt she was always being humiliated: people made her say stupid things, she was made to dress up as a rabbit with a long funny tail attached to her tutu, she was treated like a little girl or told off for behaving like a spoilt star. It was true that she kept arriving late, but it was because she was frightened, she suffered from appalling, gut-wrenching stagefright. She was obsessed with the idea that one day they'd find her out, expose her.

She called herself an orphan because she had lived in orphanages. But she wasn't an orphan: her mother was alive, but had rejected her, which was even worse, a wound that would never heal. By becoming Marilyn, and inventing the 'child-woman', she had replaced her mother's lost love with the adulation of the crowd. But it was an empty, abstract love, directed not at the real person but at her childish, perverse image. She was trapped, condemned, she acted like a child out of a kind of death wish. 'Marilyn's secret,' as Montand would say later on, 'was that she would have liked to have been a great actress, like Katharine Hepburn, Jean Arthur or Myrna Loy. But with her little-girl voice, it was very hard for her to play proper dramatic parts. She really did have such a tiny little voice, a squeak! And she knew that she'd never be able to climb any further up the ladder.' Nobody could have saved her, a cruel truth that Arthur Miller would have to face, discovering at the same time the limits of what one person can do for another, the limits of love.

Simone Signoret had got to know Marilyn without her make-up on, unadorned. The Montand couple were staying in the bungalow next to the Millers at the Beverly Hills Hotel. Today these bungalows, Nos.20 and 21, are mythical places, staging-posts along the 'visit to the homes of the stars' so popular with tourists in Hollywood.

The tenant of No.19 (or so people whispered) was Howard Hughes, the wicked movie mogul. The Montands were in the middle of the citadel. Marilyn told Simone how worried she was about a wispy lock of hair on her forehead: she kept on having to dye it. She ran herself down in a masochistic way. 'Look, they all think I've got lovely long legs, but I've got knock-knees, and I'm squat!' In fact, she was genuinely beautiful, but in a simple, naked, touching way. 'Like one of those beautiful peasant-girls of the Ile-de-France that people have been sighing about for centuries,' as Simone wrote later, in her magnanimous way.

A few years ago I saw a disturbing cartoon in a newspaper. A woman is making herself up; her eyes grow bigger, her mouth turns red, her cheeks start to glow. For a moment she looks at this image, which is so unlike the 'real' her, then, in a panic, she takes some cotton wool and wipes it all off. But her whole face is wiped off along with the make-up, leaving just the outline: her eyes, nose and mouth have all been rubbed out. This must have been how Marilyn felt after taking her make-up off – the feeling of having lost her face, of not existing any more.

In *Nostalgia*, Simone manages to talk about her with genuine affection. She felt a sort of pity for her pathetic rival; she knew both of Marilyn's faces; she knew that the painted face attracted a certain kind of man in an irresistible way, as a decoy attracts birds. 'Can *you* think of many men who wouldn't have responded to Marilyn's charm?' She couldn't feel genuinely threatened by this decoy; yet the threat was a very real one, since it came from the other side, from the 'real' Marilyn, the lost child that a man like Montand could not help wanting to take under his wing.

Montand and Marilyn were filming *Let's Make Love* with the

delightful George Cukor directing. The French actor was charming but above all reassuring, since he, too, suffered from terrible
stagefright and, not speaking any English, couldn't understand
his own cues. So she was not the only one who was scared.
With Montand as her partner, Marilyn became well behaved and
disciplined; she even arrived on time, like a real 'pro'. Then, the
filmhands went on strike, and the shooting stopped for a time.
Simone Signoret left for Italy to star in a Pietrangeli film called
Adua E Le Compagne, while Arthur Miller had appointments to
meet in New York.

That was how Montand and Marilyn found themselves alone
in adjoining chalets waiting to start working together again; the
ghosts of their absent partners hovered over the rooms. As could
have been foreseen, they started to share 'their loneliness, their
anxieties, their jokes, their memories of being poor children'.
Marilyn, the self-styled orphan laughing hysterically to stop herself from sinking into despair, Montand, the unemployed urchin
and local Lothario from La Cabucelle. They were bound to fall
in love.

The gossip-columnists had a field day, the newspaper offices
were buzzing. Twentieth Century Fox decided to exploit the
romance for all that it was worth in their publicity campaign.
The whole world's cameras focused on Bungalows 20 and 21,
spying on the comings and goings of the couple from the moment
that they pulled back their curtains. Struck to the heart, Simone
Signoret had to face a barrage of calumnies, insinuations and
indiscreet gossip.

She took up the gauntlet. In spite of her grief, she didn't forget
the things she already knew about Marilyn; she didn't forget
that her rival was a pitiful, lost girl. In any case, she was sure
that Montand would come back to her. In *Nostalgia*, she has
the finesse to close the episode with a few affectionate lines:
'She will never know how much I *didn't* hate her, and how
I understood that story, which only concerned the four of us,
though it seemed to obsess the whole world in a troubled time
when there were far more important things going on.' And she
describes the little square of champagne-coloured silk that Marilyn
had given her one day because it matched her dress: 'It's a bit

frayed by now, but if you fold it in the right way, you don't notice.'

The danger was over, Montand was back with her, in the same old way. But the wound would never heal: the gnawing jealousy, the humiliation, the terrible obligation of having to present a good front to the world's Press when all she wanted was to creep away and cry in private, would all leave their indelible mark. She could face and handle the pain, but the wound would be deep and lasting, because it was linked with a wound of a different kind – ageing.

It was at this point that Simone Signoret started to grow old. Ageing is inevitable, but she made an act of defiance out of it.

On the telephone, we can hear the voice of a woman at the end of her tether. On the other end of the line, a man is leaving her. He says nothing, but listens to her pathetic litany, waiting for her to fall silent before going on to join his new love. The woman speaks into nowhere, rambling on as if her faltering words could push away the spectre of deathly silence that haunts her.

An interminable, unbearable monologue. Suddenly she's cut off; she calls him back at his home, he had said he was there. But his valet answers, 'No, Monsieur isn't here, he's at the restaurant.' She calls the restaurant, her lover answers, and from that moment she knows that he is lying. He is with the other woman, and his one aim is to get rid of her, and join her triumphant rival. She goes on talking, babbling on to fill the emptiness, to exorcise what she knows must happen. Gradually she sinks into the void, her voice trails off into silence, a desert of silence, represented by whole lines of dots in Cocteau's text. At last she puts the phone down, and darkness falls.

Simone Signoret recorded Jean Cocteau's *La Voix Humaine* in January 1964. With self-deprecating humour, she describes in *Le Lendemain, elle était souriante* how she got ready on the day of the recording session, using all the techniques of a seasoned film actress to get under the skin of her pathetic role. She lists in cruel detail her recipes for breaking down resistance and for 'cooking up synthetic grief'. An early dinner of two hard-boiled eggs swallowed standing up in the silent kitchen. All make-up off: put on an old dressing-gown, get out the box of Kleenex

Aged six, with her mother

On the Pont Neuf, in the centre of Paris, near the entrance to the
Place Dauphine

(Left) Simone with her daughter Catherine Allégret

At home in the Place Dauphine, in the 'caravan' where she put down
roots

In *La Ronde*, directed by Max Ophuls

With Laurence Harvey in *Room at the Top*, the film that won her the
Oscar

With Yves Montand, early in their marriage

The Oscar Ceremony

Inseparable from Montand, she follows him on tour

With Marilyn Monroe

With Jean Gabin in *Le Chat*

With Serge Reggiani in *Casque d'Or*

With Alain Delon in *La Veuve Couderc*

With Yves Montand in Arthur Miller's *The Crucible*

(Top right) With Jean-Paul Sartre

(Middle right) With Lech Wałesa in Poland

(Bottom right) With Claude Mauriac and Michel Foucault

With the television personality Bernard Pivot

With Adam Rayski, Irene Allier and Catherine David, at the *Nouvel
Observateur*

Her last great role – the writer

The Last Days

. . . What she doesn't say is that it was useful to have had a similar experience herself, and that to have had the terrifying mental picture of Montand in the arms of the most desirable woman in the world helped make these cheap actor's tricks all the more chillingly effective. Just as Edith Piaf needed unhappy love affairs to reach the pinnacle of her art, Simone had learned the hard way how emotional experience helps actors to flesh out illusion.

In this resonant part, in which she remains invisible, Simone's voice evokes her physical presence with an incredible intensity. A sigh, a strangled cry, an unfinished sentence, a snuffle as she blows her nose . . . The woman's agony shows through as the expressive voice rambles on, occasionally breaking. In her gravelly tone, we hear the surge of hope, soon to die away, the last coquetry, the growing sense of vertigo and panic. Then we see her face in our mind's eye, and we picture her in her little room on the first floor in the Place Dauphine, her hair in curlers, her face smeared with anti-wrinkle night cream, lying on the bed like a limp doll, her arms stretched out towards the telephone on the floor, her cheeks blotched with tears mingling with the cream.

I had just been listening to Simone Signoret's recording of *La Voix Humaine* when, leafing through Arthur Miller's memoirs, *Timebends*, I came across his account of a phone call from Marilyn. One day, when he was on a trip to Nevada, Marilyn had phoned him late at night; she was desperate. She was filming, she couldn't cope, she felt badly treated, humiliated, lost. 'Oh Papa, I can't make it!' she cried. This was the kind of cry for help that leaves men feeling impotent and defenceless. 'An abandoned voice crying out to a deaf sky . . . I kept trying to reassure her,' he wrote, 'but she seemed to be sinking where I could not reach, her voice growing fainter.' For the first time, listening to that voice, he had felt that she might end up committing suicide. His intuition had been so strong and his frustration at not being able to help her so acute, that he had passed out: and he had dropped the receiver and sunk down on to the floor of the telephone booth as Marilyn's frightened voice continued to reverberate down the receiver in the middle of the Nevada desert.

CHAPTER THIRTEEN

By the age of forty, in 1961, Simone Signoret felt that she had led a full life. The best part – films, love, international fame – seemed to be over: 'The real discoveries – the way up the professional ladder, the taking stock of myself, the loves and the friendships, the important books, the irreversible choices – all those were played out during the first forty years.' She had been loaded with praise, fêted and wounded . . . After all those peaks, she could not imagine what was left to aspire to. She was 'somebody', people respected her. The hands of the clock were moving on, and she prepared to grow old gracefully, quietly looking back on the pleasures and buffetings of the past.

She had no idea that the 'fateful forties' would turn out to be just another stage. Her destiny was far from being completed; the main part was still to come. She had a full quarter-century left to tackle, when her life-course would lead her into further and deeper experiences than she had dared to expect.

She was not one to settle back into the dreary prospect of reliving the past, a defeatist who gives up enthusiasms or challenges. There was still plenty to do, horizons to discover, battles to fight, important films to act in. She had not yet completed her full cycle of re-births; she still had to serve her apprenticeship in the craft of writing, which, even more than political commitment, would be her main interest in middle age.

Nevertheless, as she sensed unconsciously, that first trip to America, with its high points and dramas, had been a turning-point. Until now, the world had been at her feet; she could shake her blonde head at it, like a young lioness. Now, she had reached her limits; ecstasy and pain had come closer than expected. The joy of winning the Oscar had been immediately followed by heartbreak. She had changed; those two extremes of emotion had affected her deeply. From now on, she could only rely on herself; she would no longer expect to find the meaning of life outside herself, from a man or from a film.

Her personality was in the process of acquiring an extra dimension. She was starting to grow old; she could feel it happening, and this new adventure, much as it frightened her, was also exciting. A new Simone Signoret would be born, strong, desperate, inconsolable about losing her youth, but also a woman of action. Film directors would offer her still more exacting roles, difficult and prestigious; heroic, tragic parts. Politically, after agonisingly revising her own position, she would become even more deeply committed, giving freely both herself and her time, pestering journalists to speak out on behalf of a Chilean refugee or a Russian dissident. And then she would discover yet another vocation: writing.

By writing books, she would connect up with her private inner self, and with her father's ancestors about whom nobody had been able to talk. Discovering writing would be linked with discovering Judaism, and carried along by her cult of memory. Thus the cinema, politics and writing would combine to make this intelligent film star into one of the major chroniclers of our times.

'For a film on the history of the French Left, what better scenario could there be than the life-story of Simone Signoret?'[1] When she returned from Hollywood, in 1961, Claude Lanzmann would bring her the Manifesto of 121, which would become a marker in the history of decolonisation. It was high-quality subversion, condemning the prosecution of the Algerian War, and defending the right to military insubordination. She felt guilty about not having taken action earlier, and she ended up by signing the manifesto, after much soul-searching and weighing up of the risks.

In 1959, an explosive book, *La Question* by Henri Alleg, came out, revealing for the first time the methods of torture used by the

[1] Pierre Billard, *Le Point*, October 1985.

French Army in Algeria. Immediately banned under government censorship, the book achieved instant notoriety, though it was unavailable in France. Like everybody else, Simone Signoret had heard about it, and had made a fuss about the way it had been treated; but she had made no effort to get hold of it. It was in Ostend, in Belgium, that she first saw it in a bookshop window. She bought three copies, but when the bookseller acidly asked her what else she was doing for the struggle for Algerian independence, she replied, 'Not much,' and flew off to New York with Montand, for his Broadway show.

On that day, as she listened to Claude Lanzmann's grave, urgent voice (with which viewers of the film *Shoah* would later become familiar) telling her about what was happening in Algiers, Oran and Constantine, she remembered the Ostend bookseller. She realised with alarm that, during her Hollywood interlude, she had rather forgotten about what was going on in her own country. It was time for her to get back to her own people, to reforge links with the Left. Montand was still in America, with Marilyn; a photo of them together, with suggestive captions, was splashed all over the world's Press. Simone was suffering, facing the music on her own. By signing the Manifesto of 121, she had the sensation of opening a new chapter, of pushing aside her private grief and joining her old friends again. She felt she was being of use, and taking risks, which she always enjoyed. She wanted to be personally involved.

It needed real courage to sign the Manifesto. In France in 1961, decolonisation was still a subversive idea. Reprisals were predictable, and virulent. 'Anyone who had signed the text, whatever his or her profession, was banned on radio, on the stage or in any kind of televised news broadcast.'[1] It was the first time since meeting Montand that Simone Signoret would take such an important decision on her own. He would be angry with her for not signing on his behalf, all the more because the absence of the name 'Montand' alongside hers would, understandably, in the circumstances, be noticed and commented on by the Press as a kind of 'moral divorce'.

[1]*Nostalgia* . . . op.cit.

True professional that she was, she took up work again, carrying her forty years as necessary baggage rather than as a handicap, firmly deciding to keep her wrinkles – 'the scars of the laughter, the tears, the questions, the astonishments and the certainties'. She preferred not to cheat about ageing, not to lie to herself. She refused to touch up the photo; anyhow, it would show. 'After you're forty – come on, let's say forty-five – you can take one of two routes: either you can cling to parts that keep you looking thirty-five or thirty-six as long as possible, or you can be like everybody else, and quietly accept the idea that forty-five puts you on the road to forty-six rather than forty-four.' She had thought a great deal about the question, and saw herself as a philosopher; but in fact she was a sophist. She vainly tried to convert her terror into resignation, and, to avoid having to face her wrinkles, she forestalled Fate. Although she imagined herself going gently into old age, she would plunge into it in a frenzy, wallowing in it and rushing towards it as if to an emergency exit. If her face withered quickly enough, the problem would be settled; she would no longer feel afraid of not being attractive enough, since she would know, once and for all, that she was not attractive any more. In any case, with their subconscious cruelty, journalists were already asking her the eternal question, 'How do you feel about growing old?'

Horrified! Old age horrified her. The actress who remembered being Casque d'Or now felt like a real-life Dorian Gray, faced day after day with this ageless image of her own perfect, smooth face as a radiant young woman. Her body was starting to deteriorate. Her face, deformed by puffiness; the swollen pouches under the tiny eyes sunk in flesh, that mass of flesh weighed down by unhealthy fat: it was a statement. Her victories were not enough to calm her anguish. Fame, the great love-affair with Montand, had brought her enormous joy. But happiness was not just there for the taking; she could not understand why things had gone wrong. She drank. She fuddled her wits with whisky, well knowing that she was methodically helping in her own destruction. Her inner flaws and secret griefs were written on her flesh like scars. But words were different. Words were like masks, they helped to push back the sorrow. By making her mind up to write, she would recapture the savour of words, and the pleasure of sharing secrets.

She never spoke of her changed appearance as a misfortune. Quite the opposite: fictitiously, she would claim that it was the result of living too well, of an excess of life's pleasures. She would even glorify in it, so that her physical alteration would bring her some of her most splendid parts. She would talk about it as if it was the result of a deliberate choice. As for the profound pain and sorrow, evident but silent, hidden behind the façade of her denials, she kept them a secret. The main thing was to protect the immortality of the myth.

In Hollywood, she would refuse the oddments of old stock that the American studios were pressing on her as is usual after winning an Oscar. Leaving Montand in the arms of the most desirable woman in the world, she flew off to Rome where Antonio Pietrangeli was waiting for her. Once again, she would be the inspiration for films. Once again, thanks to the Oscar, she was excellent box-office.

But there was little self-deception or complacency in her estimation of her own fame. Simone Signoret had never been a sex-symbol. She had became a star because of a whole series of exceptional qualities – a strong will, intelligence, beauty, charisma, professionalism – but above all because of her extraordinary capacity to feel and communicate passion. What gave her star-quality was her ability to give of herself, her fiery sprit, her indomitable energy. But she did not possess the sex-appeal, the glorious fragility or exquisite femininity of a Marilyn, Ava Gardner or Bardot. This was probably why she had always come second: 'When I started in films, there was Michèle Morgan, Danielle Darrieux, Micheline Presle; then after that there was Martine Carol, then Françoise Arnoul. Meanwhile, over in my corner, I was getting older. Then there was Bardot, who left everybody else standing. After that there was Moreau and the French New Wave, and me and the English New Wave. Then there was Girardot, and there I was getting older and still in the same place: second.'[1] Possibly. But the comparison was artificial because she was not

[1]Interview with Mathieu Lindon, *Libération*, 26 January 1985.

just an actress, but also a woman involved in real events, whose creative energy would not be fully expended in her work for stage or screen.

After *Adua E Le Compagne*, she acted in the first film made by the budding young director, François Leterrier. This young philosopher, who had improvised in a Bresson film, had become assistant to Louis Malle and Yves Allégret; in other words, he was one of the family. For *Les Mauvais Coups*, an adaptation of a Roger Vailland novel, he had decided, as a good disciple of Bresson, to offer one of the main parts to a non-professional. He installed himself with Simone on the terrace of the Café de Flore, a key place for observing passers-by, hoping to find his hero. He found him – Reginald D. Kernan, a forty-five-year-old American doctor who, in the film, would be the unfaithful husband of a 'sarcastic, drunken, tortured' Simone Signoret, who is drowning in alcohol her grief at being deserted.

She continued with René Clément's *Le Jour et l'heure*, a fine film about the Resistance. This is the story of a middle-class woman content to lead an uneventful life until, through her love for an American parachutist, she is suddenly swept up into the underground movement. This was an ideal part for Simone, the frustrated Resistance heroine. She gave one of her best performances in a film where the action centres on those decisive, apocalyptic moments when outside events transform a life into a destiny, and when a person's true character reveals itself in the flickering light of a bombing. For René Clément, it was 'the day and the hour of a meeting, the day and the hour in which a woman becomes aware of her responsibilities, the day and the hour in which she decides to move from "no" to "yes" and to commit herself, even to the point of self-sacrifice; the day and the hour when she performs a tiny little act that will affect her whole life.'[1] Simone Signoret knew from her own experience that life could suddenly rock on its foundations. She empathised with this simple, courageous woman, divided between the cosiness of everyday things, and the call of adventure. While making the

[1] Quoted by Joëlle Montserrat, op. cit.

129

film, she made friends with René Clément's young assistant, Costa-Gavras. Later, she would live through several significant experiences with him. It would be a long time before Simone Signoret started writing her memoirs; but she had already felt the urge to put pen to paper, and at the end of 1962, at the Théâtre Sarah-Bernhardt, Pierre Mondy directed her adaptation of Lillian Hellman's play *The Little Foxes*. For the daughter of that skilled interpreter, André Kaminker, translation was like a royal road, an art in the fullest sense: 'What does translating mean? For a bilingual actress, it is not very different from acting in a foreign language, or from just plain acting. A good interpreter, or actor, is somebody who is totally faithful to the author's way of thinking. It's odd that, in French, we use the same word, "*interprète*", for an actor and for someone who translates texts. To my mind, translating a text involves exactly the same kind of passionate desire to reproduce exactly – down to the last word, nearly – the thought processes of the author.'[1]

She had not acted on stage since *The Crucible*, seven years before. For six months, in *The Little Foxes*, she would play the appalling Regina, a pitiless, greedy woman on the watch for any physical weakness in her rich husband with a bad heart. 'With her face swollen with ambition, and her icy stare, Simone Signoret is the personification of predatory greed.'[2] Lillian Hellman had written this provocative play in 1936: the action takes place in the Deep South at the turn of the century, and demystifies Margaret Mitchell's myth of gracious Southern living. It was like a remake of *Gone with the Wind*, told from the other point of view, through the eyes of 'somebody who remembered that her own grandparents had owned, bought and sold slaves'.[3]

It was the first and last time that Simone Signoret would act in a play for which she had written the script. As author of the adaptation, she found that she could not properly relax. In the middle of a scene, she would notice with anguish that she had carelessly moved or wrongly spoken her lines. She could not help surreptitiously

[1] *Une Saison à Bratislava*, preface, op.cit.
[2] Bertrand Poirot-Delpech, *Le Monde*, 7 December 1962.
[3] *Nostalgia* . . . op.cit.

observing her fellow-actors, Marcel Bozzuffi, Raymond Pellegrin, and Suzanne Flon, instead of quietly giving them their cue. 'I didn't want them to spoil my lovely translation.' But by translating *The Little Foxes*, she was unconsciously practising to be a writer. It would take her another ten years to take the plunge and become an author in her own right.

In July 1964, Catherine passed her 'Bac'. Like her mother, she intended to become a professional actress. Then, lo and behold, Costa-Gavras, the young assistant-director whom Simone had met during the shooting of *Le Jour et l'heure*, offered Catherine a part in the film he was preparing, a thriller based on a novel by Sébastien Japrisot. When they read the screenplay, Montand and Signoret found two parts that suited them, and offered to play them, thus doubly guaranteeing the success of their young friend's film. From then on, *Compartiment tueurs* became a family affair in which the actors agreed to be paid by taking a share in the production. This was how Catherine Allégret would make her début – not by standing on her own feet at last, but under the aegis of her parents. In the shadow of those two giants, she was bound to be invisible; it was probably not the ideal way of starting on a career in films.

But, very likely, none of them was aware of it. They enjoyed working together. For Signoret and Montand, the double-act took them back to *Les Sorcières de Salem*, and they loved it. Besides, Montand was at last discovering the pleasures of acting in film; for the first time, thanks to his close friendship with Costa-Gavras, he felt completely at ease before the cameras. Up until now, he had dabbled in film work, but had reserved his main forces, and his talent, for his one-man shows. This time, he would feel like a real actor, in the fullest sense of the word. Later, again with Costa-Gavras, he would give his finest performance in *L'Aveu*.

Simone Signoret continued her double life. She was having two separate, parallel careers, in France and in the Anglo-Saxon countries. In 1964, she went back to Hollywood to play the role of the 'Contessa', a wealthy Spanish morphine-addict, in Stanley Kramer's *Ship of Fools* with Vivien Leigh and Lee Marvin. John Kennedy had been assassinated the previous year, Lyndon

Johnson was standing against the reactionary Barry Goldwater in the election campaign, and American teenagers were smoking their first joints. Simone found herself back in the *dolce vita*, with walks along the beach with Katharine Hepburn, candle-lit dinners at Vivien Leigh's house, weekends with Lee and Betty Marvin, and long conversations with Jean Renoir who lived in the hills and laid on a glorious orgy of nostalgia for her by showing her an old print of *The Crime of Monsieur Lange*. 'On screen flickered all my little world, my world of the Café Flore, when all those people were thirty years younger and I hadn't met them yet.'

Then the British called for her again. In 1966, she acted in Sidney Lumet's *The Deadly Affair*, a spy story adapted from John Le Carré's thriller *Call for the Dead*. It was a complex, well-constructed tale in which the spies – as always with Le Carré – are men tortured by doubts, vulnerable, and aware of their enemy's strong points.

But the London public that had made such a fuss of the French actress would not forgive her for playing an Englishwoman and for encroaching on the sacred ground of Shakespeare. It had, in fact, been her own idea to accept the part of Lady Macbeth, opposite Alec Guinness, at the Royal Court Theatre. This was going too far; she had over-estimated her capabilities and her command of English. As Lady Macbeth, she was as out of place as Susan Hayward or Marlon Brando would have been in a Racine tragedy. It was a painful experience. Simone Signoret found herself up against the impenetrable barrier between her mother-tongue and other languages. She was not British, she would never possess those automatic reflexes, she still had a light French accent, and her tempo and intonation were both slightly, but fatally, wrong. It was a fiasco.

Simone Signoret had not only set herself an impossible challenge; on top of this, she had come on the scene at the wrong moment in British theatre history. The critics were engaged in bitter political in-fighting with the director William Gaskill, who felt that he was being unjustly victimised. She found herself parachuted into the centre of a debate whose issues were largely above her head, a quarrel between 'Ancients' and 'Moderns' in the Shakespearian kingdom. William Gaskill's modernist production, which was supposed to be 'blowing the dust' off Shakespeare, seemed to the critics to be 'devoid of colour, life and any atmosphere of terror'. The borderline between minimalism and emptiness, sobriety and poverty, is a narrow one, and Gaskill had apparently crossed it in the wrong direction, like many avant-garde directors in the sixties. Defending their freedom of opinion, the critics got their own back by listing their grievances in full. Caught in the slipstream, Simone Signoret received more than her fair share of brickbats. This presumptuous Frenchwoman was an easy target: 'a cone-shaped matron with a Medusa's head', 'a catastrophe'. *The Times'* notice fell like a guillotine blade: 'Simone Signoret's first appearance is magnificent, with her slow, stately gait and her mouth like a wide wound. But this impression disappears as soon as she opens her mouth.' But in spite of everything, the production would be a sell-out. Controversy sells tickets; Simone Signoret as Lady Macbeth had become a crowd-puller.

She gritted her teeth; she was in a tight corner. But the show had to go on. Every evening, she would return to that hell, knowing she was inviting yet more ridicule. She spent days trying to improve her morale, not to give in to panic, not to pack her suitcases and run. She went forward in the front line, facing the fire. The *Macbeth* episode would leave a terrible scar: whenever she looked back on it, even twenty years later, she could feel herself blushing.

CHAPTER FOURTEEN

After the painful Lady Macbeth episode, she went back to Hollywood to act in Curtis Harrington's *Games*. America had once again changed. The mood was grim and tense. No more candle-lit dinners or lolling about in the sun; no more fantasy; the main topics were Vietnam and the black problem. The Watts riots had shown that the old fires had only been temporarily stamped out. America was in turmoil; the young seemed out of control; teenagers burned their Vietnam draft papers in public. California was busy inventing new frontiers to conquer: in Hollywood, producers were growing long hair and beards, to be in the swim. McCarthyism was ancient history.

Meanwhile, France was bored, as Pierre Viansson-Ponté would write in a prophetic article published in *Le Monde* in April 1968. Cohn-Bendit already had his sights trained on Johnny Hallyday.

In May 1968, Simone Signoret stayed on the sidelines of the party. She was in Saint-Paul-de-Vence when the demonstrations really started. At Cannes, the Film Festival was interrupted daily: Truffaut, Malle, Godard and Polanski returned to Paris. But Simone Signoret decided to stay on at the Colombe d'Or. She had her reasons. Like a great many people, she was thrown by this extraordinary event, which fitted no pre-established pattern. She did not want to climb on to a bandwagon; she preferred to think things over quietly, in her corner, and to do her own private soul-searching in the light of the student revolt: 'I wanted to be able to consider a profound revision of everything, alone, without a lot of talk, without people's opinions, without pressure. I wanted to take a good look at the things that would argue our case if we, my generation, were to be put on trial by this youthful, judging generation.'[1]

It was no accident that she chose the metaphor of a trial. Charges, speeches, evidence: she would be more and more drawn towards the idea of justice, by the Utopian concept of a game of Truth where the different pieces of the dossier, finally spread out for all to see, would make possible a definitive judgement, on herself as well as others. The slow process of a trial, even if only imaginary, seemed to her to be vital to the workings of art, a way of finally exorcising the ancient demons of guilt that haunt all human beings who live in society, and from which nobody is ever really free. As they built the barricades on the Boulevard Saint-Michel, the students were, in effect, putting their parents' generation on trial – the generation of Munich, Marshal Pétain, collaboration, the war in Indo-China, the Algerian tragedy, the Cold War and the Bomb. But there is no escaping history, any more than escaping from time; and the trial would stop short, grind to a halt and repeat the same old story. Yet there really was something new here – a party feeling, a popular gaiety in the streets. May '68 was *joie de vivre* in pictures. Of course, the party spirit did not extend to the political sphere; *joie de vivre* is no match for the rationality of the State. Volatile, fleeting, capricious and fragile, it is not substantial enough to justify a war. Hence the creative, cultural dimensions of that extraordinary revolt.

Of course, she would have liked to go back, to join the crowd, to shout slogans and be part of the march of history. Montand was in Paris, and she would have enjoyed sharing the adventure with him, once again. But she knew, only too well, that this was not her struggle. She belonged to another generation; she did not want to be like those society women who try to imitate teenagers. She was clear-headed. When she was twenty, she had been hired as a secretary by Jean Luchaire, a well-known collaborator. With this dubious past, she was hardly the right person to advise twenty-year-old girls. If she went back, she might be forced to do things she would regret: 'If I missed some things, I'm pretty certain I also avoided some of the stupidities I surely would have

[1] *Nostalgia* . . . op.cit.

135

committed.' And then, because she was famous, they would try to use her, to enrol her on their side; she knew herself well enough to realise that, in the heat of the action, carried away by emotion, anger and the general feeling in the air, she would obey orders and take up positions. She foresaw the ridicule that would rebound on the heads of the ageing teachers and political has-beens who, as they waved their arms along with the students, imagined that they were recapturing their youth. 'I practically keeled over when I discovered that these middle-aged intellectuals had suddenly become revolutionaries.'

And that is why Simone Signoret was not on the barricades in the Latin Quarter in May 1968.

For an actor, the alternation of dreams with waking life is mirrored by the interplay between filming and ordinary existence. While she was acting in a film, Simone Signoret would put everyday life on 'hold': she would go into retreat, and joyfully escape into the fantasy world of the cinema, the 'dream factory' in which time was suspended. Her priorities would be reversed, turned inside out like a glove. On set, as a true professional, the strong-willed personality would become a paragon of docility. Temporarily freed from the exigencies of ordinary life, she enjoyed the role of daughter of the regiment, or strolling player: 'When I arrive on set, I often intimidate people, but within forty-eight hours, they're asking me to sweep the studio floor.'[1] Petitions to be signed, friends, conversations with Montand, would all shade off into a kind of artistic blur. In the foreground was work: different faces, different men, different conversations, different desires. But above all somebody else was in control. Unreservedly, uninhibitedly, with the agreeable sense of work well done, she would return to this communal womb, where she could feel deliciously irresponsible. Work and pleasure were effortlessly mingled; her material needs were seen to without her having to worry about them, she worked to a strict timetable, and even her personality was 'programmed' by the script. The woman of action who spent her time making decisions reverted to the blissful days of infancy. For a few weeks,

[1]Interview with Mathieu Lindon, *Libération*, 26 January 1985.

CATHERINE DAVID

she would abdicate her free will: she gave up being the queen mother, the one who takes charge, leads and organises, who helps preserve the delicate status quo among family and friends. She became as malleable as putty in the hands of God the father, her director.

This explains how, in August 1968, she could forget completely about the May events which she had missed. She accepted a part in Chekhov's *The Seagull*, directed by Sidney Lumet with whom she had worked in *The Deadly Affair* two years before, and discovered the wild beauty of Northern Europe for the first time. The play's mixture of passion and refinement, the lucid beauty of Chekhov's text, the director's intelligence and the cheerfulness of the crew left her in a state of peaceful beatitude. She had retired from the world. 'There are people who take LSD in order to go on trips. We grew high on Chekhov, and after that the world could collapse.'[1]

The Swedish summer is a glorious but short-lived season. It was still summer, in all its poignant finery, but already there was a nip in the air, a sense of foreboding about the approaching winter. They lingered on, luxuriating in the sun. Meanwhile, Montand was singing at the Étoile, and for once Simone was not there to reassure and support him, and wipe the sweat off his brow. With a clear conscience, she delegated her groupie duties to Catherine. Sidney Lumet had forbidden her to make the Stockholm-Paris round trip for her singer's first night, and she had given way with a good grace: 'It's Arkadina who would have been in Montand's dressing-room before and after the performance, not me.'[2]

She enjoyed the party to the full, drank *tchaï*, adjusted her beautiful costumes, waved her fan. But the emotions she felt while playing the part were extraordinarily intense; she had a physical sensation of the violence that sometimes hides in secret between the words of a text. On top of all this, the actors lived as closely as a family, like circus people. There was always somebody to drink or chat with, to carry on the dream. 'We had all lived under the same roof, we had shared the same bread and salt at every meal for two months. As the countdown approached, towards the end

[1]*Nostalgia* . . . op.cit.
[2]Id.

137

of the filming, we were in the process of going completely mad with shared tenderness and mutual understanding.'[1]

Autumn 1968 brought a sudden change of scene. After the poignant world of Chekhov, Simone Signoret found herself transported to Frankfurt in 1935, to the murky atmosphere of the rise of Nazism. For their new television programme, *Festival*, her friends Pierre Lazareff and Éliane Victor, two pillars of 'Cinq Colonnes à la Une', had invited several famous actors – notably Michel Piccoli and Michel Bouquet – to choose parts they had always dreamed of but never had the opportunity of playing.

For the moment, Simone Signoret had difficulty in finding an idea; she did not think of Thérèse Humbert, the financial adventuress whose picaresque escapades her grandmother had described to her, in the 'Tout-Paris' of bankers and notaries at the turn of the century. Later on, she would make a television series about her with Marcel Bluwal. For the time being, she felt no regrets, no repressed longings to play Jeanne d'Arc or Marie-Antoinette. A great reader of Zola, she certainly wished that Carné had called on her for the role of Gervaise in *L'Assommoir*; but she had made a rule never to cast herself in any role. After reading Catherine Guerard's charming novel *Renata n'importe quoi*,[2] she had a momentary desire to film the story of a cleaning woman who extends her Sunday day-off and starts wandering through the city on a metaphysical journey through scented squares and gas-lit boulevards. But she soon thought better of it. To give of her best, somebody else had to 'take charge', as she liked to put it: she needed to be desired and dreamed about by a director.

But, this time, she had to follow the rules of the game, the premise of the television programme; she was committed to finding a subject. Accidentally, she came across a play by Berthold Brecht called *La Femme Juive*, the story of a German-Jewish woman married to a German doctor who is infected with Nazism. Uneasy, influenced by the ideology of the time, he regrets having married this compromising woman from the shadows, and is worried about losing his job at the hospital. She decides to leave, to

[1]*Nostalgia* . . . op.cit.
[2]Gallimard, 1968.

emigrate to Holland and sacrifice herself. For Simone Signoret, it was a way of re-connecting with Brecht's theatre, after the *Mother Courage* that she had set off to film in East Berlin back in 1953 had fallen through. This time, the connection worked.

'A slow camera-pan takes us through the window into Judith's apartment. We are in Frankfurt on an evening of 1935; we can hear the tram bells, and the noises and cries of the street. This busy background lends a grim reality to Judith's drama, as do the middle-class décor, and the colour.'[1] Alain d'Hénaut, a young director whom Simone Signoret had known as a child, made a magnificent film of this tragedy of a couple whose lives are destroyed by history, bringing out the very best, the most profound and subtle side of her acting. 'Simone Signoret lives through this drama with a sobriety and intensity that make one clench one's fists,' went on Jacques Siclier in *Le Monde*. Her choice of subject for her first appearance in a television film would foreshadow, by a few years, Simone Signoret's gradual, if belated, discovery through Pierre Goldman and the combatants of the MOI,[2] then Moshé Mizrahi and Jean-Claude Grumberg, of her secret loyalty to her Jewish roots, which, up until then, had apparently played no part in her life.

It would also be an excellent preparation for her part in Jean-Pierre Melville's *L'Armée des ombres*, one of the three or four jewels in her actress's crown. Jean-Pierre Melville was an outsider, a bold freelancer in whom the New Wave, at the beginning, thought they had found a precursor, but who always ploughed his own solitary furrow, away from fashions and conformism, in his search for a perfect form. 'There's only one kind of film-making: yours. Why don't I do it? Because I don't know how to,' Jean-Luc Godard would say to him one day.

For twenty-five years Melville had been dreaming of bringing to the screen *L'Armée des ombres*, a novel by Joseph Kessel which he had read in London during the war, in 1943. The former Resistance fighter was profoundly moved by memories of this period: 'Looking back at my past, I realised the charm that

---

[1]Jacques Siclier, *Le Monde*, 30 April 1968.
[2]La Main-d'Oeuvre-Immigrée, the foreign Resistance movement.

"bad" memories could possess. As I grow older, I think back nostalgically to the period between 1940 and 1944, for it formed part of my youth.'[1] This sentence could well have been uttered by Simone Signoret, with her cherishing of memories of her youth, and her sensation of having been born in the early-forties, in those times of deprivation and laughter, among the eccentrics of the Café de Flore.

Gerbier, the main hero of the film, played by an inscrutable, desperate Lino Ventura – all the grimmer on screen from having quarrelled with Melville at the start of the shooting – personifies three or four of the great Resistance heroes, among them Jean Moulin. Gerbier is an austere, sombre man, in the grip of despair. During the long periods of waiting that precede action, he immerses himself in books with enigmatic titles like *Transfinite and Continuous*, written by the head of his Resistance cell, Luc Jardie (Paul Meurisse, turned mathematician and philosopher), a character based on Jean Cavaillès.[2] Among the other characters whose destinies interlock in an atmosphere of silent heroism is Mathilde, an Antigone of the Resistance. Mathilde is a woman with steely eyes and unwavering courage, who goes behind the Gestapo lines in an attempt to rescue her captured comrade.

Mathilde is an extraordinarily moving character because her heroism has one weak point: her love for her daughter. In spite of warnings, she cannot bring herself to throw away the photo of her daughter that she carries next to her heart; and, when things start to go wrong, the Gestapo use this photo as a way of putting pressure on her. When she is released, her comrades, who can't be sure that she hasn't talked, decide to kill her. She has only just been freed, when, her eyes still blinking in the light of day, she sees them driving towards her and understands that they are going to kill her, in spite of the veneration in which they hold her, because they have no choice. Such is the law of the Resistance. The range of expressions that Simone Signoret allows to play over Mathilde's face at that moment – the mixture of surprise, terror and understanding, as she stand transfixed on the white pavement – is unforgettable.

---

[1] *Le cinéma selon Melville*, Luis Nogueira, Seghers, 1974.
[2] Philosopher and logician, one of the original founders of the French Resistance.

CATHERINE DAVID

With *Le Jour et l'heure* and *L'Armée des ombres*, Simone Signoret gradually added to her collection of 'personae' the emblematic figure of Resistance heroine. In people's collective imagination, this image, juxtaposed with her image of committed left-winger, fitted her extraordinarily well and became confused with reality – a notion that pleased but also embarrassed her. Not having worked actively for the Resistance was one of her main regrets, and those heroic parts would represent a kind of ghostly appropriation of a role she could not play at the time, and a belated way of compensating for a painful gap in her life.

The great adventure of Costa-Gavras's film *L'Aveu* was about to begin. After acting in *L'Américain*, directed by her old friend Marcel Bozzuffi, the story of a man who returns to France after fifteen years in the States to find that he cannot readapt, Simone Signoret found herself acting once again with Yves Montand, her opposite number in *Compartiment tueurs* and, most memorably, John Proctor in *Les Sorcières de Salem*. *L'Aveu* is in a way symmetrical with *Les Sorcières*, an equally political film made in the middle of the anti-McCarthy fever. This time, the Montand-Signoret duo were fully committed to denouncing the show-trials of Eastern Europe. The book by Artur London, one of the three survivors of the Slansky trial, is one of that succession of great testimonies that finally opened the eyes of Western intellectuals to the terrible truth about the 'socialist paradises'. Signoret's role – Lise London – is secondary to Montand's: he plays Artur London himself, the former Communist deputy-minister tortured by the KGB, a scapegoat whose sufferings the film unveils, layer by layer.

But even at this late stage, and in spite of a series of revelations, Simone Signoret still felt a reflex of loyalty to the Communist party, which held her back from making the final leap. Acting in this film would mean once and for all crossing through the looking-glass, over to the so-called wicked ranks of anti-Communism. It would mean committing what could still be considered a major sin. Finally she made up her mind, and from that moment she teetered, then took the plunge, suppressing her disgust at the role of Lise London, the wife who breaks ranks with her husband at the worst possible moment. The release of *L'Aveu* would be a marker in French political life, and a triumph for Yves Montand the actor. 'I have to say,' wrote Henri Chapier, 'that faced with Yves Montand's extraordinary, selfless spontaneity in this film, it is difficult to talk of "acting", given the way he surpasses himself as a human being reliving a page of our history.'[1]

Simone Signoret would not meet the leaders of the May Revolution until the seventies, when the gradual fading of the dream would make activists on the far-Left look like has-beens in the twilight. The Public Order Act hung over their heads like a sword of Damocles. Alain Geismar, Michel Le Bris and Jean-Pierre Le Dantec, among others, were convicted of incitement to violence and of threatening the safety of the State. In the factories, this was the heyday of the '*établis*' (entrists), militant Maoists who would sign on as skilled workers in order to destabilise the system of production. Robert Linhart has described their epic tale in his book *L'Établi*.[2]

At the Renault factory, the '*établis*' were spotted, and sacked. To attract the attention of the Press, three of them started a hunger strike, to which the public were indifferent. Sent by Sartre, Jean-Pierre Le Dantec asked Simone Signoret to help them; and she visited them nearly every day, as Sartre already was doing, in the Saint-Bernard chapel where they had installed themselves in Billancourt. On their behalf, she mobilised her friends Costa-Gavras, Régis Debray, Michel Drach and Chris Marker. Simone Signoret was not a Maoist; she was not a child of May '68; she was protesting on behalf of Human Rights. She was dismayed by the public's indifference and the silence surrounding these three young people whom she saw growing weaker by the day on their camp-beds.

But she did not lose her sense of humour. She compared herself with one of 'those Russian ladies who took revolutionaries into their *châteaux* before 1905'. She felt slightly ridiculous at being dropped off each day by taxi in front of the little chapel: 'I went to visit my hunger-strikers in the way charitable ladies in

[1]*Combat*, 29 April 1970.
[2]Minuit, 1981. 'Établi' means a wooden work-bench.

old-fashioned novels went to see their poor.'[1] In short, she was having fun doing the 'silly things' she had not done in May '68. But the Press did not react; and there was a backlash in public opinion. The Maoist militants were trying to fan the flames of a fire that had already died out. At the Renault factory, there was a total stalemate.

Things would change dramatically a few days later, when an eighteen-year-old demonstrator, Pierre Overney, was shot at point-blank range by a guard, Jean-Antoine Tramoni. Immediately the Press were after the story; in fact, the papers talked of nothing else. Simone Signoret would discover the awful truth about 'media events': 'Having lived day to day with people's total lack of interest in those grievances, I had suddenly realised that someone had to die in order to rouse the Press – and the idea terrified me.' She would not forget the lesson. Having realised that to mobilise the Press one has to dramatise the event, she would learn how to dramatise. In the teeth of the evidence, the Communist Party simultaneously accused both the police and the far-Left groups of being *agents-provocateurs*. François Mitterrand wrote in *L'Unité*, 'René-Pierre Overney wanted to change life, in his own way. Well, he's done it.' Simone Signoret went to Pierre Overney's funeral at the Père-Lachaise on 4 March 1972, along with the 200,000 other people who were present at the beginning of the end of an era that began in 1968.

Gradually, political commitment would become a way of life for Simone Signoret, a sort of priesthood. Her energy was boundless. On the one hand, there was Montand, the arguments, the crises, the moments of recaptured tenderness, Catherine who was growing up and becoming an actress, one or two films a year, and friends with whom she would talk for hours about the weather or the state of the world, or the neighbour's cat or a cross-stitch in her knitting, or a petition she was hesitating about signing, or a book she half-wanted to write. There were the refugees from all over the world, hoping for her help, telling her about the sufferings of their people. Then there were the journalists; she harried them with

[1] *Nostalgia . . .* op.cit.

requests, and questions, and they would ask favours in return. 'We must do something for . . .' 'And for . . . have you thought about what?' People would listen to her; she was that kind of person. She was demanding, passionate, convincing. The causes that she chose to support, and put her weight as a celebrity behind, were often just ones. Her choices were guided by her emotions, but her emotions were based on a clear conception of justice and human dignity.

CHAPTER FIFTEEN

Living a stone's throw from the Palais de Justice, almost on its steps, Simone Signoret would occasionally fantasise about the dramas that were played out in its dark and dusty courtrooms. She was fascinated by the contrast between the trappings, the ritual, the precise juridical terminology, and the nakedness of the emotions and dramas that were re-enacted there. In the closing pages of her memoirs, she talks about the Palais de Justice with a solemn reverence, as if the obsessive presence of this real-life theatre where destinies were decided had been not just a part of neighbourhood geography but a metaphor for her own terrors, the Kafkaesque terrors that grip us all when bureaucratic authority enters our lives.

'It takes the big trials, however, for the restaurants on the Place to hang out their "Full" placards and remind us that every day inside the edifice there are accused, accusers, the guilty, the innocent, the witnesses, the false witnesses, the judges, the juries, the Peeping Toms, the clerks and the policemen. Every day just up the road from us . . . Strangers in the Place always seem to be strangely troubled. We don't even notice them any more. We know they're only there in transit. In a little while, they'll go up that great stone staircase.'[1] It was on the steps of the Palais, or the Place Dauphine where 'the gates of Justice opened majestically on that peaceful provincial little square'[2] that she would set the bleak meeting between Elie Guttman and Volodia, the lost cousin, who

---

[1] *Nostalgia . . .* op.cit.
[2] *Adieu Volodia . . .* op.cit.

had been sucked into the abyss of Stalinism. Simone Signoret saw a definite link between heroes and victims. She would be moved to tears by men who seemed marked for death, fighting to the end to stay true to themselves.

On Monday, 9 December 1974, at the Paris Assizes, the trial opened of a man who felt that he had a 'mission to leap clear of the banality and materialism of the times'. The man in question was a Polish Jew, an atheist and philosopher, a revolutionary and sensualist, violent, and desperate. His name was Pierre Goldman. He felt himself accursed, convinced he would end up on the scaffold; and, in his inspired lunacy, he behaved like a man who 'longed for this final confrontation'. On 20 September 1979, on a wet pavement in the 13th arrondissement in Paris, Pierre Goldman would be shot three times in the back, in the name of 'police honour', by three mysterious killers who would never be traced.

But on that December day in 1974, Pierre Goldman was on trial for the alleged murder of two female assistants in a chemist's on the Boulevard Richard-Lenoir. A long and painful story ensued. He was sentenced to life imprisonment, found guilty without a shadow of proof. On the evidence, Pierre Goldman was convicted because of his reputation as a left-wing fanatic, and his professed vocation of revolutionary adventurer. Through him, the State was setting its sights on a whole generation, a whole way of thinking, a '*milieu*'. Then the verdict was quashed by the Court of Appeal; and two years later, in Amiens, a new trial ended in acquittal. In the meantime, French intellectuals had been mobilising themselves.

Simone Signoret came along to the trial as a neighbour; like many others, she was fascinated by Goldman and his dare-devil bravado, his intelligence, his integrity, and his despair. 'I caught sight of Simone Signoret. Her presence particularly moved me, since I knew that she wasn't there just for the legal spectacle, or the artificial splendour of the tragi-comedies you see in the courts. I looked at her, and she looked at me. Her face was crumpled with emotion. Looking at her, I thought of two films that I had loved, *Casque d'Or*, whose inner meaning and beauty I only fully understood years after seeing it, after I had been in prison, and *Le Jour et l'heure*, which I had seen in Warsaw with my mother, who had wept and said, "My son, that's exactly how it was, that actress is me." Every time I looked at Simone Signoret I thought of my mother, and, in a way, she symbolised my mother's presence for me throughout the trial.'[1]

Now that Pierre Goldman has faded into a myth belonging to a past age, it is difficult to remember what a network of friends he had around him, firm, indissoluble friendships proportionate to the trials and sufferings he had to undergo. For Pierre Goldman was more than just a cause to fight for, or a figurehead: he was a tragic hero. His story involved several actors in the flamboyant political melodrama described by Patrick Rotman and Hervé Hamon in their book *Génération*.[2] When the trial opened, *Libération* ran a banner headline: 'Pierre Goldman, our friend.' For those who came of age at the same time as the end of the Algerian War, the people's revolution in Cuba, the battles between the French Communist Party and the UEC[3], Godard's *Pierrot Le fou*, for those whose revolutionary zeal had been steeped in the internal battles between 'Italian' Communists, Trotskyists and Maoists, Pierre Goldman embodied the romantic intensity of a struggle gone astray, condemned to failure and derision.

Dedicated to carrying provocation to its absolute limits, he often overstepped the law, carrying out hold-ups, and knocking about Latin America searching for the Revolution but never finding it. A great rum-drinker, he never stopped lending money to his friends and only felt really at ease with his West Indian cronies with whom he went on wild drinking sprees.

In spite of earnest entreaties, he would obstinately refuse to serve as standard bearer for a Left which he regarded as infantile, 'pornographic', incapable of the 'serious, real violence' that he felt to be necessary in order to transform the student revolt of May '68 into revolutionary action. 'I am not your symbol or your mirror!' he would cry to those who wanted to follow him and make him their leader. Nevertheless, from intellectuals like Régis Debray to Marc Kravetz and Serge July, from Bernard Kouchner to Georges Kiejman, Marianne Merleau-Ponty and

[1] Pierre Goldman, *Souvenirs Obscurs d'un Juif polonais né en France*, Le Seuil, 1975.
[2] Two volumes: *Les Années de rêve, les Années de poudre*, Le Seuil, 1987 and 1988.
[3] Union des Étudiants Communistes, the student organisation of the French Communist Party.

Simone Signoret, this paradoxical anti-hero would never cease to attract a fraternal loyalty, a mixture of affection and fascination that gave his friends the feeling that they were sharing, once again, an historic adventure. As Marc Kravetz would write in *Libération*, echoing this shared feeling: 'It is rather absurd to claim, from where we stand compared with where he stands, that his struggle is our struggle, and that we recognise ourselves in his misdemeanours. But it must still be said, for his sake, our sake and the sake of those who are trying his case, that the man now standing in the dock at the Paris assizes is our friend and our brother.' Pierre Goldman was one of those people who provide dreams with a ballast of reality, and help give an epoch its unique quality.

He was a key figure in Simone Signoret's life, one who represented a new stage of experience and personified the questions that she tirelessly addressed to the world around her. Like Jo Langer, Pierre Goldman gave her a sense of belonging.

She identified, obscurely, with the wanderings of this 'exiled Jew without a promised land'. Like her, he was intransigent, passionate, driven by a sense of quest. She looked at this youth who was not even thirty years old, a Jewish child born in turmoil and fear in 1944, of parents who were in the Resistance. By defying death like a modern Achilles, choosing a short, glorious life rather than a long and boring existence, Pierre Goldman was joining the line of MOI combatants of whom his father had been one, 'the new Asmonians, the new Maccabees, those children of the people of the Book who took up arms to write the sacred history of the Jewish revolt'.[1] Simone Signoret did not realise that this little-known but dramatic story, which had been a cornerstone of Pierre Goldman's childhood, would be the inspiration, a few years later, for the characters in her novel *Adieu Volodia*. She felt maternal towards Goldman and longed to save him.

'I became involved with the Goldman affair accidentally at first, later on passionately, but I do not intend to go into all that here . . . Enough to say that, after going along to the Paris assizes next door to me, on an afternoon in December 1974 because people had told me about the opening of the trial of a young man whom I had

---

[1] *Souvenirs obscurs . . .* op.cit.

never met, who was facing charges about which all I knew was that they were not proven, I did not miss one single hearing over the days that followed, right up until the last one which ended at about half-past midnight with a sentence of life-imprisonment.'[1] As it did to most of those who followed the hearings, the verdict seemed to her to be an irredeemable scandal. This, then, was how a man could be condemned, without proof, to spend his whole life in prison.

In the end, from her point of view, it made no difference whether Goldman was guilty or innocent. It was the miscarriage of justice that was intolerable. In Hollywood in the sixties, Simone Signoret had had long discussions with Walter Wanger, a producer who would move heaven and earth for the release of the famous Caryll Chessman, condemned to death without proof for murder and rape. She admired Wanger's energy, which was fuelled by his firm conviction of Chessman's innocence. But she already felt sure that this conviction was only secondary in the struggle for justice. The determining factor was the absence of proof. 'You never know whether the people you're siding with are really innocent or guilty. Most of the time, you are siding against those who think that they have the right to side against the accused, when they have no right at all.'[2]

What was intolerable was the deliberate deafness of the jury, the 'good men and true' who were supposed to judge with the help of their soul and conscience and to represent the French people, but who had not the least idea of the passions that drive a man like Pierre Goldman. 'Nine of my fellow-citizens, the jury, in my name and yours, were able, without asking a single question and consequently without asking *themselves* a single question, to swallow piecemeal all the half-truths, improbabilities, and flagrant lies dished up by the gang of prosecution witnesses who were paraded in front of them . . . Those nine people voted for "Life" (because they could not think of anything else to do, or so we are told), and then went back to sleep in their own beds at home. I have never forgiven them.'[3]

[1] *Le Lendemain, elle était souriante*, op. cit.
[2] *Nostalgia* . . . op.cit.
[3] *Le Lendemain* . . . op.cit.

In his own book, Pierre Goldman transforms the surreal moment when the sentence was pronounced into an instant happening, a flash-photograph in words.

'I looked at Langlois.

'Marianne.

'Marc.

'My best friend (who was sitting with the journalists).

'As soon as Braunschweig started speaking, Philippe Boucher stood up, pale, drawn and distraught.

'I looked at him.

'I looked at Simone Signoret.'[1]

The narrative continues, like a litany, cry or prayer. He looks at them, sees their emotion, and the love they feel for him: a rare moment in a man's life, uplifting in a paradoxical way. After that, nothing; just the dark, and the loneliness of the cell where he would write his poignant *Souvenirs Obscurs d'un Juif polonais né en France* (*Obscure Memories of a Polish Jew born in France*).

Heroes had always fascinated Simone Signoret. In Greece in 1964 she had created a furore by talking to journalists, as she got out of the aeroplane, about the dead patriot Beloyanis, a hero of the Greek resistance who had been shot by the monarchists, and whose photograph she had at home in the 'caravan'.

She had come to Greece to play Bouboulina in Cacoyannis's *Zorba the Greek*. She was forty-three years of age at the time, and Bouboulina was fifteen years older. 'I honestly tried. I had all sorts of props: a false bottom and false sagging breasts and cotton inside my cheeks, and a fake gold tooth as well as a plastic wart . . .'[2] She had tried hard, for several days, but then they had to fake a photograph of her looking ten years younger, strangely beautiful, evoking Casque d'Or. The contrast was too brutal; she was not yet ready to make herself ugly, as she would be at the time of Madame Rosa. She gave up the part of Bouboulina.

So the only memento of her trip to Greece would be this spectacular episode: 'If you arrive in Athens in 1964 for the first time in your life, having firmly decided not to get mixed

[1] Pierre Goldman, op.cit.
[2] *Nostalgia* . . . op.cit.

150

up in things that are none of your business, and you're made to pronounce the name Beloyanis just as soon as you step off the plane, it's about as diplomatic as arriving in New York for the first time ten years earlier, and when they ask you, "Do you know any famous Americans?", you reply, "Yes, the Rosenbergs." Or, if the same question were asked in Moscow, you reply, "I only know one Russian, and that's Trotsky!" [1]

A blown-up photo of the smiling Greek patriot, a carnation pressed to his lips, appears in Costa-Gavras's film, Z. It is like a sign, a wink in Simone's direction. She had never met Beloyanis, but he belonged to her album of souvenirs, her 'family photo', like her brother. Like the Rosenbergs, or Slansky, the MOI freedom fighters or Pierre Goldman, he was part of her life story – 'one of us'. Simone Signoret included him automatically among the ranks of those exceptional people who enjoy the sombre privilege of bearing other people's destinies on their shoulders.

Seeing her, day after day, so attentive during the first Goldman trial, Raymond Thévenin, the law reporter, had an idea for a television series in which Simone Signoret would be in her rightful place, sitting on the Bench rather than in the visitors' gallery. Playing the character of Elisabeth Massot, 'Madame le juge', in six episodes written and directed by a galaxy of writers and directors, she would soon experience the rare pleasure of combining her actor's craft with her passionate interest in the workings of the judiciary.

In Le Lendemain, elle était souriante, she describes the second Goldman trial in Amiens in 1976, which ended in an acquittal. With the precision of a budding novelist she charts the dramatic high points, staging the discomfiture of the witnesses as they were caught lying in flagrante delicto. It was in Amiens, between two hearings, in the main reception room of the hotel where she was staying, that she would try in vain to finish editing her memoirs, 'this "Thing", nearly six hundred pages long, which I had been lugging around with me far too many months'. Looking out of the hotel window at the wall opposite, she would spot a graffito in red paint that would remind her of another graffito glimpsed

[1] *Nostalgia . . .* op.cit.

151

in New York, with the 'moving, absurd and incomprehensible' message: 'Nostalgia Isn't What It Used To Be'. At least she had found her title; but the book would not be finished until after *Madame le juge*, in the heat of a Parisian July.

To start filming *Madame le juge*, she had to leave Amiens the evening before the verdict, and she heard the result in Aix-en-Provence, where she had just met up with Claude Chabrol: 'I went to sleep that night feeling happy about justice in my country, and I told myself that it was a good omen for tackling Elisabeth Massot's first case of conscience the next morning.' She did not, however, forget that in the Aix-en-Provence courthouse where she was preparing to take up her 'magisterial functions', Christian Ranucci[1] had just been condemned to death. She saw Gabrielle Russier's[2] ghost pass by – the woman accused of a crime of passion that drove her to suicide, climbing the main steps under Mirabeau's marble gaze. The Palais de Justice was the supreme stage for tragedy. 'After all, I was an actress, and it was quite normal for me, when I found myself in a setting, to wonder how the plays were staged in it.'

In those huge, cavernous halls, amidst the colonnades and the mosaics, she could easily let herself be taken over by her new 'lodger'. In the foreground of her capacious memory were the images of the second Goldman trial: the ritual, the costumes, the line-up of witnesses, the deadpan faces of the jurors, the solitary defendant, the uncanny silence of the spectators during the tensest moments. What theatre! A tragedy in two acts, with a temporary happy ending. The first act had ended with a life-sentence; at the end of the second act, hanging at the end of the hotel telephone in Aix-en-Provence, she experienced, vicariously, the rush of raw emotion that comes from participating in extraordinary events. Her hero had been saved. Three years later he would be gunned down in the street, like a dog.

At this period, she would battle on all fronts in the theatre of life. She threw herself feverishly into her political activities, as if with

[1]Condemned to death and executed in 1976 for the murder of an eight-year-old girl.
[2]A schoolteacher from Marseilles who committed suicide in 1969 after being convicted of the corruption of a minor. (She had had a love affair with a sixteen-year-old pupil.)

a mission to change the world and the whole of human nature, as if afraid of leaving a cause out. Perhaps these ceaseless battles were a way of escaping from herself, and her past. She was always available, except when she was working on a film. Then she was dead to the outside world, nobody was allowed to ask her to sign a petition: the guardian angel of Human Rights would turn a deaf ear to the noblest of causes.

But at other times, she was receptive, ready to listen at the other end of the line. A dissident who needed rescuing from jail, a hunger-strike, a complaint against the police, a conviction without proof, a wrongful extradition . . . every time she mobilised herself, she would put all her weight behind it. When the Chilean refugees asked for help, when the Vietnamese fled from dictatorship, or when Lech Walesa was imprisoned, people would turn to her as they did to Sartre, Foucault, Maurice Clavell and Claude Mauriac.[1] Gradually, her perseverance earned her moral weight and authority.

When people asked her about her political activities, Simone Signoret would deny that her action was 'political'. She had never belonged to a party, she was not a militant, she was not obeying orders. She was fighting for a particular concept of justice. In her own way she was a forerunner of the great campaign for Human Rights that would fill up the void left by the collapse of ideologies.

In his turn, Alain Krivine, leader of the Communist League, would be sent to prison. And once again, Simone Signoret protested, on a point of principle: 'I know nothing about the schisms that divide the various Trotskyite movements, and I'd even go so far as to say that I couldn't care less. I had never met the young man they had just thrown into jail, but I really didn't see why he should be in prison.'[2]

This was how, one day, she found herself kicking her heels with Michel Piccoli and Serge Reggiani outside the gates of the Ministry of Justice, after trying to get an official delegation together to plead Krivine's cause. Finally, after a long wait in the bar of

---

[1]Left-wing intellectuals, who were close friends of Sartre.
[2]*Nostalgia* . . . op.cit.

the Ritz Hotel, they were received by the Minister's Principal Private Secretary who pointedly listened to their claim that it was wrong to imprison anybody for anti-racism. Looking ridiculous does no harm, when generosity is the reason. Clear-minded, Simone Signoret was well aware that the officials listened to them because they were celebrities. She was also aware that, every time she put herself in the firing line, she risked being suspected of self-promotion. Jauntily, she accepted the risk: 'You must have the courage to be taken for simpletons who use dreams to give them a clear conscience.'

Barred people, exiles, representatives of victims of dictatorships on the other side of the world, knew that their door was open. They all came to the Place Dauphine with their sufferings and their petitions. 'When I was little they told me that tramps would leave mysterious signs on the doors of farms. They were intended for other tramps, their pals, following the same itinerary. They meant: "These people give", or "These people are mean", or "Here they give if you work". It was a sign language of crosses, lines and circles cut into the door with a penknife. The door of the "caravan" undoubtedly bears some invisible symbols.'[1]

Sometimes, there were too many of them, and the Montands did not know where to turn. Hungarians, Czechs, Chileans, Brazilians, American-Indians, Poles . . . When Régis Debray, released from prison in Bolivia, returned to Paris, he chose to live in the Place Dauphine in the room on the fifth floor. When Allende was assassinated in Chile, Montand decided to give a one-night concert at the Olympia, after five years of silence. When Bernard Kouchner launched Operation 'Île de Lumière' to try to save the boat people drowning in the China Sea, Montand and Signoret were by his side. When Lech Walesa was arrested in Poland, they wore the 'Solidarity' badge. In 1982, Simone Signoret went to Warsaw and Gdansk with Michel Foucault; his last political act. She felt all the more concerned about the imposition of martial law in Jaruzelski's Poland when she recalled how, nearly thirty years earlier, the entry of the Russian tanks into Budapest had marked the end of her illusions.

[1] *Nostalgia* . . . op.cit.

By denouncing the empire of the gulags with a virulence born of disillusion, Montand would soon become one of France's top-earning stars at the box office. In 1984, 55 per cent of French television viewers would tune in to hear the singer 'sounding off' on *Dossiers de l'écran*. He was totally candid about his past affiliations, but insisted that his position remained unchanged on essential questions like intolerance, injustice and humiliation. For the benefit of the young, he reminded his audience that, when he was young, Communism had been an ideal shared by many of the brightest and the best; and he described how he was devastated when forced to admit the impossibility of Marxism in practice: 'It was like rejecting the person I loved best in all the world – like rejecting my own father.' He used his former faith in socialism to add fuel to his attack on the deadlocks and massacres of the regime that had pretended to be an earthly paradise. Alain Jérôme, seeing a politician beside him in the studio, asked the burning question: Would he stand in the forthcoming presidential elections?

Don Quixotes of the media, Montand and Signoret tilted at contemporary windmills with untrammelled enthusiasm. Yet by involving themselves so personally in the misfortunes of the world, and having been petitioned by so many different people, they occasionally risked seeing themselves as oracles and allowing themselves to be carried away. When he gave an interview on the gulags to Louis Pauwels' conservative *Figaro Magazine* in 1983, Montand took the extra risk of going too far in the other direction and of laying himself open to the charge of having gone over to the Right. Wiser, truer to herself, and certainly more genuinely 'political', Simone Signoret stayed in the background. For the first time, she disowned Montand in public, not fundamentally, but because there were limits she should not cross: 'Sometimes Abbott appears without Costello,' she told the *Nouvel Observateur*. The *Figaro Magazine* stood for an ideology that Montand had fought against all his life. She knew from bitter experience how the media can distort impolitic or maladroit remarks. She would try to protect Montand from the mistakes of an ageing man reliving his youth, and to stop him from being carried away; afraid that he would suffer a backlash from all the adulation that surrounded him. Better than anyone, better than Montand himself, she knew his vulnerability, his anxieties, the inner tension that led him to make rambling speeches punctuated by sweeping gestures, and she was aware of the longing of a self-taught man to be recognised by intellectuals. Of all the heroes that fed Simone Signoret's dreams, only Montand was nobody's victim but his own.

I am guessing, playing the novelist; probing the myth. I admire her capacity for always being available, for friends, or for causes to fight for. I admire her talent for co-ordinating, for being a group-leader thanks to the compelling physical presence that made her the centre of attraction, wherever she was.

Simone Signoret kept up with everything. She never missed a news broadcast or a scandal or a revolution. 'She was the kind of person who starts telephoning at dawn, often to discuss what she'd seen, read or heard. There's never been such a television and radio *aficionado*, or a more intelligent one: she listened to everything, saw everything, from the news programmes on televison in the evening to the early-morning bulletins on radio.'[1] She would telephone newspaper editors on behalf of Pierre Goldman, or the hunger-strikers, for Angela Grimau (widow of Julian Grimau, assassinated by Franco), for Geismar, Le Dantec, Krivine, for Jean-Paul Kauffmann, a hostage in the Lebanon, or to ask for help in getting Chtcharanski out of the gulag at Perm, or to attract attention towards two Frenchmen imprisoned in Poland, or for Sakharov, or for victims whom the media ignored like Madame Stein, the lady who lived in the same building as Chapour Bakhtiar, the former Iranian prime minister, and who was assassinated by mistake instead of him. Nobody mentioned her. On television, Bakhtiar did not say a word about her, but contented himself with making the ' "V" for Victory' sign: 'Just think about it: the story of Madame Stein, her sister and her little boy, the story of the Shah's prime minister's next-door neighbour, a lady who had nothing to do with Iran – on top of everything else her name was Stein – who is murdered by Khomeini's thugs. I'd make an hour-and-a-half-long documentary about her, which would make people cry. Well, nobody gives a damn: extraordinary, isn't it?' At such moments, Simone Signoret was a visionary. She could

[1] Anne Sinclair, *L'Événement du Jeudi*, 3 October 1985.

156

not get used to the gap between reality and its representation in the public marketplace.

In her last years, she was so active, appeared so often in the papers or on television, was so often mobilised, questioned, and petitioned, that the void left by her death is still enormous. This void extends beyond her physical presence. Of course, we have changed epochs, but in truth we have already changed centuries.

CHAPTER SIXTEEN

In 1970, Simone Signoret began the series of great films of her maturity with *Le Chat*, directed by Pierre Granier-Deferre. Puffy-faced, limping, and yet vulnerable, she is trapped in a hideous private hell opposite that old rhinoceros Jean Gabin, who is absorbed in his own unspeakable suffering. Adapted from a Simenon novel, *Le Chat* is the grim, hopeless story of a marital battleground. Set in a little suburban house isolated in the middle of a huge building site in an area being developed, amid the noise of diggers, roaring bulldozers and grinding chainsaws, it focuses on the merciless hatred between the old typographer and the ex-trapeze artist who are locked in deadly, yet perversely enjoyable, enmity. The viewer feels that this hell has been going on for years, maybe for a lifetime. Trapped in his infantile vanity, Gabin finally wins the war, but his wife dies in the process, and he is incapable of surviving her.

The double-act of these two heavyweights, both grumpily refusing to become 'lovable monsters', gives an odd, looking-glass effect, and a feeling of connivance between actors that surmounts their profound differences. They look strikingly alike, following the classic pattern of old couples: 'I don't run trotting horses at Vincennes, and I don't raise cattle, and we don't agree on a great many things. But we agree on one thing, and that's vital: how you act in a film together.'[1] Signoret felt enormous admiration for him, mixed with affection. 'It was beautiful to look at him and catch in his eye the deserter in *Quai des Brumes* and in his

[1] *Nostalgia . . .* op.cit.

smile the smile of Captain Maréchal in *La Grande Illusion*.'[1] Gabin
had insisted on Signoret being in the film, and had turned down
every other partner. He respected her. Though he hated climbing
stairs, he meekly agreed to walk up three steps off-screen to give
her a cue. He considered *Le Chat* to be one of his best films.

She formed another mutual admiration society with Alain
Delon, another lovable monster: 'A gentle madman trying to act
tough – and a generous madman too. We're happy when we're
together, because we work very well together.'[2] With him, she
embarked on *La Veuve Couderc*, another Simenon novel adapted
by Granier-Deferre. Like Gabin, in political, human and all other
terms, Delon could have come from a totally different planet.
She had known him as a young man, when she was married
to Yves Allégret. Now they were partners, of different ages but
equal powers.

In *La Veuve Couderc*, Signoret plays a fifty-year-old peasant
woman, still desirable in spite of her girth and her grey hair.
It is hard to believe that *La Veuve Couderc* was filmed after *Le
Chat*. It was a miracle of make-up. The pathetic Clémence in
Le Chat seems ten years older than the elegant countrywoman,
as tasty as a slightly over-ripe fruit. The set is subtly poetic: a
canal, barges, a lock, two houses, one on each side, and merciless family feuds in between-the-wars France. The widow
Couderc, living alone in her farm, is harried by the hatred of
her dead husband's family, who are after her inheritance. She
gives work to a commercial traveller, Alain Delon, whom she
guesses to be wanted by the police. Gradually, a bond of love
forms between them, which adds right-wing fanaticism to the
family vendetta. It is the time of the Fiery Crosses[3] and the Sixth
of February,[4] the heyday of the French far-Right. The widow
Couderc has given her heart to the traveller, and, when the police
track him down, she knows what she has to do. Self-sacrifice
goes without saying, and she will die with him in front of her
burning house.

[1] *Nostalgia* . . . op.cit.
[2] Id.
[3] Neo-Fascist organisation of the thirties, led by Colonel de la Roque.
[4] A mass right-wing rally was held in Paris on 6 February 1934.

159

The most surprising thing about the film is the chemistry between Alain Delon and Simone Signoret. It crackles on the screen. Yet with Simone, Delon was strangely submissive. It was hard to believe – but he looked frightened. Could it be that the ageing lioness actually scared the wild animal with his shining pelt? 'She called me "kid", just like Gabin, and I called her "Auntie",' Alain Delon would say on the day after her death.

The sense of complicity between them would have a bad effect on their second film together, just after *La Veuve Couderc*: *Les Granges brûlées*. The shooting of this Jean Chapot film was so dramatic and violent that Signoret would never talk about it. Yet it is quite well made, a story of ice and snow in the mountains of the Jura. The discovery of a woman's bloodstained corpse near a lonely farm triggers off an investigation by the examining magistrate, Alain Delon. Patient and conscientious, he tries to understand this world of obstinate peasants, and to penetrate the cache of family secrets kept by the mother, Simone Signoret, a silent block of repressed emotion. As in *La Veuve Couderc*, they exchange extraordinarily intense looks.

She was being offered still more parts that fitted her image of a tough, capable woman, and powerful heroine. But the film she made next was *Rude journée pour la Reine* (*A Rough Day for the Queen*), with René Allio. The story is unnecessarily complicated, but Jeanne's personality, her fantasies and anxieties are unforgettable. She is a cleaning-woman who has been battered by life, a timid, frightened, simple person tortured by anxiety about delivering a letter in secret to her imprisoned son's fiancée. Jeanne is an 'anti-Signoret', a natural victim, one of the losers you will not find in family photos, a poor, vulnerable creature who escapes into fantasies of grandeur. She imagines herself to be, in succession, the Empress of Austria, the French President's wife, and the heroine of a women's magazine story . . . Simone Signoret had a special affection for this humble, vaguely mythomaniac 'lodger' of hers, with her hair-curlers and shop-soiled raincoat. During the filming, Jeanne actually succeeded in making Simone a nicer, gentler person: 'After my daughter Catherine saw the film, she said: "Now I know why you were so gentle, unaggressive and kind at home! You were Jeanne!"'[1]

In order to become Jeanne, she agreed, as for *Le Chat*, to make herself look ugly and even older than she really was, to accept the challenge she had refused back at the time of Bouboulina. Now that she was the same age as Bouboulina, she was no longer afraid. She refused to have a face-lift. In fact, she forestalled the idea: 'I'm clever enough to know, that at fifty-two years old, I could have a different silhouette, a different kind of face, if I wanted. So, if my being the way I am can be of any use, why not let Jeanne benefit from it?'[2]

She would never be graceful again. *La Veuve Couderc* was the last film in which she would look attractive. In 1974 there would be Patrice Chéreau's *La Chair de l'orchidée*, a strange, obscure work in which her imposing shape would make a few unforgettable entrances, then Alain Corneau's *Police Python 357* where she plays an all-powerful paralytic who rules the world from her bed.

By deliberately playing up her loss of physical attractiveness, she was unconsciously preparing the way to finding another means of expression that would soon become as important to her life as the cinema. She would fight against the passage of the years by writing.

[1]Interview with Michel Delain, *L'Express*, 26 November 1973.
[2]*Femmes d'aujourd'hui*, December 1973.

CHAPTER SEVENTEEN

I would never have wanted to write about her and her world, or to have involved myself so obsessively in what I believe her life-story to have been, if she had not been a writer, if writing had not been her longtime dream, a craft she pursued with timidity, perseverance and difficulty, and finally with the enthusiasm that she put into all her ventures. It was a sort of consecration, the ultimate proof of her real worth, of her own, personal capacity, as the daughter of André Kaminker the interpreter, of being more than just the interpreter, however brilliant, of stories written by other people.

For a long time she had thought she would be content with acting. She loved 'playing the actress' and stirring up emotions, and she gave herself unreservedly, with the generosity mixed with narcissism that creates great actors, wanting to combine the best of herself with the pleasure of being watched and admired, without which there can be no good entertainment. Without false modesty she enjoyed the 'joy of being looked at that all we actresses feel when the camera comes very close'.[1] In her youth, she had experienced the intoxication women feel when they see other people's eyes reflect the moving, fragile grace called beauty, which cannot be described but silently displays and offers itself to the beholder. During the war at the Flore, Jorge Semprun recalls, he dared not talk to her, but would look at her passing by, regal, blonde, exotic, 'as beautiful as the day, or as the night (why should day be more beautiful than night?)'.[2]

[1]*Nostalgia . . .* op.cit.
[2]*La vie continue*, Denoël, 1983.

162

She was intelligent enough to enjoy her own beauty, but not vain; she refused to mistake beauty for personal worth. She fully realised not only that she herself had nothing to do with it, but also that time would work its ravages, and that she would have another life to live, another journey – the journey through the looking-glass of appearances. Realism does not exclude regrets, and occasionally, during bad patches of her middle-age, she would openly envy young stars on their way up. When people talked about Isabelle Adjani's beauty at a dinner party, she would rasp, in a bass voice thickened by alcohol, 'Did you see me in *Casque?*' But losing her beauty did not represent a lost paradise, as it did for Greta Garbo, or a vanished kingdom where life had been so golden that the rest was grey and mediocre by comparison. For Simone, it represented the memory of past pleasures, of basking in the sunshine of a glorious spring, of being admired, desired and envied. It was the sweet, nostalgic memory of a lost sovereignty that she replaced with another rougher, more exacting power.

Even if we had a snapshot taken of Simone Signoret every day, at the same time, the strange feeling we experience when we look at the image of Casque d'Or alongside Madame Rosa's would remain the same. Reaching the truth is just a question of acknowledging this strangeness, analysing it deeply; and remembering that there is always a touch of mystery about how a person still looks like himself or herself at different ages. A mysterious something surviving physical changes – the continuation of personal identity, that very concrete abstract idea. In Signoret's case, the transformation was radical, and enormous in its implications. On a postcard that I have pinned in front of me, I can scrutinise the haughty little face of Gisèle in *Macadam*, with her bowler hat, her kid gloves, the cigarette dangling between two fingers, and her frilly shirt and riding jacket. Beside the card, there is a photograph of the elderly woman whom I knew all too briefly, with wispy grey hairs brushing her forehead, and a little gold ring in her ear; in her eyes the naked stare of near-blindness: a woman without artifice, but not without passion, disarmed, serene, hopeless, and alone. Can it really be the same person? The resemblance is incontestable, but how can one define it?

Returning, near the end of her book, to the time-span that she had covered in *Nostalgia Isn't What It Used To Be*, she herself is surprised: 'I began walking hand in hand with myself at the age my mother took me for my Joan of Arc haircut to hairdressers who didn't singe their tongs, and I've followed myself across all those borders that came later. Last night I left in my typewriter a forty-year-old bleached blonde. I was so deep inside myself, inside that bleached blonde (what a bore, one's memory!) that I was astonished when I glanced in the mirror this morning and met there a person a bit too plump, greying, not to say white-haired, who looked back and said, "Hello there, that's me!" when I was about to brush my teeth.'[1]

In autumn 1976, the publication of *Nostalgia Isn't What It Used To Be* was one of the big literary events of the year, a huge volume of nearly four hundred pages which would sell hundreds of thousands of copies. Its success was all the more spectacular for being unexpected; it sold far more copies than other actors' memoirs. Yet this unstructured hold-all of a book had been composed in defiance of all the academic rules. The author never stops making digressions and playing around with chronology. The chapters succeed each other erratically, following a plan that reflects her impulses and her wish to linger in the 'little stations' of her memory. Her dialogue with Maurice Pons, the first stage of her journey, disappears and reappears with no apparent reason, interrupted by long monologues. Yet this free-flowing structure is the expression of a deeper kind of freedom, and the narrative is carried forward by a lyricism, a sense of fun, and pleasure in story-telling which sweeps aside all considerations about form. For Simone knew how to tell a story. It was one of her passions; she was an inspired gossip, she took you by the hand and would not let go.

She had given firm instructions to Le Seuil, her publishers, not to put any photographs in the book; these were not the memoirs of any ordinary actress, her aim was not to put a set of images together but to reflect on her experience; she was writing a twentieth-century chronicle, a book for adults, without pictures. But, above all, it was a real book, initially based on tape-recorded conversations, but written on her own, like the work of professional authors.

There is something heart-rending about how Simone Signoret felt obliged to insist to the public and her critics that she really was the author. She was about to wage a ferocious battle imposed on her by the current vogue among French publishers in the seventies for 'taped books', a fruitful source of profit which, while the fashion lasted, helped publishers to top up their failing lists, and allowed people who enjoyed fabricated scandals to give full rein to self-righteous indignation.

Looking back on a debate that received so much space in literary gossip-columns, it would have been a pity if at least some of the views gathered in this way had not been published. After all plenty of non-professionals have important things to say, which deserve to last. There is nothing dishonourable about using a 'ghostwriter'; the only justifiable criticism is the hypocritical habit of leaving the ghost's name off the jacket. Basically 'ghosting' is very much like the age-old practice of scribes in ancient times, who sat cross-legged in the marketplace with their wax tablets or papyri, waiting for passers-by to entrust to them the commercial or romantic messages that they could not write themselves. The scribes did not put their own signature on their clients' letters. Even if the modern scribes of 'taped books' are able to write their own business letters or words of love, they lack the modicum of skill needed to write a proper book.

Simone Signoret possessed this modicum; what she had long lacked was confidence. One can understand it. It is almost impossible, in France, for a film actress to try her hand at writing without running the risk of exposing herself to the sneers or patronising indulgence of the literati. Yet she had always enjoyed writing, scribbling bits of a novel or fragments of a journal. 'Now and again, opening a cupboard drawer, Montand would come across a bit of paper and read it, and he'd say, "This is funny!" And then, whenever I've had serious problems, I've always liked to put them down on paper. Everybody has his own way of coping: some people go to the café, others to psychoanalysts' couches. I don't lie down on an analyst's sofa; my couch is writing!'[1] At school in Neuilly she had been good at writing essays, and she had had no problems in passing her 'Bac' in philosophy at Vannes at the beginning of the war. Spelling and grammar had no secrets for her.

But she had to choose: writing or films. 'When I made my début, there was no question of doing several things at the same time: one was an actor, and that was that. People tended to distrust jacks-of-all-trades, those who could paint a little, sing a little, write a little. If I wanted to be an actress, it was better to forget that I wanted to write. And to make other people forget it, too. If, like me, you started your acting career in the role of a pretty little tart in *Macadam*, it was better not to tell people that you had been good at essay-writing. It was even better to pretend to be illiterate.'[2] Later, she too would catch herself feeling irritated when a young actress at the start of her career walked around the set with a fat philosophy book under her arm. Spinoza and *Cinémonde* do not go together.

By choosing the cinema instead of writing as a career (if indeed she made a conscious choice, which is unlikely), she was affirming her desire to be a twentieth-century woman; she was also distancing herself from her lonely childhood as an only daughter living in Neuilly in a 'displaced' family. She would re-live the pains and pleasures of that solitary existence during the long days spent in front of her typewriter at Autheuil, with the pages of her manuscript slowly piling up on the left side of the table.

Everything started in Nice on 10 May 1977, between eleven o'clock and noon, during the literary festival, Le Salon du Livre, with a live broadcast on the hot topic of the day, 'ghostwriters in literature'. At the time, the programmes hosted by Anne Gaillard, the consumers' Mata Hari, were a kind of media marketplace where occasionally injustices were made public, and even set right. But sometimes a passion for justice can be carried too far, and on that day, Anne Gaillard's guests on the television programme *France Inter*, probably excited by the gossipy atmosphere of the

---

[1] *Elle*, interview with Françoise Tournier, 8 June 1981.
[2] *Marie-Claire*, interview with Pierre Démeron, September 1979.

festival, overstepped the line. The tone was set by Marie Cardinal, herself a former ghostwriter ('exorcised since', as Pierre Georges joked in *Le Monde*): 'The other day I saw a famous French film star on television. Everybody was enthusing about her book, which is excellent, by the way. She did not write a line of it.' And the critic Jean-Edern Hallier took up the tune: 'As far as I am concerned, the main trouble with ghostwriting is that the public are taken in . . . some publishers systematically fool their readers. They present Daniel Gélin's book as a book by Gelin, Morgan's book as a book by Morgan, or Signoret's book as the work of a great writer. It's dishonest.'

As so often happens, his malice touched a raw nerve. In plain language, Maurice Pons was being accused of undercover 'ghosting'. And it is true that he played a decisive role in both the gestation and the birth of Signoret's book. Initially, there had been long conversations, organised at the request of the Lacoutures – 'sitting in a circle on the carpet, around the god-like tape-recorder, like worshippers kneeling before their idol'.[1] Over long days of relaxed friendship, and breakfasts together in the big sunny house at Autheuil, Maurice Pons played, in turn, 'cop, father-confessor, psychiatrist, biographer, historiographer, commissar, secret agent, crouching scribe, examining magistrate, bride's witness, and godfather'. In his preface to *Nostalgia*, he makes no bones about how something that had started with a fascinating game of words had gradually developed into 'the slow, mysterious and exciting transmutation of thoughts into writing', and finally into a book of which he was neither the 'co-author nor the re-writer' but the 'first listener, and the most assiduous reader'.

Maurice Pons' introduction was necessary because of the conditions in which the project saw the light of day, and Simone Signoret approved and accepted it after reading and re-reading it. It was a pleasant tale of friendship and trust, where each player had his cards on the table. But in this age of suspicion, a spark can set off a small fire and clouds of evil-smelling smoke. Maurice Pons' introduction, the questions that Simone Signoret retained in the final version of the book, the news items in the Press . . . not

[1] Maurice Pons, in his preface to *Nostalgia* . . . op.cit.

much is needed to fan malicious gossip. And then, of course, everybody knows that actresses can't write . . . Simone Signoret the writer was a prime target, all the more vulnerable because she was famous, all the easier to wound because her book was well-written and successful, an idol with feet of clay.

Calumny can stick for a long time in the public's mind. I have met several people who are genuinely convinced that Simone Signoret didn't write a line of *Nostalgia Isn't What It Used To Be*. Perhaps they would never have asked themselves the question if Simone Signoret had not reacted like a lioness defending her cub. Sometimes a dignified silence is better than a pitched battle which can only, at best, end in a Pyrrhic victory. She was well aware of this, of course. 'I've known for a long time that by correcting one news item with another, you run the risk of attracting attention to a news item nobody has read.' But for a woman of her mettle, there was no question of turning the other cheek. She needed a fight, proof, and a complete retraction. Technically, victory proved easy: *France Inter* was sentenced to pay a fine of 1.200 Francs, plus 6.000 Francs damages, for libel.

But this was not enough; she felt impelled to write a second book, *Le Lendemain, elle était souriante*, which was intended to set the record straight, and prove her innocence, and her talents as an author in her own right. It was like a speech for the defence. Yet all the publicity surrounding the libel case, and then the second book, had the paradoxical effect of prolonging suspicion and giving it substance. If she had not defended herself so well, the matter would probably have been just another of those flash-in-the-pan scandals that Paris feeds on, from Balzac to Carmen Tessier, which only mildly dent reputations.

She had decided, in *Le Lendemain, elle était souriante*, to ram the point home and to prove that she knew, at first hand, the 'joys, anxieties, ecstasies and sorrows, and the solitude, too, of a writer at his table'. It was a strange idea, when one thinks about it; she should have known that writing, like love, defies proof.

She could have let the matter lie there. But at that moment of her life, she was possessed by such resentment and bitterness that she felt the need to hit out, in a private vendetta aimed at almost everyone who had crossed her path and who had helped her overcome her anxieties. *Le Lendemain, elle était souriante* is the pathetic journal of a woman who has been flayed alive.

It was as if the spark that would finally ignite the exquisite torments of creative writing could only be conjured up by raging anger: 'I did not know, yet, that I would enjoy writing; that I was preparing myself for days when I would not enjoy myself at all. I did not know, yet, that I was moving towards something I had never experienced – the necessity of being alone.'

'I absolutely do not know why I started writing,'[1] Simone Signoret would say. She used to install herself at her writing table at half-past nine each morning, after a shower and coffee drunk while listening to the news. Then she would settle down to the daily grind, working away at the white page as she used to work away on her face at her make-up table, in the happy days when she acted in films, smoking Gauloise cigarettes. She had started writing on impulse, like suddenly going away on a trip, 'with the delicious guilt of a runaway'. Yet she was working as hard as any civil servant, totally concentrating on her task.

Without the providential slanders of Anne Gaillard's programme, we would probably know far less about the little rituals she had invented to keep her going, which she listed to make us believe her claims: the silly tricks that keep writers going during their long and lonely vigils, the intimate ceremonies invented to keep ourselves sitting at a table with enough courage to fill the pages.

Writing caters for all kinds of minor eccentricities. Everyone has secrets they can't own up to, and their own magic formula. There are some who tidy their desks for hours before they can write a line, others who telephone their friends to tell them that, at last, they are getting down to it. Others copy out their address book over again; nightbirds wait up until three o'clock in the morning for inspiration, and go to bed exhausted at dawn. Simenon would sharpen his eighteen pencils every morning and lose 800 grammes of perspiration per chapter, Balzac swallowed litres of coffee, Freud smoked cigars on top of his cancer of the throat.

---

[1] Interview with Françoise Tournier, *Elle*, 21 January 1985.

SIMONE SIGNORET

At my paper, on a day when people are letting their hair down, you hear some good stories. Chantal puts an old bra on top of her T-shirt and shuffles about in carpet-slippers, Marie spreads out all her notes higgledy-piggledy on the floor and crouches down in the middle of the scattered pages, Emmanuel scribbles phrases on Métro tickets, Maurice smokes mint cigarettes and drinks whisky, Claire does the washing-up and hoovering, Mariella runs six times round the park, Catherine takes a siesta under the table-legs, on the carpet, amidst the smell of dry dust. 'The important thing was not to leave the room I was working in. It was a place that Montand had fixed for me, with windows facing the roof – I can't even see the countryside. There I would be, completely isolated, without anything to distract me, my nose up against the white wall. And when, at a certain moment, you're looking for something and you can't find it, you'll end up seeing things on that blank white wall.'[1]

The urge to write is powerful but volatile, like an alcohol that evaporates, a mirage that retreats as time advances; or like a guardian angel.

We live in a paradoxical time, when the written word invades us from every side, yet slips from between our fingers. In theory dethroned by the reign of the image, writing continues to extend its influence on people's minds. By crossing from the razzmatazz of the silver screen to the solitary confinement of writing, Simone Signoret delved deeper into the complexities of her time. In the cinemas, she lent her regal shadow to the parade of fantasy-figures. But when she wrote, it was no longer her image that she projected on to the page, or her inimitable voice that was heard in her choice of words.

The image faded away, revealing the real person. Under the pressure of writing, the mirror broke, and the image was scattered like a thousand splinters of glass in a kaleidoscope. She could play about with her image, dress up as somebody else, escape into different identities. After trying to destroy this image by maltreating it and letting her face grow misshapen, she had finally found a way of reducing it to the status of mere illusion. She had

[1]Interview with Jean-François Josselin, *Le Nouvel Observateur*, 25 January 1985.

derived enough pleasure from changing her appearance to be able to turn away from it without regrets. By writing, she would finally plant roots in the deepest part of herself. At last, she was removing the veil. She wiped off her make-up, and her face did not disappear. On the contrary; another image took shape, complete, finished, three-dimensional, not deformed by the flat cinema screen. The real Simone was created by writing, the Simone one would like to see alive again now.

It was not an easy decision; she had only made up her mind to write under pressure from her friends. They interpreted the strange law of an epoch by which glory on screen would seem incomplete without a journey through the austere paths of writing. And she launched herself much more recklessly into this new career than people had expected, in spite of the sedentary life that it involved, and the beginner's uncertainties.

Yet this was still only a stage in the journey, the beginning of a dream coming true. It would need many more years, and yet more encouragement from friends to take her to the next decisive step towards fiction which, with poetry, is one of the two paths leading a writer to creative freedom.

CHAPTER EIGHTEEN

From now on, her life would be divided between the cinema – or television – and writing. 'It's been like that for several years. As soon as I stop acting, I feel the urge to write.'[1] When filming interrupted the writing of her books, she would lug her typewriter around everywhere with her, in the hope of adding a few pages to the unfinished manuscript in between two scenes. But it was impossible; she could not do things by halves. She never could, and the older she grew, the stronger her capacity for concentration became; inherent in her very being, it came from the intensity of her desire, whatever its object. She did everything with the same professionalism, and threw herself into each experience, whether it was a meeting, a film, a contest or a book, with the same intensity and gravity. When she entered a particular field of activity, everything else dipped below the horizon. From the beginning, totally absorbed in acting in a film, she had been oblivious of ordinary life around her, and not even her passion for writing affected this absorption. Now it was reversed: while she was fully engaged in writing, nobody could talk to her about her next film. Alain Corneau learned this the hard way when he came to see her at Autheuil to discuss *Police Python 357* when she was in the middle of a journey in *Nostalgia*, somewhere between East Germany and Czechoslovakia.

In 1977, after much hesitation, she embarked on the formidable venture of playing Madame Rosa in *La Vie devant soi*, an adaptation

[1] *Elle*, 21 January 1985.

by Moshe Mizrahi of Émile Ajar's prize-winning novel.[1] She was suspicious of the mysterious Ajar; nobody as yet knew that he was Romain Gary. She found his novel rather too closely inspired by a short story by Peter Feibleman, called *Fever*, which she had discovered in Hollywood; it had so fascinated her that she had longed to translate it and have it published by Gallimard. In her view, Madame Rosa's story was very like the story of Feibleman's heroine.

But above all, it was a challenge, a way of testing her limits. She knew that by accepting this pitiless role she would be delivering the final *coup de grâce* to her image of former days. Casque d'Or had turned into a fat old wreck. Strapped into her flowery dress, outrageously made up, crowned with a ridiculous frizzy perm, Madame Rosa had reached the last stage of physical disintegration. The ghost of Bouboulina loomed unmistakably out of the past. By becoming the pathetic Madame Rosa, who had been so cruelly treated by fate, half-destroyed by loneliness, stifling from physical and moral deprivation, Simone Signoret was casting away every shred of false modesty or coquetry. The hardest part was facing Montand's look, his horror and incredulity at the transformation of the woman of his life into a mountain of quivering flesh.

To put acting before everything else, she needed a director like Moshe Mizrahi, she had total trust in him, but he was not a close friend. Claude Berri and Costa-Gavras had both offered her the part of Madame Rosa. But she had felt that, because she had known them so long, she would not be intimidated enough; she would be in danger of wanting to keep up appearances, and of not making herself ugly enough. Moshe Mizrahi told her to wear flower-patterned dresses that were too tight and made her look even fatter. She tried the dresses on, looked in the mirror, saw a caricature of herself, and resigned herself to it. Henceforth, for the sake of a role, she would be capable of anything. With Mizrahi, she felt incapable of cheating; she was merciless with herself, drained the cup down to the bitter dregs. Faced with this inflexible determination, Mizrahi in turn was struck by her sheer professionalism and conscientiousness: 'Sometimes she gave

[1]Mercure de France, 1975.

herself so completely in the retakes that I was afraid she would wear herself out.'

She became Madame Rosa with a combination of courage and passion. After Brecht's *La Femme Juive*, she was playing the part of another Jewish woman, but, this time, she wore inside her wrist the branded mark of the former Auschwitz deportees. The mark is never seen in the film, since Madame Rosa's forearm is hardly ever uncovered. But she insisted on wearing it: 'I needed it under my nightdress and under the cardigan that covered it up.' The official number was 17 329, and had been given to her by her make-up assistant Maud Begon, a former Resistance fighter and survivor from Ravensbrück. 'She was the only one of us to know that Madame Rosa, deported in 1942, was perforce one of that little band of people whose only identification mark from then on was a number in which the two first figures could only be sixteen or seventeen thousand.'[1] Because she wore this fateful number, carefully washed and powdered each morning, Madame Rosa would leave a deeper mark on her than any of her other roles; and not just Madame Rosa but the phantom of the millions of Jews exterminated by the Nazis, of whom Simone Kaminker could so easily have been one, as she well knew.

Her old regrets about not having fought in the Resistance did not fade away; far from it. In a way, she used this 'sense of shame' as a starting-point from which to go further and deeper in her journey of self-exploration. Her meeting with Madame Rosa, under the eyes of Moshe Mizrahi, would be a crucial stage in the slow maturation that would lead her, in her remaining years, to regain movingly the Jewish identity that she had neglected for so long.

After the filming, out of superstition and respect for those whose tattoos were indelible, it would be several days before she scrubbed at the little patch of skin. 'The 1, 7, 3, 2 and 9 faded away gradually of their own accord, changing from blue to mauve, from mauve to grey, until they became little marks illegible to anybody except me.'

The following year she made another film with Moshe Mizrahi,

---

[1] *Le Lendemain, elle était souriante* . . . op.cit.

CATHERINE DAVID

Chère Inconnue, which shows the same strange time-shift that made her look younger in *La Veuve Couderc* than she did in *Le Chat*. Though she had not become attractive again, at least she looked less like a caricature of herself. But soon illness would change her once again.

In May 1980, Granier-Deferre's filming of *L'Étoile du Nord* had to be delayed: Simone Signoret had been admitted to hospital. For somebody who had never been ill, it was the first warning, a red alert. 'They thought I had cancer, and they made a meal of it. After I'd had my gall-bladder removed, they ought to have been reassured. But I had to take six months off to rest.'[1] In fact, it was very probably the first manifestation of the cancer that would carry her off five years later. The Simone who emerged from this ordeal was much thinner, a grave-looking grandmother, finally cured of alcoholism. A year and a half later, she played the part of the tragic Madame Baron, a Charleroi landlady madly in love with one of her lodgers, Philippe Noiret, a dangerous criminal and murderer, but charming and good-natured, who enchants her with his stories about his journeys in the Far East. Along with Michel Drach's *Guy de Maupassant*, in which she played a cameo role as the writer's mother, *L'Étoile du Nord* would be her last cinema film. The final count-down had started. But she still had a few crucial adventures to live.

When in 1982 she agreed to record the voice-over for Mosco's film on the MOI, the 'terrorists in retirement', she had no inkling that this experience, which might seem unimportant in cinema history, would prove so crucial. The unsung heroes of the Resistance, whose epic story she would discover with emotion, would enable her to cross the final frontier that separated her from creative writing.

Simone Signoret is sitting in my kitchen, opposite me; she only has a few more months to live. Her hair is grey, cut short, she is wearing a sky-blue shirt, the same blue as her eyes, which are nearly blind. She no longer has the puffy face of her tragic films,

[1] Interview with Jean-Claude Maurice, *Le Journal du Dimanche*, 28 March 1982.

175

she is beautiful again, thinner, as though purified: she is her old self once more, she has regained her old nobility. The structure of her face is once again visible under the fine web of wrinkles, she is old, but 'in the way that Casque d'Or would have grown old. Not like Madame Rosa. Old in the way that the girl I glimpsed fleetingly at the Flore back in 1942 should logically have grown old', as Jorge Semprun writes in *Montand, la vie continue*. The cancer that is doing its deadly work has also brought her this ephemeral gift, a final reconciliation with her image.

On this spring day – her last spring – she has an appetite, she is happy to have the opportunity of chatting, she talks about the Rosenbergs in America and Slansky's trial in Prague with the same old fire, since she is talking about herself, and her past mistakes. Her memory is amazingly precise, her mind lively and quick. She cannot forgive herself for having been one of those intellectuals 'of goodwill' who, while fighting to save the two 'spies' who refused to confess their crime to the FBI from the electric chair, turned a blind eye to the show trials of Eastern Europe, out of loyalty to a certain idea of the Left. She still blames herself for having believed Eluard's dreadful *mot* about the innocent and the guilty. Her heart sinks as she thinks of victims, like Artur London or Oskar Langer, who were ground down by the Soviet party machine with the blessing of sincere Westerners who should have helped them, but were prevented by their ideological blinkers. 'Here, on the one side, were people who, after being told that they could stay alive if they would only confess to being spies, ended up being electrocuted. On the other side, they were executing people who confessed to crimes they had never committed! At the same time!' As always, she's surprised and indignant. Her eyes flash feebly, lit by the past but turned towards the twentieth century.

Today, the twentieth century is in my kitchen: Adam Rayski, one of the leaders of the MOI, the Resistance organisation formed by the wartime Communist Party for foreigners – Spaniards, Italians, Poles, Armenians and Jews like Rayski. Simone Signoret came to *Le Nouvel Observateur* to talk to Adam Rayski, whose book, *Nos Illusions Perdues*, had just come out. It was a good title for the memoirs of a man who had been pushed to the limits of his endurance by the absurd paradoxes of his time.

Born in Poland, he had taken asylum in France in the thirties, and became first a member of the Communist Party, then one of the Resistance organisers for foreign immigrants in Paris. It was then that he was faced with the terrifying ambiguities of the Party leadership that had taken refuge in the provinces. The foreign resistants, left unprotected in the capital, knew that they were being denounced and shadowed. But when Rayski asked to withdraw to Lyons, the answer was that 'we don't put Party officers in cold storage'. A month later, as could have been foreseen, twenty-three MOI combatants were arrested. On 21 February 1944, they were shot at Mont Valérien, and forgotten, with their outlandish names and unorthodox origins, for forty years.

Adam Rayski and Simone Signoret had met in 1982, at the time of Mosco's film. This extraordinary document was the first to break the silence about these unknown heroes. She had been overwhelmed by the story of the handful of foreigners, mostly Jewish, whose families and friends had been deported, alone in an alien, terrifying city, with their impossible accents, holding bombs with hands that were used to cutting and sewing, with the courage born of despair.

The Communist Party leaders must have had this sorry story on their conscience, since, by exerting discreet pressure, they managed to prevent the television channel Antenne 2 from showing the film for several years, although it had co-produced it. Kept under wraps under the presidency[1] of Maurice Ulrich in 1979, buried by Desgraupes and Héberlé on various pretexts, it would not be broadcast until 2 June 1985, very largely thanks to the efforts of Simone Signoret; this would be her last campaign, fiercely fought and won a few months before her death. In a classic article by Jean-Pierre Ravery, the Communist newspaper *L'Humanité* prevaricated: 'To appreciate the enormity of the decision to show Mosco's film on television, you only have to imagine a TV channel agreeing to promote a theory that General de Gaulle was responsible for Jean Moulin's death.' But Colonel Passy, one of the great leaders of the Gaullist Resistance, quietly gave his view to the journalists of *Le Point*: 'This film does justice to history.' In

[1] Of the ORTF, the government-controlled radio and television office.

the meantime, thanks to Marin Karmitz, the movie was shown in a cinema in Paris.

It was a strong, fair-minded film, which asked serious questions without giving cut-and-dried answers. Was it true or false that the immigrant Resistance had been sacrificed to other priorities by the Party leaders, insisting that they remain in Paris, although it amounted to suicide? Had the internal power-struggle to impose Communist influence in the core of the French Resistance temporarily taken priority over the fight against Hitler? Had the subsequent long silence on the subject of the MOI martyrs anything to do with their foreign-sounding names? Those who felt under fire could judge whether these questions were awkward or not. By interviewing the survivors of this tragic episode, Mosco was lifting a corner of the veil from a little-known period of French history. For Simone Signoret it was a revelation, a shock to the system that would reverberate through her last years, providing the characters and settings for her novel *Adieu Volodia*.

Amazed and moved, she wanted to meet the MOI survivors traced by Mosco. She longed to make the acquaintance of the shadowy figures who threw home-made bombs into German cinemas and tramped the streets of Paris, constantly risking their lives, at a time when she herself, already a 'regular' at the Flore, was starting her career as a film extra in Jean Boyer's *Le Prince charmant* and *Boléro*, with no notion of the hell that the members of MOI were going through in the same city, at the same time.

At her request, Mosco took her to the sweatshops where the survivors continued to tailor coats and sew linings into jackets: well-behaved old Jews who still shivered with terror when they remembered the war. They were classic victims, with the heart-breaking humour created by the absurd feeling of having escaped death by accident, survivors who could never shake themselves free from the period, or forget the war or Nazism. Some events are everlasting; some dramas are too momentous to be absorbed by memory.

In a drawer, among cotton-reels and crooked scissors, Adam Mitzflicker still keeps the old revolver that he fired at Nazi officers under the plane trees. He is still amazed at himself at having been able to handle such a bizarre instrument, so little-suited to a peace-loving Jew. 'I was supposed to kill my first German with a hammer. I couldn't do it, I wasn't a murderer.' Laughing, he explains how, in those days of penury, they went about manufacturing Molotov cocktails.

Simone Signoret had dined with Mitzflicker, Kogitski and Rayski, had heard their life-stories, and had suddenly felt she was finding her own family again – uncles, brothers. In late-middle age she became more and more aware of her hidden roots. It had taken many years, experiences, meetings and disillusionments to confront her Kaminker ancestors. Three years later, when Adam Rayski telephoned her with the news that he had written his book, she told him, 'Me too; I've finished my novel, and it's about people like you.' What she did not say was that, through the novel, she had succeeded in finally repairing her relationship with her father, in reconciling herself with the dead man whom she had never really known.

But before dedicating herself to this slowly maturing grand project, she wanted to make an old childhood dream come true. In the far-off Neuilly period, as they strolled together under the acacias, her Signoret grandmother had told her the true story of Thérèse Humbert, the high-flying adventuress who, when the Dreyfus affair was at its height, managed to persuade Parisian bankers that she was on the brink of receiving a colossal inheritance of hundreds of millions of gold francs. Thérèse Humbert had lived in grand style for over twenty years, juggling with bills of exchange and charming her creditors.

Her grandmother, who passed herself off in Neuilly as the wife of the 'great actor Gabriel Signoret', had no assets except her pathetic little fantasies. She had a limitless admiration for the high-class mythomaniac. Thérèse Humbert turned her dreams into action, built castles in Spain on quicksands, and so enjoyed the game of chance that the whole world complied with her desire. Her personality had fascinated Kiki just as it had fascinated her grandmother, and she had promised herself that, later on, she would make a film about her.

Thanks to the talent and friendship of Jean-Claude Grumberg, whose play L'Atelier she had admired, Thérèse Humbert was made into a television film in four parts, directed by Marcel Bluwal.

The making of the film was like a party, a consecration that gave Simone's creative instinct full rein in an original, flamboyant way. Mythomaniac of genius, actress on the stage of real life, queen among crooks, Thérèse Humbert was a novelist, after her own fashion, but she made fiction out of her own life, a true novel in which her contemporaries – lawyers, speculators, financiers – were characters without knowing it.

Just like Simone Signoret, Thérèse Humbert is always at the centre of events. Leader of the gang, *capo* and alter ego of Law the banker, her charismatic character is the focal point for the complicated intrigues of this subtle fable about the theatre of power and the unreality of money in a society founded on credit – or in other words, on gullibility, and make-believe. In the tailor-made part she had always wanted, of grand but wicked lady, Simone Signoret superbly displays the full range of her talents. As she put it, she was 'putting on the style', and viewers asked for more.

After the filming was over, as always she felt drained, deprived, and abandoned. 'For several years now, I've turned to writing when I felt orphaned after finishing a film.'[1] Orphaned by Thérèse Humbert, she once again felt the urge to write. As yet she did not know what her novel would be about, but the fictional material was there, ready to serve. She had met her future characters by going to see the MOI survivors, and she had found part of the background for the novel while making Thérèse Humbert, when she would go to Pigalle every day to have her sumptuous costumes fixed in the dressmakers' workshops.

For Simone Signoret, telling her life-story had meant conforming to yet another genre, permitted by the code of the day: an actress telling her memoirs, with memories of shoots, pen-portraits, love-affairs, political commitments. Writing a novel was different. As the Argentinian writer Ernesto Sabato says, 'Fiction is the only truthful way of describing the human condition.' In writing *Adieu Volodia*, Simone Signoret revealed herself even more profoundly than in *Nostalgia Isn't What It Used To Be*. She showed us – secretly – more of herself in her novel than she had in her autobiography.

[1]Interview with Jean-François Josselin, *Le Nouvel Observateur*, 25 January 1985.

CATHERINE DAVID

Nostalgia is really about Montand. From the very first pages, the narrative builds up towards the magical moment of their first meeting. After that, it's not her life but their life together that she describes.

In *Adieu Volodia*, Simone's confidences are no longer about her personal life, at least in its visible aspects. They are about her father's ancestors, about what she knew and did not know about them, and imagined they were like. She describes what had been passed on to her, a mixture of memory and forgetting. Knowing nothing about her father, she needed to invent to find him, to listen to the 'people within'.[1] Clearly to get as close as possible to the truth, *Adieu Volodia* could only have been fiction.

'I never knew where, when, how and from what *shtetl* my father originally came. I never knew, because nobody ever told me; at home, they never mentioned it, and I didn't ask any questions. Perhaps my father's own father didn't talk about it either . . . Perhaps, subconsciously, this grandfather, who came from an unknown little ghetto in a place whose name I don't know, and never will, planted seeds that germinated in my mind. Yes, that must have been what happened, but I don't know how.'[2]

I had had a very similar experience myself. My father was about the same age as hers; in his family, wartime memories were only communicated through a sort of reticence that took the form of humour. People didn't talk about events of the past, or, if they did, they made them into funny stories. The tales of the exodus that occasionally surfaced during my childhood were often scenes from farce, with my angry uncle chasing his wife through the vineyards with a sulphate-spray, the lung-pâté that went on breathing, the rickety pig that was nicknamed 'Adolf'. The all-too-real anxieties, the spiteful neighbours, the changes of identity, the panic-stricken departures at dawn just before the Gestapo arrived, were all tucked away in the recesses of the family memory.

Simone Signoret had spent a good part of her life acting out stories made up by other people, and giving flesh to imaginary characters; she had turned visions into reality, and had been a

[1]Claude Roy, *Le Nouvel Observateur*, 25 January 1985.
[2]Interview with Françoise Tournier, *Elle*, 21 January 1985.

181

conduit for emotions, memories and desires that had come from elsewhere. 'I felt I was only good at describing what I knew about personally, at following my memory.' Fiction was still an impossible fantasy, a formless desire, an inaccessible Promised Land. 'When people asked me, "What about fiction, then?" I would reply, "I have no imagination."'[1]

But writing had been part of her life since *Nostalgia*, and there was no question of giving it up. After *Thérèse Humbert*, she went back to the grindstone, to the white wall and the typewriter; like going on the wagon after a drinking spree. Her first project was for a sort of fictional sequel to *Nostalgia*, which would describe an imaginary episode.

Even after writing the most detailed autobiography, there nearly always remain dark areas, stories that have been forgotten, or buried memories that can provide subject-matter for a new work. Only someone who spent their whole life writing about that life, like Simone de Beauvoir, could feel, as death approached, as Beauvoir described it to me, that they had drained their memory, and transferred everything into the written word. At the opposite extreme, Arthur Miller, after putting the final touches to *Timebends*, the flowing narrative in which he had believed he had gathered up all the threads of his long life, describes his surprise at realising that he still had enough memories left to write another volume as fat as *Timebends*. Memory is indeed inexhaustible, and Signoret's more than most people's. She would talk about it with a sort of amazement, as if it were a very heavy piece of luggage, growing still heavier, which she had to carry. 'One day I pull out a Henri II dresser, another day a yellowing photo, and the memories start marching through my head. It's frightening, and exciting. Nothing, I can forget nothing.'[2] She thought she would continue in the same vein as *Nostalgia*, delving into her reserves, telling 'a personal story of my own, a story of rediscovery, which would span from 1943 to 1979'.[3]

But the source had been exhausted; not memory itself, but the

[1]Interview with Danièle Heymann, *L'Express*, 25 January 1985.
[2]*France-Soir*, 5 April 1980.
[3]Id.

desire to go back to the past and relive old stories had dwindled. She was ready for a new exploration, in another past that she had not experienced at first hand, in memories which were not her own but which nevertheless concerned her personally. 'I wrote ten pages. Fine; it went fine. Up until the moment when I brought them, the heroine and a man who was called "he", to the door of a shabby little cottage above Grenoble, I'd been trying to remember the colour of the wood and the shape of the doorknob. I started to stall. What was the colour of the wood? It was only then that I understood that I had fallen into my usual rut and that I was trying to write an account of my own life, and that I would bore myself to death since I already knew the ending. I wrote down, "Behind that door, somebody was waiting for them, smiling." The door stayed shut.'[1]

She had come up against the great barrier, boredom. Certain writers can foresee what they are going to write, down to the last detail, and go ahead and write it. They give up any idea of being surprised and construct their books like architects following plans for apartment blocks, conforming to the programme they themselves have set up. Their writing is merely the formulation of pre-existing thought, a 'mode of expression', or accurate transmission of a message. The door stays shut.

Simone Signoret had realised that writing was another way of making her own films. 'If I've been good at describing people, it's because I've played them all – parents, children, friends. The headiest thing of all, for actors, is suddenly to feel you're totally in control: when you're writing a book, what's exciting is being your own director, your own stage-designer, your own make-up lady, your own dresser. And above all, your own producer. You're also in charge of feelings.'[2] She threw the first ten pages into the wastepaper basket and started playing around with words and images, and the faces of the MOI survivors introduced to her by Mosco. 'Little by little, the story followed its own course, with a life of its own.'[3] It was a story that would develop gradually,

[1]L'Express, 25 January 1985.
[2]Interview with Jean-François Josselin, Le Nouvel Observateur, 25 January 1985.
[3]Interview with Françoise Tournier, Elle, 21 January 1985.

forming its own ramifications, and creating a densely peopled world of its own, and finally a long novel of 570 pages, a testament in fiction form.

She invented a childhood for them, and ancestors in Poland and the Ukraine. Maurice, Zaza, the mothers who did fine-sewing work at home, the 20th *arrondissement* in Paris between the wars, Dr Pierre's face on the blind wall of a house, the Julien Damoy grocery shop, the *quiches lorraines* from the Blé d'Or in Quimper, the local schoolmaster, the little girls skipping, the sweatshops . . . she invented a daily life for all of them, complete with games, secret memories, ancient terrors, allayed anxieties, and comforting illusions about the future of the beautiful country that had been so welcoming to these foreigners and refugees, and had given work to these Jews, as the means of survival, along with an identity card. She started writing without a plan or method, or a preconceived idea, and without knowing the ending, so that she could find it out herself in due course, to keep up the suspense that was the driving force behind the narrative.

To her surprise, the characters started to come to life under her pen, much as film characters become alive on screen when the lights go down. As first witness and first reader of the pages as they came out of her typewriter, she avoided the boredom of a set plan, and of transcribing her memory; she was cutting a new path, lifting the curtains that concealed the backdrop. The miracle repeated itself day after day: she could not stop writing, and she would continue writing for eighteen months in her little study under the eaves, in front of the white wall, in spite of her failing sight, bending closer and closer over the pages, re-reading what she had written with a magnifying-glass, working till she was exhausted, but with the joy one feels when surprising oneself. 'The greatest danger I felt myself to be in was of not being able to stop. I could have gone on writing till I died . . . But I would have liked my characters to go on living.'[1]

She delved into her memory. Like *Nostalgia*, but less obviously, *Adieu Volodia* is like a hold-all, filled with private jokes for friends, reminiscences, and supporting characters dotted around

---

[1]Interview with Françoise Tournier, op. cit.

CATHERINE DAVID

the story like photographs slipped under a mantelpiece mirror. We meet Visconti in the guise of a handsome Italian assistant, Jacques Becker, Danielle Darrieux, Jean-Pierre Aumont, Marcel Duhamel, Pierre-Richard Wilm, Renoir's stage-manager, and the man 'whose name was Prater or Prévert, but whom everyone called Jacques' . . . Nicole Roginski, the beautiful Jewish mytho-maniac who only speaks Yiddish when making love, invents Slav ancestors for herself from St Petersburg, and tells lies with an affrontery inspired by Thérèse Humbert. And when, during the war, Zaza Roginski has to give up her job as script-girl, it is because, like Simone Kaminker, she could not obtain the notorious COIC card . . . We even find memories of Montand's youth in the novel: 'Things I pinched from him without knowing it . . . Like when I make one of my characters go home with his brand new naturalisation certificate and say, with tears in his eyes, "That's it, we're French!" That's how it happened with the Montand family.'

She would list the novel's autobiographical elements, though incompletely, of course, after publication. 'Because of this novel, I more or less psychoanalysed myself.'[1] That does not mean that *Adieu Volodia* is what is called a *roman-à-clef*. In a *roman-à-clef*, the original models are clearly defined in advance, whereas Simone Signoret would usually only discover the links between fiction and life after finishing the book, like a surprise encounter with an old friend on a street corner in a foreign city. To quote her own words, 'I put a fantastic amount of my own life into this book, yet I didn't realise it until much later, when it was finished.'[2]

She had noticed some of the messages from the unconscious, and some of the enigmas and coincidences, but many would remain hidden, even from herself. And that was how it should be. Authentic novelists who draw on their experience of life are never completely in control of what they dredge up. The autobiographical features of a novel are not necessarily events, love affairs, sorrows, betrayals, journeys or bereavements. Of course, the solemn elements that lend life its rhythm can be transposed and translated into fiction; but a novelist can easily write a story which

[1] Interview with Pierre Démeron, *Marie-Claire*, March 1985.
[2] Id.

185

truly has nothing to do with his own life, but which will contain that fleeting image glimpsed through a train window, or the face of a sleeping tramp, the perspective of an avenue lined with chestnut trees or the imposing shape of a cargo-boat moored in a port. Perhaps images like these, coming from unconscious memory and the interstices of life, but in an informal, invisible way, give a novel its special tone of voice and unique truthfulness.

Though she herself made a cult of memory, the heroes of the novel are 'young parents with amnesia'. They are Jews from the Ukraine and Poland, who have settled in the 20th *arrondissement* and want to spare their children the weight of their memories, filled as they are with pogroms, arson and screams. The parents of Maurice Guttman and Zaza Roginski have made a solemn oath never to mention the terrible recollections that they shared: 'They would not be like their own parents or grandparents who, by the ghostly light of tallow candles, had obsessively listed every detail of the pogroms of their time, comparing them with those of the night before, from which they had just escaped . . .' As a good novelist, Simone Signoret found a way of giving them a generic name to designate their persecutors, the name of Petlioura.

The *ataman* Petlioura was the governor of independent Ukraine from 1918 to 1920, during the dark years of civil war that succeeded the October revolution; his name was still associated, in the memory of Polish and Ukrainian Jews, with the dreadful massacres perpetrated by the bands of *pogromtchiki*. The immigrant Jews whom Simone Signoret met in Paris had retained the image of an anti-Semitic torturer who 'after massacring thousands of his Ukrainian fellow-citizens between 1918 and 1920, had gone on, in the van of the Red Army, to massacre thousands of Poles, particularly in the Lublin region'.

Petlioura's name serves as a 'signifier' in the novel, in the psychoanalytical sense, one of those concentrations of language which, as solid as a nugget of uranium, link the generations by con- serving fragments of memory and ancient meanings that become still more mysterious, and more pressing. That is how Petlioura's name, by being buried in silence, becomes a kind of bugbear for the children, 'Pète-Loura', a masculine Fairy Carabosse, and even a rallying-cry, aggressive and teasing, in their games. Without ever interrupting her story, or labouring the point, Simone Signoret succeeds in showing how secrecy, in certain families, far from making people forget, can become a twisted conduit for transmitting memory; a phenomenon she had certainly experienced herself, in the silence that had weighed so heavily on her father's family.

'Write on my father's tomb, dear Anna, that his son Shalom has avenged his father's blood.' This is the message that a certain Samuel Schwarzbard sends to his wife in 1926, before going out to assassinate the *ataman* Petlioura in the Paris street where he has taken asylum. Petlioura pays for the massacres committed in his name, and for those committed since the beginning of time by the hordes of Cossacks, Tartars, Poles, Hungarians and Ukrainians. But other incalculable massacres are already being prepared during the years of 1926 and 1927, just when the Guttmans and Roginskis, who had taken refuge in Paris, think they have finally found a safe asylum for themselves and their children.

It is at Samuel Schwarzbard's trial that Elie Guttman is finally able to meet Vladimir Guttman once more, 'handsome, kind Volodia', the cousin whom he had thought dead, because he had had no news of him for years. Simone Signoret makes Volodia one of the eighty witnesses called by the lawyer Henri Torrès to help in Samuel Schwarzbard's defence. They have come from Poland, the Ukraine, Europe and America to describe, like the witnesses at Barbie's trial, the past atrocities committed by Petlioura's men. They have come to testify that, by executing an assassin who had gone unpunished, Schwarzbard committed an act of just retribution. And, in fact, Samuel Schwarzbard is acquitted.

Monsieur Florian, the children's headmaster, one of the far-seeing schoolteachers occasionally produced by the Third Republic, has read Vladimir Guttman's name in the newspaper among those of the witnesses called in the Schwarzbard trial, and comes to tell the children's parents. Volodia is still alive: he escaped from the great Jitomir pogrom, and has made the journey from the Ukraine to Paris, hoping to see his cousins once again, to hug and kiss them, and meet their children.

But nobody knows his address, not even Maître Henri Torrès, the defence lawyer who brought the witnesses to Paris. Vladimir Guttman has come in a group, with an interpreter and four other

187

witnesses; and everything is subtly organised to prevent them from seeing him properly. It is only on the very day of his departure back to the Ukraine that an official meeting is organised 'at the café-restaurant, des Trois-Marches, Place Dauphine, in front of the Palais de Justice'.

For Simone Signoret, the Place Dauphine meant home, the 'caravan', the little Parisian square where she lived, her village, whose inhabitants, trees and stones were as familiar to her as the drawers in her bedroom chest. She deliberately chose this intimate, personal place as the setting for the abortive rendezvous of the two cousins Elie and Volodia Guttman. It was as if she wanted to bring Volodia, the far-off cousin, into her own home, on her own territory, in the shadow of the law courts where people's lives were settled, in order to render all the more heartrending the central scene over which hover, in silence, the ghosts of those who, in 1957, prevented her own meeting with Jo Langer.

Carried away by her magnificent subject, Simone Signoret wrote away with a febrile, passionate concentration, and, as the pages piled up beside her, her eyes grew weaker and weaker.

Friends dropped by, and she would shyly hand them pages she had just written: 'Could you just glance at them?' She had none of the coyness of timid beginners who jealously guard their copy like a secret treasure in danger of evaporating in the open air like the antique frescos in *Fellini, Roma*, which fade when people look at them. 'I'm not mean about showing what I'm doing.' Not only would she let people read her work in progress, she needed them to read it; it gave her the strength to go on. As always, friendship acted as a springboard to let her pause and get her breath back. Of course, her friends read her drafts and joined in her amazement, reassuring her that, yes, *Adieu Volodia* really was a novel in gestation, a viable product.

Her country neighbour, Yvette Étiévant, whom she had known ever since those carefree days when the common people of Thebes intoned Jocasta's name at the Théâtre des Mathurins, was her most loyal reader at the time, and it was when Yvette told her one day that she had been thinking about Maurice and Zaza, the Guttmans and Roginskis, during the week at her Paris office, that Simone finally felt confident about the novel. Her characters were alive for others, not just for herself, which meant that they would survive her; that is what really counted. From this point of view (keeping things in proportion, of course) she was as obsessive as Balzac on his deathbed when he called for Bianchon, the doctor in *La Comédie Humaine*, because, he felt, *he* would be able to cure him.

From Jo Langer to Volodia, via the heroes of the MOI; the story had come full circle. The breach that had opened, without her knowing it, at the Hotel Alkron in Prague would never close up again. Because of her sensation of irremediable loss with regard to Oskar Langer, which only served to increase the feeling of being dispossessed that had haunted her since childhood, she had finally found a way of linking up again with the memory of her ancestors, and of using the time regained to find her dreams; and she could finally be a writer in the truest sense. As Adam Rayski told her on that spring day of 1985 (paying her what is perhaps the greatest of all compliments for a novelist), 'The further you go in your fiction, the nearer you get to the truth.'

This is why many Polish Jews recognised themselves in the characters of her novel. I know this from my own experience: my daughter's father, Isi Beller, told me so, and, far more important, told *her* so, on that famous day when she was there in our kitchen, happy to share our food, and to join in the conversation, asking questions, as inquisitive as a novelist or intimate friend. Almost immediately, he had the urge to confide in her and to talk to her about his parents – about his father Chaïm, the furrier turned painter who appears in Mosco's film, about the noise of the sewing machine he used to hear at night as a child when his father went on stitching up fur coat sleeves before he started, in late-middle age, painting the colourful, violent images of his vanished *shtetl*. The Roginskis and the Guttmans in *Adieu Volodia* could be his family, too. She listened, and wanted to hear more: 'What about the war? How did you survive? Did your parents tell you about life in the Polish *shtetl*, or were they amnesiacs too?' She wanted to hear everything; she never tired of adding new life-stories to her own.

I'm talking about the Simone I met (and long to have known better) on that March day in 1985, her body shrunken but her passion intact. She had fulfilled her destiny. Her books had been written, her fame was at its height, she had never been so loved, and so respected by the public.

And then, quite suddenly, she started to talk about her eye-disease, the infirmity that had attacked her, like a curse. She could hardly see at all any more, except around the edges: she had kept her peripheral vision. She could not focus any more. As I listened, I thought what a cruel trick fate had played on a woman whose look had made her famous; and I thought of old Tiresias, who saw things so much more clearly with his blind eyes.

It had come on gradually, while she was writing the book, like an invasive fuzziness, a veil. She fought against a fog that grew more dense each day. She bought herself a pair of thick spectacles, then a magnifying-glass, and she would bend right over the table so as to see the paper better. But she went on writing. When they sent her the proofs, she could still see well enough to read over the 566 pages, correct the literals, and pass the proofs for press. 'The day I sent the parcel of proofs back to my publisher, that was it: I couldn't see any more, at all.'

She did not say as much, but clearly she felt she had 'fixed' things so as to go on seeing until the book was ready. It was as if she had a mission to fulfil. At that late period, she wrote some magnificent pages, among the finest in the novel, in which (as has not been sufficiently appreciated) the action is framed by two anti-fascist assassinations, Petlioura's by Samuel Schwarzbard, and the murder of three Ukrainian army officers by Maurice Guttman, son of Elie, Volodia's cousin.

After having accomplished his act of vengeance, Maurice takes to the *maquis*. 'As he walked, he reflected on how at the same time on the day before, he had been simultaneously preparing to kill, readying himself for the possibility of his own death. Today, the men whom he had most likely killed were nameless bodies, and he himself was alive, but unknown . . . They would be replaced by others, who would go off elsewhere to have a drink at the end of their working day. He had nearly finished his own day. He breathed in lungfuls of cold air, but he did not feel cold, he stared at the snow above him and, higher up, at the sky, which was so incredibly clear that it was royal-blue, no, periwinkle-blue, and at the sun, which had turned slightly red but was still so high in the sky that it would not have set by the time that Maurice arrived.'

Simone Signoret had almost finished her own day on earth. With her diseased vision, she had captured the incredible colours of the snow, sky and reddening sun, the colours of the wings of death; and she had seen through the absurdity of a struggle that produces nameless corpses and silent survivors. It is lucky that she felt it necessary, absolutely necessary, to go on seeing enough to write that passage, to give us that message.

Later, on the set of *Apostrophes*, the television literary programme, Bernard Pivot asked her whether she had 'astounded Montand' with her novel. She gave an affectionate laugh, with the touch of shyness that would sometimes overcome this strongest of women when she was asked to talk about herself on television, without hiding behind the mask of a screen character. She replied that she did not know whether he had been astounded; but surprised, yes. After all, he had shared her life for thirty-six years, and the question he asked himself was, 'Where on earth had all that come from?' He had not realised that she had so much imagination. The truth is that the people closest to us remain, luckily, unknown to us, or partly so.

Her advancing blindness did not prevent her from playing her last television role in *Music Hall*, with her partners from *Thérèse Humbert*, Jean-Claude Grumberg and Marcel Bluwal. In this musical with a tragic plot, Yvonne Pierre, director of a Parisian theatre in 1938, fights to save her revue at the height of the Munich crisis, just as the Jewish refugees from Germany come knocking at her door, as Judith in Brecht's *La Femme Juive* might have done after leaving her husband in Frankfurt. Simone Signoret was nearly totally blind by then, but she was such a true professional, and so used to acting in films, and had such a natural instinct for acting, that she behaved quite normally on the set. 'When I hear the clapper-board, it's like seeing.'

But that was not the worst of it. She had cancer, as she knew, and she had good reason to think that the prognosis was bad. She had told Marcel Bluwal and his wife Danièle Lebrun, but they were the only ones in the crew who knew about it. As always, she put up a good front, appearing on the set from seven in the

SIMONE SIGNORET

morning, and staying on till the evening. Oddly enough, she felt that work pushed her illness back, kept the cancer at a respectful distance.

Dissociation, the phenomenon whose strange power she had discovered in *Casque d'Or*, would work its last miracle in *Music Hall*. She wasn't ill, because she was Yvonne Pierre, a woman in rude health who shouted at people at the top of her voice, and belted out old songs. 'I was hardly in pain at all, I was playing a character who was full of vitality.' Just as she had forced herself to go on seeing for a little longer so as to finish *Adieu Volodia*, she was determined to finish *Music Hall* in spite of the discomfort, delaying her operation until the filming was over with her usual determination. Her suitcases were packed; fastidious as always, she never left any loose ends.

The operation took place in August; but she knew that the illness was terminal. She died on 29 September 1985, in the big white house at Autheuil where she had laughed so much, loved so much and written so much. 'She died bravely, just as she lived,' her daughter Catherine would tell the reporters. 'I am at peace,' Simone herself told Jean-François Josselin a few days earlier. She did not say it to be portentous: she was just stating a fact. She was amazed at feeling so peaceful after all the turmoil, as she prepared for the last great leap.

At her funeral a crowd of anonymous faces pressed at the iron gates of the Père-Lachaise cemetery. There they all were, standing round the grave, round Montand, ashen-faced, and Catherine, who looked so like her mother: everybody who was anybody from the art world, and from the worlds of books and politics. She was sixty-four years old. It seems like yesterday.

CHAPTER NINETEEN

She wrote, 'I have no nostalgia,' as if to exorcise a familiar demon, as if nostalgia had been a lifelong enemy, a temptation to struggle with. She wrote this, but had proved the opposite to be true, in every page of *Nostalgia Isn't What It Used To Be*.

The truth was that nostalgia was her secret passion. Anything could conjure up its bitter-sweet taste – pleasures as well as pains, the Neuilly market, the German Occupation, or the filming of *Casque d'Or*. Aware of the precariousness of things, she would feel a pang of nostalgia for moments of happiness while she was experiencing them. Nostalgia is just another form of desire directed towards what we have irrevocably lost.

Nostalgia is the disease of the times. We write our memoirs, produce encyclopaedias, classify archives, cover the planet with museums and retrospectives; we are constantly commemorating, celebrating, and piously collecting fragments of ancient relics. We are forever putting memory into a bottle. Academic disciplines that focus on the study of the past have multiplied; no other civilisation has had this mania for archivism. We fool ourselves into thinking that our gaze is fixed on the blue line of the future, on technological progress, inflation, economic growth, literacy, world peace. But in truth we are contemplatives. We are obsessed with the past, it takes over our behaviour and thoughts, we delight in feasting on its remains. For the past is indeed another country, as they say, yet another place to escape to from everyday life, and we cling to its fragments like someone desperately trying to recapture the scent of a faded bouquet. No civilisation has been quite so eaten up by nostalgia, so full of people who spend their time dreaming of being elsewhere. In this, Simone Signoret was a true contemporary.

She was acutely conscious of the passage of time, and, in this her judgement was faultless. She could physically feel time passing through her body and, day by day, leaving its indelible mark. There was no point in fighting against an enemy like this: she had surrendered. Time then quickened its pace: within a few years, the sensual Alice Aisgill from *Room at the Top* had become a fat old woman with a heavy body, sinking under its own weight, like Madame Rosa, 'with all the kilos she carried, and only two legs to support them'.

She would have liked us to believe that she was not nostalgic: not true, not true. Memory was her sixth sense; she had worked at it, constructed it, trained and perfected it. She never forgot a face, she hoarded details, anecdotes and dates. Nostalgia needs material to nourish its yearnings. Simone Signoret's memory was like a brimming reservoir, on which she would draw when nostalgia took her by the throat, like a ghost from the past, and she would feel the need for an image, a name or a story to give it meaning. It was only right at the end, when she knew that she was going to die, that she may have finally vanquished the demon and given up that final, heart-rending pleasure.

I am listening to the radio, while I look down at the children playing behind the curtain of trees. The bell rings; it is time to go back into the classroom. The news presenter announces that Montand has been taken to hospital with influenza; it's a media event that will reverberate through many subsequent news broadcasts. Montand is a monument in the French landscape; one cannot tell whether he would have had quite such a glittering career if he had not been Signoret's husband. On her journey to the top, she could not have borne for her husband to be just a train-bearer, and to have had a less prestigious career than hers. She added her forces to his, and the journey towards the centre became an ascending spiral, a cyclone.

Today, as I write, Simone Signoret would be sixty-nine years old, like Montand, she would be in good heart; she would fuss about his influenza. She haunts some of my dreams. Last night

I saw her laughing, it was a good sign, she loved a good laugh; after all, she had been sacked from the Théâtre des Marthurins for uncontrollable giggling, and Montand had won her heart for ever by making her laugh till she cried. Montand had always included the art of making women laugh in his repertoire of amatory tricks. As a young hairdresser's assistant in the Marseilles slums, he would whistle as he shampooed the women's hair, and hum bits of songs, juggle with the hair-rollers, and tell jokes. He had enjoyed plenty of laughs with Piaf as well; she found him 'a scream'. Simone Signoret was a good match for him, the slightest thing would set her off. She took a profound, childish delight in laughing, the untrammelled pleasure of those uncontrollable fits of giggles when you're at the back of the class and the teacher disappears behind a blur of tears. *Nostalgia Isn't What It Used To Be* is studded with stray remarks about her love of laughter. In Eastern Europe, she had laughed with Henri Crolla, Montand's guitarist, who made bad puns on Russian names. She had laughed while swapping make-up tricks with Marilyn; she had laughed on her walks on the beach with Spencer Tracy and Lee Marvin. She had had a fit of nervous giggles with the actors rehearsing Lillian Hellman's *The Little Foxes*, when the playwright came to Paris on the night before the dress-rehearsal and poured contempt on the production. 'The wild uncontrollable giggles that only children have, or actors who are half-dead with fatigue, stagefright and genuine anxiety.'[1] For Simone Signoret laughter was a release; there was no substitute for it, it was almost like an orgasm. It possessed all the virtues: it was a profane kind of ecstasy, an innocent form of drunkenness which helps disarm adversaries, weld friendships, alleviate anxiety, and make life easier all round. In the acting profession, moreover, laughter is like a working tool, a safety-valve necessary to creative concentration: 'If you don't laugh together on a film, you will never be able to make people cry together.'[2]

I have spent months living with her ghost; it has become an obsession. My loneliness has made friends with hers: in my little study perched in the trees that have woven a green curtain in

[1]*Nostalgia* . . . op.cit.
[2]Id.

front of the lycée Fénelon, she has played every part for my sole
benefit – friend, sister, mother and confidante; she has been, in
turn, evasive, intrusive, open-hearted, irritable, unpredictable, and
fascinating. Seen through her singular vision, certain happenings
would suddenly make sense and come together; and chronology
was forgotten. Following in the tracks of this remarkable person,
I made the only journeys that really matter – journeys in time.
In the morning, she found her first white hairs; two hours later,
she passed her 'Bac', next day she went to Overney's funeral,
breast-fed Catherine, acted in *Casque d'Or* or danced with Gary
Cooper. It felt as though a mad projectionist were showing the
film reels in random order. She attracted questions of all shapes
and sizes, like a magnet. She used to quote Giraudoux's saying:
'If I'm not careful, my life will develop without me.' She was
careful. She would smile, enigmatically, as if to indicate that,
in every life, there is a mysterious ingredient which escapes the
biographer.

Sometimes she would drop her defences and allow herself to be
taken off-guard. It was then that one saw her other side. Another
Simone would appear on the reverse of the coin, a diabolical,
devouring Signoret, an object of fear, full of driving ambition
and the primitive energy of a wild beast asserting its domination
over the jungle. 'A civilised tigress', as her friend Claude Roy puts
it. This Simone was like a force of nature, occasionally abusing her
power to eliminate rivals: short-tempered, authoritarian, hard to
get on with, capable of bad faith, pettiness and spite, even cruelty,
not always kind to humbler people. 'She doesn't like bores,'[1] to
quote her daughter Catherine. As vindictive as an elephant, with
as long a memory, she never forgot to get her own back for a
slight, and there could be no appeal against her sentence. During
a shoot, she would sometimes choose a scapegoat on whom to
vent her aggressive streak. Although she was a star, she had
remained an 'ordinary' person, rough and ready, even, but that
did not prevent her from being self-obsessed, jealous of her own
power and influence, conscious of being a VIP and expecting

[1] *Simone Signoret*, by Philippe Durant, Favre, 1988.

to be treated like one, irritated when she was not immediately recognised, pitiless towards her enemies, ready to use her influence to break a director's career, or savagely accusing the publisher of a book on Montand of lining his own pockets. Simone Signoret was a woman of iron, sure of her own views, impossible to argue with, somewhat misogynistic, and extremely adept at promoting her own image.

The nearer one gets to somebody, the more the contradictions multiply and become apparent, disclosing a secret tension that forces one to suspend judgement and take all the data at one's disposal into consideration. As La Rochefoucauld said, we are sometimes as different from ourselves as we are from other people. As happens with all of us, Simone Signoret occasionally behaved like somebody she would normally have detested. And probably, as, again, is the case with all of us, she occasionally detested herself in earnest, and blamed herself for her faults, her cruelties, her sins of omission, and her faithlessness towards her own conception of life. She made many enemies in the course of her career, as is inevitable with those who, living beyond the norms of ordinary life, attract the envy of those who have not had the opportunity or the energy to forge an exciting life for themselves. But in some cases, she was only reaping what she had sown.

There lurked within her a dull rage, which came from her childhood, an unresolved sense of resentment that resisted all the gifts life had lavished so abundantly on her. This rage would occasionally be ignited by an insult, or betrayal, or an act of cowardice – or what she perceived as an act of cowardice; but she succeeded, mainly by channelling it into political combat, in giving it a purpose and making a revolt, a motive power for action, out of it. But the anger remained, gnawing at her from within, and her relationships with those closer to her were often burdened with this hidden violence, which could so easily flare up and lurked like a grenade hidden beneath the smooth surface of everyday life.

All her close friends knew Simone Signoret's hidden side, and I cannot help thinking that this is one of the reasons for the wall of silence that they have built around her memory. Nobody could be close to her without coming up against her dark side at one time or another. Nothing escaped her inquisitorial gaze, the instinct that drove her to look inside people's souls, call it what you will, love or voracity, curiosity or indiscretion, friendship or appropriation. Perhaps this pertinacity was one of the secrets of her acting, for she would grab hold of her screen characters with the same energy and total concentration, looking into their secret nature, their memory, their intimate feelings, until they were hers, captives of her vision and her passion.

In countless interviews she would challenge the cliché that an actor 'gets under the skin' of his or her character. She found this a scandalous idea, a misconception which she never stopped correcting by explaining that the opposite was the case, that it is the character who 'gets under the skin' of the actor. After all this insistence on her part, I found myself wondering why this idea was so important to her, given that it is only a matter of metaphors. It is true that a film or stage character is an abstract being without flesh or blood apart from the actor's; but another metaphor perhaps provides the answer.

For what enters a woman's body, makes its nest there, and stays there until the work in gestation comes to birth? A child. In ceaselessly returning to the fact that it was the other, the 'lodger', that inhabited her and not the other way round, Simone Signoret was asserting herself as a kind of mother. While she was acting in a film, she was pregnant, heavy with child. Indeed, she used to describe how 'monstrously puffed up with egotism' she would be during shoots. Usually so available to others, she would envelop herself in her part and become as indifferent to the outside world as pregnant women. In the best cases, when the director was able to play the part of father-figure, someone who gives a meaning to life, she would turn into mother and child at the same time, a new Simone related to the older one, neither completely the same as the other, nor completely herself.

With those she loved, she was not just possessive: she would take them over. She could not bear them to fail her in any way, but insisted on their lining up behind her positions, and answering her questions. You had to submit, or quit: everything had to be shared, all or nothing. Faced with her exorbitant demands, her friends would occasionally make a bid for independence; afterwards they would have to defend themselves, and then the sentence would sometimes fall. As in ancient Greece, banishment was the supreme punishment: 'You're no longer part of the family.' From then on, the curse was on you, you could burn in hell: you were as good as dead. The tribal loyalty of the Montand-Signoret clan ceased to function. In private life, Simone Signoret applied the terrible law of revolutionary groups, or of the criminal underworld: for us, or against us.

Montand let her reign unchallenged at the heart of the clan, in a systematically inbred, matriarchal court. Subtle hierarchies defined everybody's position, measured by the extent of their intimacy with her. This was her Madame Verdurin side. The way people were classified changed from one period to the next, but the system never changed; observers of Parisian life found it a mine of ethnographic interest. In the front ranks were the people who were really close to her, the companions of her daily life, Catherine, Marcelle and Georges who ran the Autheuil house, Henri Crolla and Bob Castella who worked with Montand, and Montand's brother Julien. Then there was the 'first circle', often her oldest friends, Chris Marker, François Périer, Serge Reggiani, Claude Roy, but also Costa-Gavras or Jorge Semprun, Montand's soulmate. Women rarely had access to the magic circle; Simone preferred them to be smiling and submissive, as Françoise Arnoul and Anna Karina were for a time, and as Colette Périer continued to be until the end. Young postulants were admitted to the second circle, intellectuals like Régis Debray, Georges Kiejman, Claude Lanzmann or Pierre Goldman who gave her access to a world that fascinated her, along with the whole crowd of Autheuil regulars, actors, artists, journalists. Jacques Becker, Pierre Brasseur, Jean-Claude Dauphin and José Artur . . . There were also, flashing across this fixed constellation like short-lived meteors, outsiders like Maurice Pons, who reached the top of the ladder in a single jump, only to find themselves, just as suddenly, thrust back into the shadows, disgraced and inconsolable. Then there were the shifting quicksands of the third circle, where everyone with whom she kept in regular touch revolved, cinema people like Alain Delon, Pierre Granier-Deferre, René Allio and Mosco, journalists like Pierre Benichou, Anne Sinclair, Bernard Pivot,

Jean-François Kahn, and television people like Marcel Bluwal, Jean-Claude Grumberg . . . And then there were the odd men out, who revolved in a different kind of orbit, people whom she had suddenly taken up but who were not part of the 'Signoret system', like the MOI survivors or her cousin Jo Langer. At the heart of this influential network, Simone held pride of place and set the tone, a tutelary figurehead of cultural and political life. One can challenge her choice of friends, criticise her behaviour, and see her incessant activity as an excess of activism, but the fact remains that she really was a 'steady point in a shifting world', as Anne Sinclair wrote on the day after her death.

She was a kind of insurance: she steered her course unswervingly through the squalls of fashion and the storms of private life, in spite of the erosion of love, broken friendships, bereavements, disappointments, and shattered illusions, in spite of the afflictions of old age, and illness, and the shadow of loneliness that weighed so heavily on a woman who needed other people so badly. For she was alone at the end, in spite of how things seemed. An uncontested queen, applauded, listened to, admired, respected, sought after, and at times intensely hated; but she reigned alone. Family life was only a fiction: Montand was absent, always away on his trips, busy elsewhere. Catherine was grown-up, leading her own life. Friends dropped by occasionally, but did not linger any more.

She had felt the need for solitude when she started to write, a devouring, imperious need. She had cloistered herself away in her little attic room in Autheuil, in front of the white wall. She had immediately realised the links between writing and solitude, and had changed her lifestyle, becoming sedentary, silent, riveted to her desk all day long. They would drag her away from it to have lunch, dreamy and preoccupied; always ready for a laugh, she now turned a deaf ear to jokes.

But gradually solitude turned into a painful reality imposed upon her. When she was not writing, she had a desperate need for human warmth, and even when she was writing, she would escape from loneliness because of her need for a reader. But people like her require the right kind of reader, that is to say one whom they trust enough not to jump on him with claws out if he tells them, braving their disappointment, that what he has just read is no good at all. I am sure that Simone took criticism badly: one would have had to be very brave indeed to tell her, as Dashiell Hammett told Lillian Hellman on the beach at Malibu, that all she had to do was start her play over again, right from the beginning.

There was one occasion, a single one only, when somebody should have given Simone Signoret that advice; and I know that some did so, without success. This was when she decided to publish *Le Lendemain, elle était souriante*. She probably had no idea of the effect that the book would have on the image of herself that she had so carefully constructed. For while claiming not to bother about her appearance, she had always taken great care with her public image. It could be that she was well aware of this, and that her behaviour was a sort of provocation or defiant challenge, as if to say, 'You admire me, but look how nasty I really am.' This was the dreadful period when her face was all swollen with drink: of evenings with friends when she would start to belch like an old tramp or drunkard, not like a woman who has just had one too many. During those years it would be her friends who kept her going, as they had to: she was Simone, and Simone was sacred. But they were fed up with her. It was only after she had become seriously ill and had stopped drinking that she became good company again – marvellous company, even. But by that time, she was an old lady.

The Press talked about her bad temper; they said she was difficult. Everybody had heard about the Homeric rows when Montand and she washed their dirty linen in public. She did not deny it, merely saying, 'I'm not always a barrel of laughs.' Probably one does not become a sacred monster without having a personality strong enough to recognise one's dark side, and give it its due. For the dark side can be also an inspiration for creative artists, and it was perhaps this internal contradiction that helped her acting talent to flourish. Her talent was like a unifying bond, which made her inimitable by transcending her faults. It struck a chord with her viewers' dark side, with their shoddy secrets, repressed desires, meannesses and yearnings for power, as well as appealing to the best in them.

Her ambition had been to live her own part of the century to the full, and to share the experiences of her contemporaries. Everything was grist to her mill: the cinema, which gave her the chance of living several different lives; the love she had borne for Montand, the man who, like it or not, represented his age and indelibly stamped it with his melodies and songs and his many different faces; friendship, which allowed her to satisfy the insatiable curiosity that gnawed at her; political commitment, which gave her the intoxicating, if perhaps illusory, sense that she was affecting world events; and finally her writing, the finishing touch on the edifice, which, by the end of her journey, would enable her to explore the secret regions of her inner life.

Now that I am at the end of my own journey, I feel that I still only half-know her. I have tried to describe both what I already knew, and what I felt to be true: 'two or three things that I know about her', to quote Godard's title. As for the rest, she retains her mystery like lovers and heroes of novels. In death, she remains as inaccessible as she was while alive. In order to identify with her, I had to explore my own psyche and draw out unconscious desires from its uncharted depths. I do not claim to judge her, for I am only too well aware that in probing her life-story, it is my own dream that I am exposing.

But others share the same dream. A portrait of Simone Signoret as Casque d'Or figures prominently on the huge Radio Télévision Luxembourg wall in Paris on which the twentieth century's most famous faces are displayed together in a colourful collage, from Charlie Chaplin to De Gaulle by way of Kennedy, Gandhi and John Lennon. At the entry to the Bir-Hakeim bridge, the traffic is held up by motorists slowing down to take a better look at the huge mirror where their fantasy-heroes and heroines are on display. But the paint is already slightly faded because of the exhaust fumes from the cars.

Soon pollution will erode the faces, and there will only remain particles of paint here and there on the big wall, Chaplin's moustache, Churchill's eye, Picasso's chin, Marilyn's ear, as indecipherable and mysterious as a prehistoric wall-painting, or a puzzle invented by a lunatic child; traces of an extinguished passion.

Among this crowd of eminent faces, perhaps a fragment of Simone's painted lips will remain, part of her eyebrows, or a wisp of blonde-gold hair. Like a signature.

EPILOGUE

Yves Montand died on 9 November 1991. He survived Simone Signoret by slightly more than six years. Not a long period, compared with the thirty-six years they spent together, but enough time for Montand to make a new life for himself and to have, by another, much younger woman, the child he had not had by Simone, a baby which perhaps neither of them would have wanted, taken up as they were by their all-absorbing passion for each other, their political activities, and the demands of fame.

In those six years, Montand saw the collapse of the old socialist order, and with it the purpose of all the battles that the couple had fought. Together, they belonged to a period when the Left still attracted innocent, altruistic passions. Simone did not, as Montand did, live to see the ambiguous outcome of their political crusade; nor was she alive to rejoice when the Berlin Wall came down, or when the Soviet Army retreated from Afghanistan, or when the Israelis met the Palestinians round the table at Madrid. But what would she have made of Walesa's career now, after all her efforts, with Montand, to free him from prison? What would she have made of the resurgence of anti-Semitism in France?

Maurice Pons never forgot the day, in the late-seventies, when he went to have tea with her in the house at Autheuil. She had stopped drinking alcohol, on medical advice, and Montand was keeping a discreet eye on her. Hearing his car approaching, she decided to play a practical joke on him. She poured tea into a whisky carafe, and replaced the teacups with glasses full of ice-cubes. When Montand arrived, she pretended to be blind-drunk, and forced him to have a glass. Pale with anger, he took a sip . . . of tea. 'When he understood what she'd done,' says Pons, 'he melted with love; and Simone laughed and laughed and laughed . . .'

In France's reaction to Montand's death, it is as though Simone had died for a second time.

FILMOGRAPHY

1941   *Le Prince charmant*
Directed by Jean Boyer, with Renée Faure, Jimmy
Gaillard, and Lucien Baroux.

Boléro
Directed by Jean Boyer, with Arletty, Meg Lemonnier,
Denise Grey, and André Luguet.

1942   *Le Voyageur de la Toussaint*
Directed by Louis Daquin, with Jean Desailly, Gabrielle
Dorziat, Assia Noris, Jules Berry, and Louis Seigner.

Les Visiteurs du soir
Directed by Marcel Carné, with Arletty, Marie Déa,
Alain Cuny, Marcel Herrand, Jules Berry, and Fernand
Ledoux.

L'Ange de la nuit
Directed by André Berthomieu, with Michèle Alfa,
Jean-Louis Barrault, Gaby Andreu, and Henri Vidal.

1943   *Service de nuit*
Directed by Jean Faurez, with Gaby Morlay, Jacqueline
Bouvier, Jacques Dumesnil, Julien Carette, and Louis
Seigner.

Le Mort ne reçoit plus
Directed by Jean Tarride, with Jacqueline Gautier, Gérard
Landry, Jules Berry, Aimos, Félix Oudard, and Simone
Paris.

SIMONE SIGNORET

Adieu Léonard
Directed by Pierre Prévert, screenplay by Jacques and
Pierre Prévert, music by Charles Trenet and Joseph
Kosma, with Jacqueline Bouvier, Denise Grey, Pierre
Brasseur, Charles Trenet, Madeleine Suffel, and Jean
Meyer.

Béatrice devant le désir
Directed by Jean de Marguenat, with Renée Faure,
Thérèse Dorny, Fernand Ledoux, Jules Berry, Jacques
Berthier, and Gérard Landry.

La Boite aux rêves
Directed by Yves Allégret, assistant director René Clément,
screenplay by Viviane Romance, Yves Allégret and René
Lefèvre, with Viviane Romance, Margeurite Pierry,
Frank Villard, Henri Guisol, René Lefèvre, Pierre Louis,
and Gérard Philipe.

1945 *Le Couple idéal*
Directed by Bernard-Roland, with Hélène Perdrière,
Denise Grey, Annette Poivre, Jacqueline Pierreux,
Raymond Rouleau, and Yves Deniaud.

Les Démons de l'aube
Directed by Yves Allégret, with Georges Marchal,
Jacqueline Pierreux, and Dominique Nohain.

1946 *Macadam*
Directed by Marcel Blistène, artistic director Jacques
Feyder, with Françoise Rosay, Andrée Clément, Paul
Meurisse, Jacques Dacqumine, and Janette Batti.

Fantomas
Directed by Jean Sacha, with Françoise Christophe,
Lucienne Le Marchand, Marcel Herrand, André Le Gall,
and Alexandre Rignault.

1947 *Against the Wind*
Directed by Charles Crichton, with Gisèle Préville,
Robert Beathy, and Jack Warner.

CATHERINE DAVID

Dédée d'Anvers
Directed by Yves Allégret, with Jane Marken, Bernard
Blier, Marcel Pagliero, Marcel Dalio, and Denise Clair.

1948 *Impasse des Deux-Anges*
Directed by Maurice Tourneur, with Paul Meurisse,
Jacques Castelot, Marcel Herrand, Marcelle Praince,
Danielle
Delorme, and Jacques Baumer.

1949 *Manèges*
Directed by Yves Allégret, screenplay by Jacques Sigurd,
with Jane Marken, Bernard Blier, Frank Villard, and
Mona Doll.

Four Days' Leave
Directed by Leopold Lindtberg, with Josette Day, Liselotte
Pulver, and Cornel Wilde.

1950 *Le Traqué*
Directed by Boris Lewin and Frank Tuttle, with Fernand
Gravey, Dane Clark, and Robert Duke.

La Ronde
Directed by Max Ophuls, with Serge Reggiani, Gérard
Philipe, Simone Simon, Danielle Darrieux, Daniel Gélin,
Fernand Gravey, Jean-Louis Barrault, Anton Walbrook,
Odette Joyeux, and Isa Miranda.

Sans laisser d'adresse
Directed by Jean-Paul Le Chanois, with Danièle Delorme,
Arlette Marchal, France Roche, Bernard Blier, and
Carette.

Ombres et Lumières
Directed by Henri Calef, with Maria Casarès, Germaine
Reuver, Jacques Berthier, Jean Marchat, and Pierre Dux.

1952 *Casque d'Or*
Directed by Jacques Becker, with Serge Reggiani, Claude
Dauphin, Loleh Bellon, Dominique Davrey, and Raymond
Bussières.

SIMONE SIGNORET

1953 *Thérèse Raquin*
Directed by Marcel Carné, with Sylvie, Raf Vallone,
Jacques Duby, and Roland Lesaffre.

1954 *Les Diaboliques*
Directed by Henri-Georges Clouzot, after the novel
by Boileau-Narcejac, *Celle qui n'était plus*, with Paul
Meurisse, Véra Clouzot, Charles Vanel, and Pierre
Larquey.

1956 *La Mort en ce jardin*
Directed by Luis Buñuel, with Georges Marchal, Charles
Vanel, Michel Piccoli, and Michèle Girardon.

1957 *Les Sorcières de Salem*
Directed by Raymond Rouleau, with Yves Montand,
Mylène Demongeot, Françoise Lugagne, Jeanne Fusier-
Gir, Jean Debucourt, Alfred Adam, Yves Brainville,
Pierre Larquey, and Raymond Rouleau.

1958 *Room at the Top*
Directed by Jack Clayton, with Laurence Harvey, and
Heather Sears.

1960 *Adua E Le Compagne*
Directed by Antonio Pietrangeli, with Sandra Milo,
Emmanuele Riva, and Marcello Mastroianni.

Les Mauvais Coups
Directed by François Leterrier, with Alexandra Stewart,
Reginald D. Kernan, and Marcel Pagliero.

1961 *Les Amours célèbres (Jenny de Lacour)*
Directed by Michel Boisrond, with Pierre Vaneck,
Colette Castel, and Antoine Bourseiller.

1962 *Term of Trial*
Directed by Peter Glenville, with Laurence Olivier, and
Sarah Miles.

210

Le Jour et l'heure
Directed by René Clément, script by Roger Vailland,
with Stuart Whitman, Reggie Whitman, Geneviève Page,
Michel Piccoli, and Pierre Dux.

1963 *Dragées au poivre*
Directed by Jacques Baratier, with Jean-Paul Belmondo,
Marina Vlady, Sophie Daumier, Guy Bedos, Jean-Pierre
Marielle, Françoise Brion, Sophie Desmartes, and Claude
Brasseur.

1964 *Compartiment tueurs*
Directed by Costa-Gavras, after the novel by Sébastien
Japrisot, with Yves Montand, Jean-Louis Trintignant,
Catherine Allégret, Pascale Roberts, Pierre Mondy,
Michel Piccoli, and Jacques Perrin.

Ship of Fools
Directed by Stanley Kramer, with Vivien Leigh, José
Ferrer, Lee Marvin, Oskar Werner, and Elizabeth Ashley.

1966 *Paris brûle-t-il?*
Directed by René Clément, with Yves Montand, Alain
Delon, Anthony Perkins, Jean-Paul Belmondo, Leslie
Caron, and Claude Rich.

1967 *The Deadly Affair*
Directed by Sidney Lumet, with Harriett Andersson,
James Mason, and Maximilien Schell.

Games
Directed by Curtis Harrington, with Katharine Ross, and
James Caan.

1968 *The Seagull*
Directed by Sidney Lumet, with Vanessa Redgrave,
James Mason, and David Warner.

1969 *L'Armée des ombres*
Directed by Jean-Pierre Melville, with Lino Ventura, Paul
Meurisse, Jean-Pierre Cassel, and Serge Reggiani.

SIMONE SIGNORET

L'Américain
Directed by Marcel Bozzuffi, with Françoise Fabian, Jean-Louis Trintignant, Bernard Fresson, Marcel Bozzuffi, and Rufus.

1970 *L'Aveu*
Directed by Costa-Gavras, with Yves Montand, Gabriele Ferzetti, Michel Vitold, Laslo Szabo, and Monique Chaumette.

Compte à rebours
Directed by Roger Pigault, with Jeanne Moreau, Serge Reggiani, Jean-Marc Bory, Charles Vanel, Marcel Bozzuffi, Michel Bouquet, and Jean Desailly.

1971 *Le Chat*
Directed by Pierre Granier-Deferre, with Jean Gabin, Annie Cordy, and Jacques Rispal.

La Veuve Couderc
Directed by Pierre Granier-Deferre, with Alain Delon, Jean Tissier, Ottavia Piccolo, Monique Chaumette, and Boby Lapointe.

1972 *Les Granges brûlées*
Directed by Jean Chapot, with Catherine Allégret, Alain Delon, Miou-Miou, and Fernand Ledoux.

1973 *Rude journée pour la Reine*
Directed by René Allio, with Orane Demazis, Jacques Debary, and Michel Peyrelon.

1974 *La Chair de l'orchidée*
Directed by Patrice Chéreau, with Charlotte Rampling, Edwige Feuillère, Alida Valli, Bruno Cremer, and Hugues Quester.

1976 *Police Python 357*
Directed by Alain Corneau, with Yves Montand, François Perrier, Mathieu Carrière, and Stefania Sandrelli.

1977 *La Vie devant soi*
Directed by Moshe Mizrahi, with Samy Ben Youb, Claude Dauphin, and Bernard Lajarrige.

CATHERINE DAVID

1978 *Judith Therpauve*
Directed by Patrice Chéreau, with Philippe Léotard,
Marcel Imhoff, Robert Manuel, and François Simon.

1979 *L'Adolescente*
Directed by Jeanne Moreau, with Jacques Weber, Francis
Huster, Laetitia Chaveau, Roger Blin, and Jean-François
Balmer.

1980 *Chère Inconnue*
Directed by Moshe Mizrahi, with Delphine Seyrig, Jean
Rochefort, Geneviève Fonatanel, and Madeleine Ozeray.

1981 *Guy de Maupassant*
Directed by Michel Drach, with Miou-Miou, Anne-
Marie Philipe, Véronique Genest, Claude Brasseur, Jean
Carmet, and Daniel Gélin.

1982 *L'Étoile du Nord*
Directed by Pierre Granier-Deferre, with Philippe Noiret,
Fanny Cottençon, Julie Jezequel, and Jean Rougerie.

FILMS FOR TELEVISION

1965 *A Small Rebellion*
Directed by Stuart Rosenberg.

1970 *Un ôtage*
After Brendan Behan.

1976– *Madame le juge*
1977 Six parts, directed by Claude Barma, Nadine
Trintignant, Philippe Condroyer, Claude Chabrol,
Christian de Chalonge, Édouard Molinaro.

1984 *Thérèse Humbert*
Directed by Marcel Bluwal.

1985 *Music Hall*
Directed by Marcel Bluwal.

213

A NOTE ON THE AUTHOR

Catherine David writes for the *Nouvel Observateur* in Paris.

A NOTE ON THE TRANSLATOR

Sally Sampson has also translated
Elia Kazan, An American Odyssey, edited by
Michel Ciment (Bloomsbury 1988).